JACK BY THE HEDGE
A Jack of All Trades novel

DH Smith

Earlham Books

Published 2016 by Earlham Books
Book design & cover art by Lia at Free Your Words
(*www.FreeYourWords.com*)

Text copyright © 2016 DH Smith

ISBN: 978-1-909804-21-0

PART ONE:
THE CAST & SETTING

Chapter 1

Jack extricated the wheelbarrow from his gear in the back of the van. Into it, he placed his tool box and sledgehammer. He put the long, yellow spirit level aside. Unlikely he'd get around to using that today. But he would need his goggles and hard hat, and he'd take the gloves in case.

Anything else?

It was a chore to keep coming and going, unlocking and locking the van for the odd tool you'd forgotten. He looked over the contents of the wheelbarrow, and could think of nothing else he'd require. Though he knew there'd be something. But not the greatest problem with the van parked near the park gates.

The streetlights suddenly went off. Officially day. In the sky were slow moving white clouds in large patches of blue. To the east, the orange-yellow wash of dawn, a low sun hidden behind the roof tops. There was a slight breeze, not a bad working temperature. With luck, it wouldn't rain today and he could get well into the job. With all that clear sky, maybe tonight he could get out with his telescope.

Jack looked at his watch. Seven thirty the man had said, and seven thirty it was now. And there he was unlocking the gate from the inside. An early start, and here they both were. Jack lifted the wheelbarrow handles and pushed the barrow the twenty metres to the gate.

The man was swinging back the wide ironwork gate. It was wide enough to take a lorry, with ornate scrolling above the vertical bars, almost gothic in grandeur, as if there were a stately home behind it and not a public park in Plaistow. The man was locking the gate in its open position and, it seemed to Jack, he was deliberately ignoring him, waiting with his wheelbarrow.

Jack knew his sort.

He was sure this was the same person he'd spoken to on the phone on Friday. An officious sod, dressed to kill any doubt, in a brown suit with a matching waistcoat, brown leather shoes, highly polished, and brown hair, too brown. A man with so well-used a face would have grey in his hair. The nose was flattened, as if for the first few years someone had sat on it.

He was making a meal of keeping the gate open, and muttered something under his breath, perhaps irritated that Jack was there watching him. Jack knew better than to be helpful, though he could see the chain was twisted. And then the man had succeeded. Jack stepped away from his wheelbarrow and held out his hand.

'I'm Jack Bell, the builder.'

The man barely glanced at him and took his hand in a cursory shake. 'Swift, park manager. Come this way.'

Jack took up his wheelbarrow and followed the manager who walked several paces ahead. The man wasn't going to chat with him. One of those. A foreman really, who called himself a manager. The suit, a Berlin Wall between him and the workers under him; a curious phenomenon, as if overalls were verminous now that he'd reached the first rank of entitlement. Some foremen he'd come across were matey, but others, offered the merest whiff of the ticket to white collardom, lorded it to the hilt.

A friend of his had gone that way. Still lived in East Ham, or had last time Jack had seen him a couple of years back. One day joshing with Jack on the job, the next with the suit and tie, friendship in the bin like a banana skin. Much as he'd hated it, Jack understood why. It was a long time coming, the foreman's job, you'd been bossed about by too many jumped up jackasses in your time, so, when it was your turn, you gloried in the uniform, and did as you were done by. Doing what you'd seen, treading on your mates, to make up for past resentments.

Jack was glad to be self employed. No gaffer to boss him about, no underlings to strut before. The disadvantage was insecurity and making sure he got paid. Though he'd get the money for this job; local councils always paid up in the end, but you never quite knew when. They didn't care you were hard up; their timetable couldn't be shifted.

Jack stopped at the collapsed wall. He'd seen it on Friday morning when he'd come in to size up the job, and, following that, had dropped in his estimate at the council office on the Barking Road. A few hours later he'd been phoned by this man, Swift. He wanted Jack in for an early start Monday.

So far so good. Jack was early.

'What hit that?' he said, indicating the wall. There'd been no one to question on Friday.

'A tractor,' said Swift sucking in his cheeks. 'The driver was out boozing at lunchtime, came back, pissed as a fart, and smashed into the wall.' He smacked his hands dismissively. 'I sacked him on the spot.'

Jack, seeing the wall, couldn't argue with that. Stupid bugger, lost his job and who knows what else? Though it could have been him. His own drinking days, his own smash ups. Job, friends, marriage, car. But not a drop had passed his lips in two years. And it had better stay that way.

The manager was staring at him, awaiting some response; Jack wasn't sure to what, as he hadn't been listening. A question, was it? So he nodded thoughtfully, bent down to run his hand along the portion of badly bowed wall, the top bricks fallen behind.

'The tractor must have been damaged too,' he said.

'A written-off radiator, bumper and mudguard. Just a year old it was. A pleasure to get rid of the bastard.

Lunchtime drinking. A driver!' He waved a hand and blew dismissively. 'But no time to chitchat. Too much on.' He looked Jack in the eye. 'Can you finish the work in two days?'

'Probably.'

'What do you mean, probably?' he bellowed, arms waving as if Jack had insulted his mother. 'We insisted on two days.'

'Suppose it rains all day tomorrow?'

'Two days,' said the manager, indicating the gate, 'or piss off.'

That was telling him with no lack of clarity. He swallowed his doubts. 'Two days it'll be,' he said, hoping he could deliver.

He hadn't done bricklaying for a while. Windows, laying paths, fitting kitchens, decorating, but his last bricklaying was a chimney breast over a year ago. Still, this was a small job, nothing complicated. He should be up to it. It was more public than he'd have liked on this thoroughfare through the park, but beggars can't be choosers. Self employment had its penalties.

'Materials supplied?' he asked, making sure.

The manager pointed out the yard. 'All there. I'll show you what and where. Bricks, sand and cement.'

'Where do I leave the debris?'

'In the yard, by the dump. We'll take it away. Don't you bother about that. Your job is to make the wall good. And nothing else.'

'Fair enough,' he said, though he was within a sliver of snapping back. What was with the man? Had his old woman run off with the milkman? Jack squeezed his nails into his palms. No fights. Sort out the job and get the man off his back.

He hated starts like this. Like some sort of serf, head bowed, holding his cap. Work, the job, concentrate. Swift would be gone soon. He turned to the wall.

'This collapsed section has to be taken out. Right?' he queried. And took a piece of chalk from his pocket and marked a line. 'To here?'

'Let me have it,' the manager barked, taking the chalk. 'From here.' He marked his own line across the top of the wall, and down to the ground. And walked to the other end where damage ceased. 'To here.' He drew another line. 'Remove all that. Got it?'

'Clear enough.'

'When that's all gone, replace it. Got it?'

'Yep.'

'Now I'll show you where the materials are, and you can do what we're paying you for. Two days.'

'Two days.'

The manager led Jack into the yard.

Chapter 2

In 2 Balaam Cottages, one of the two park houses, Liz was at the table in the kitchen spooning muesli and banana. The weekend had been a good one. She'd seen her parents on Saturday, then yesterday been out with her painting group over Hampstead Heath. She'd had a number of goes at capturing leaves floating on a pond in watercolours, and one had worked well, caught the bronze and yellows, the reflections of cloud and trees and the tinges of death. The others she'd torn up.

She gazed out of the window, at the sky and trees. There was still an orange edge to the day. Difficult to catch in paint, the sun up and unsure, shadows longish, dawn oozing away through the half bare, autumn trees.

Or should she photograph it and work from that? But that always felt a cheat, second hand. If you are going to photograph then photograph – and leave it there. Paint from the original. She could surprise herself in her puritanism.

Friday, she'd found some death stalk mushrooms in the shrubbery. She'd like to paint them growing out of the leaf mould. So ordinary looking, the white stalk, the umbrella top with a touch of yellow-green. So delicate, so deadly, surrounded by the empty husks of beech nuts. She'd picked a couple and had them in a display on her sideboard on a sheet of pale yellow card amid leaves of red, yellow and crinkled brown, with purple sloes, chestnuts, ash twigs with their black, match-head buds.

Liz wasn't sentimental about nature. Everything died in the end. That didn't kill the beauty of the season. Maybe added to it, the temporariness of things. Everything has its day. She couldn't but glance in the mirror. No grey hairs yet in her red hair, her freckles were fading again. She looked her years, mid 30s. Her sister though looked maybe five years younger than her actual age.

And so what?

Except she didn't believe the so what. Looks mattered. It's the way we are. We look, we size up, make snap judgements. Petty it may be, but we don't live long and maybe don't learn much.

She shook her head, all these thoughts of ageing. Autumn always did this, the falling leaves, the shrivelling plants, the desperate squirrels gathering before the hard frosts. Though she loved the season. A good one to go out and paint, if it didn't get too chilly.

There were three of Liz's pictures in the room, framed landscapes, one of the park at the height of summer, a seascape, and a woodland with bluebells. They'd been up too long; change and change about. The Hampstead pond could go up. And maybe a couple more autumn ones. A park project she could do, perhaps, the four seasons. Display them outside when she'd done them. Go over Ian's head, he'd simply say no art, and speak to the Parks' Superintendent.

Annoying Ian was a game of hers. He'd snap at her, she at him. Childish really. But she couldn't let him win all the time. A pity to have him, the park's manager, living next door. It lessened the perfection of this place.

But at least Rose was gone. Two days now.

Her sister had left most of her stuff here, having gone on Saturday when Liz had been at their parents'. To return to a note. And to her own space again. Rose had been an invasion. She had completely taken over the bathroom with

7

her clubbing gels and face paints, the stink of them; Liz was still cleaning them away. Rose would come in at god knows what hour in the morning with another stranger and leave the kitchen a mess for Liz to find in the morning, after she'd done the battle of the bathroom. Friday was the last straw. Four in the morning, she'd had to yell at Rose and her spaced-out lover to tone down their love making. What on earth were they doing to each other?

Liz, herself, had been a year at art school – and had her share of substances and lovers, but fifteen years on she could not live with Rose's wildness. She'd hoped she could calm Rose down. And thought maybe the company would be good for herself. Their mother had asked her to help Rose six months ago, to give her some stability as plainly their parents couldn't. Her depression, her strange choice of company. So Liz had leaned on Ian to give her sister a job, when he and she were still an item. And then, when her sister had lost her flat, she'd offered her a room.

It'd been heartless to turf her out. But she had to, for sanity's sake. She never knew what she was coming home to. Who was there, doing what to whom. This was Liz's haven. She needed her quiet space. Fine, keep an eye on Rose, lend her money, help her stay in the job – but she could not live with her.

That had to be her boundary.

Rose would plead to come back; she knew that. Would promise anything in terms of behaviour. But Rose was Rose. Scatty, dragging the detritus of the club scene behind like Marley's cashboxes. No. Liz must paint the word on her forehead, on the front door. It had been hell getting her out. She was not letting her back in again.

She washed her spoon, bowl and coffee cup, and left them to drain on the rack. She'd be back for lunch, listen to the radio for half an hour, perhaps sketch. Her enclosed life. Rose's one success was in making her feel lonely. Rose attracted company like hanging meat, mostly the wrong sort for the wrong reasons, completely out-decibelling Liz.

In a cottage, in this lovely park. But alone.

She could try online dating. Wasn't that what the isolated did? But the strain of it, sending photos into the ether, to end up in the mailbox of someone hiding behind an avatar, a made up identity to be deciphered and only arduously rejected. Oh, give her real people in real places.

Monday's resolution.

Liz went into the hallway and sat down on the low stool by the door. There, she took off her slippers, put them neatly by the wall and slipped into her overalls. Under them, she wore shorts; trousers were too hot with overalls in her greenhouse. She did up the bib. And then put her veggie boots on. She would not wear the skins of dead animals. These were a plastic, simulated leather, that the makers swore was breathable. Whatever that meant.

Liz put on her jacket but didn't zip up. She merely had to walk across the grass to the park compound. As she opened the front door, it occurred to her she must change the locks. Rose still had a key. She'd get that off her, but, to play safe, also change the barrel of the lock.

The morning hit her, as it always did, hardly believing the luck of living here. So much sky, the greenery, the trees, the bank of clouds, white and grey and cream. A magpie and pigeons were searching the grass, there was a breeze fluttering the fallen leaves. So mild for mid October.

Rose rolled her sleeping bag up tightly. She cursed. It was such a bastard getting it back in its bag. You had to roll it ultra tight, make sure it stayed tight and then force it in. Why didn't they just make the bags bigger? Later, she'd have to sneak over to Liz's place and get some of her clothes. Maybe ask big sister nicely if she could use her washing machine. She must find a room somewhere but it was such a chore. All those poky rooms, so expensive; they wanted deposits. And all those soppy rules about noise and visitors.

Why was living so difficult?

You had to work to buy space. Every square yard had a price tag on. And those who had it, had too much of it, locked their doors on you. She was 30 today. Well, she wouldn't be buying any cakes. Only Liz knew and they were barely speaking after Friday's row. Her sister had that whole house for just one person, while she slept in a cupboard, overalls for a mattress and bundles of paper towels for a pillow.

Saturday, she'd tried the shower. Totally cold. Not again. Today just a crude wash. Everyone stank at the music clubs anyway. You covered the sweat in a patina of scent and deodorant. Though she couldn't do that forever. She'd have to suffer the hell of this shower again.

Just not yet. It was a work day. And she knew the bastard would have her vaccing again.

Rose locked her stuff in the cupboard and pocketed the key. There wasn't a mirror but she assumed she looked alright. Bit scruffy, but so what? This was a park, not a dress shop. She was hungry but would have to hang out until lunchtime. She'd go to Greggs down the road for something, unless she could cadge a bite from Liz – and perhaps put some laundry in at the same time and get some clothes. And even have a shower there.

It might be possible to move back in. In stages.

Small stages. Or risk another almighty row with her sister, who could be worse than their mother. Not that she'd seen her mother for eighteen months. Lord God save her from those third degrees in the suburban semi.

When do you stop being treated like a child?

Carefully, she looked out of the window. Across the

bowling green was the entrance of the park compound, now open. There was a man out there working on the broken wall. Damn. Not that he mattered, but she couldn't simply come out of the pavilion, too likely she'd be seen by one of the park's staff coming in to work. The way, she'd worked out, was to climb out through the back window, not the front door, too public, then duck down and sneak along the hedge and on to the drive. She'd have to wait until everyone was in. A little while yet. Oh, there was her sister. She pulled back in.

Liz had crossed the main lawn and was nearing the bowling green, where the builder was knocking at the mortar between the bricks with a hammer and chisel. He was wearing a yellow hard hat and safety goggles.

'Lovely morning,' he called, raising his hat slightly.

'Beautiful,' said Liz. 'We haven't had a frost yet, though I like the sharpness.' She looked over his work. 'Are you going to put the old bricks back?'

'I've been thinking about that,' said Jack. 'The bricks in the yard are the wrong colour.'

'Most of those could be reused,' she said, indicating the bricks he'd knocked out.

Jack picked up a brick and shook his head. 'It would take me ages to knock the mortar off all of them.'

'But it would look so much better,' she insisted.

He nodded. 'It would. But the manager wants...'

'Knocking on the head,' she interrupted with a laugh, 'with that hammer.'

Jack smiled. A long smile that faded into the intensity of his stare.

She held the look, thinking: Oh. His eyes, the curl of hair sticking out of the helmet, his hands on the hammer and chisel. A hit out of nowhere. She wasn't used to this. Not for a long time. Had Rose made her vulnerable?

11

'Do you work here?' he said at last, without looking away.

'Yes,' she was able to manage. 'There.' She pointed, her arm still able to move. 'In the greenhouses.'

Neither spoke for a few seconds, eyes liquid light. In slow motion, he put the hammer onto the top of the wall.

She said hesitantly, 'You can come over when I open up. No, come for a tea break. Ten thirty.' She took a couple of steps away and gave him a shy wave. 'I really must go, the manager gets shirty if anyone's late.'

'I've met the creep,' he said, almost normally. 'See you for tea.'

She turned away, crossed the drive and went into the yard, her stomach swirling like a roll of tumbleweed.

Chapter 3

The job was simple enough. Begin by separating the broken wall from the good wall and then, when the broken wall was isolated, knock it down and take it away. Then build a new section in the space. Easy enough in theory.

But what bricks to use?

The sun had come out again. Looking up at the skittering cloud, he guessed it would be going in and out all day. Sunshine always enlivened him. Fallen leaves drifted along the drive in the easy wind. Jack had rolled up his sleeves, warm enough with his steady chopping.

A young woman suddenly appeared. Had she come out of the hedge? He dismissed the thought. He just hadn't been looking. She was pretty, slim with blonde hair emboldened with red streaks. Tight jeans.

All these distractions on a Monday morning.

'Where did you come from?' he called as she approached.

'I've just been born,' said Rose, giving him a broad smile. 'Aged 30. Isn't that clever of me!

'What, 30 years in an egg?' he said with mock surprise. 'How did you learn to walk and talk? Where did you get clothes from?'

'Actually, I was born yesterday,' she said with a chuckle. 'I nicked these clothes from a charity shop, and I've spent all night reading an English dictionary.'

'You've done well,' he said. 'Bit of a cockney accent... that's surprising.'

'It was a cockney dictionary,' she said.

'Are you really 30?' he said.

'Don't worry,' she said, eyebrows raised, 'I'm not under age. That's if you were thinking of taking me out for a birthday treat.'

Jack's legs hollowed. She was looking at him as if she wanted to eat him up.

'Where would you like to go?' he said.

'Your place.'

'Mine it is,' he said, the chisel sweaty in his hand.

'I shall keep you to it.' She tapped him lightly on the nose. 'Must go. Work to do. But I won't forget. Your place. Tonight.'

She turned, she waved. And was gone into the yard.

Jesus Christ. What was going on today? Two offers in ten minutes. He shook himself. Was there something sexy about a yellow helmet and hammer and chisel? An aphrodisiac combination.

He hadn't even thought to get a name from either. The last one didn't hang about. Rather tarty, but a body that sent ships sailing. The first more classy, though. Something about her, the way she looked at things. And the look between him and her, not simply sex, but a flash of discovery, like a rocket going off. Freckles and red hair. They'd locked, he was sure of it. The essence of speed dating. Of course, as likely to be wrong as right. But then you had to make sure. In her greenhouse, she'd said, for tea. Hot and steamy under the fronds.

He always ran on like this. A look could do it. And then he was in bed. Then with a flash, it could be five years later. Happiness and security, as in a fairy tale.

It hadn't worked that way with Alison. There'd been love to begin with, but that had fizzled out with his drinking. Drowned, like one of those villages with just the church spire showing above the lake. He'd been like the tractor driver, smashing into his life. Divorced, on the streets, robbed and beaten up, before he staggered into Alcohol Halt.

Two years ago.

Chip mortar, take out a brick, put it on the heap. Take apart and build again. Which of the two women? A delightful thought. Might be neither, but let's begin the week hopeful. One, not both, that wouldn't work. Though which? He'd have to play it along, until one sang true. Come and see me in my greenhouse. The starter for ten. How could he refuse? Not that he knew much about plants. He imagined her with a watering can, a sort of Mary, Mary, midst banana palms and pineapples, coconuts and rubber trees. There he was again, making a video of her and him, wearing pith helmets in the undergrowth, parrots screeching and monkeys dangling from the branches.

And then the second, inviting herself back to his place. That must have been a joke. A tease she said to everyone. He'd best be wary there. Do not assume. Get confirmation in lipstick.

The manager had come out of the yard and was at the gate, standing hands on hips, frowning, looking in one direction up the drive and then the other as if waiting for someone. Jack, as if observed by a teacher parading the classroom aisle, became conscious of his work, though he'd been getting on with it anyway. Of his hands, his tools, of the chipping and the bricks, and the man just a little way off with the power.

Next time he looked up, the manager had gone, presumably back into the yard. Jack stopped for a second, relieved not to be watched. That fierce sternness. You knew he was looking for a criticism.

But what to do about these bricks? Reuse the old ones, or go for the new? Two days.

Chapter 4

The mess hut was full. All the workers were seated, some already in their green bibbed overalls, Ian at the head of the table with the signing-in book in front of him. He always came in at 8.00 precisely and drew a line across the page. Anyone signing under it was late.

There were tall lockers along one wall. A deep butler-sink in the corner, a shelf for an electric kettle and a microwave, with a fridge underneath, and above the china cupboard. And that was it apart from the central table with benches along the sides and a couple of separate chairs at either end.

There was one name under the line. Ian would rather let it go, but he had to give a reprimand or be seen as unfair.

'Bill,' he said. 'You were late this morning.'

Bill was in his 50s, with little hair, and what he had greying. When outside he wore a flat cap which was on the table under an arm, a rare occurrence as he mostly wore it inside too. But he was breathing heavily, having come at quite a pace.

'Sorry, Ian.' He shrugged uncomfortably. 'First, had to fix a washer at home, dripping tap. Couldn't leave without fixing it. Then on the way here I had a puncture. You know that bloody bike. If it's not one thing, it's another. And so I had to walk in.'

Bill was pally with the manager, too pally most thought, and they watched, pleased to see him picked on for once.

16

'We don't pay you to have punctures,' said Ian, tapping the book with his pen. 'Be here on time tomorrow.'

'Everything happens at once.'

'I don't expect it of you, Bill. At your age, you should be an example.'

He stopped, he was making too much of this. Bill was rarely late. Ian was pretending a calm he didn't feel. The morning was bubbling over; she was here, almost directly in front of him. He could hardly avoid looking at her. He had things to say to her, but business first. The builder was working on the wall, good, but the marquee hadn't arrived. He'd gone out to look for them, but no sign.

'Your job starts at eight o'clock prompt,' he went on, unable to stop himself. Liz's eyes were rolling. Didn't she realise, he had to be the manager? There must be standards. Anyone other than her and he'd have them for silent insolence. She knew she could do it because of what had been between them. Got her sister a job, then broke it off with him.

The circle of workers were waiting. He forced himself to calm down. Stress, the doctor had said; it'll kill you. But things happened. Even Bill this morning. You wonder who you can depend on.

There was a knock on the door.

Bill, the nearest, rose to open the door. There stood a well built, youngish black man with a docket in his hand. He poked his head round the room and gave them a smile.

'Your marquee,' he said.

'You're late,' said Ian, tapping his watch.

The man shrugged. 'Traffic.' And dodging a further reprimand added, 'Where'd you want it?'

Ian bit his lip. Insolent, but then he didn't employ him, and everyone was watching. Get him out and moving.

'Unload your gear by the tennis courts,' he said. 'I'll be out in five minutes and tell you where to put it.' And, as an afterthought, added, 'And mind your manners, or I'll report you.'

The man gave a mock salute to those at the table. 'Up the workers.' And left them.

Bill shut the door.

'Right,' said Ian, still irritated at the young man's response, but leaving it behind. 'Right,' he repeated, 'you all know what that marquee is for. At least I should hope everyone knows what's happening this week...' He waited for a reply.

'The Mayor's tree,' said Zar.

'Exactly. Someone's awake on a Monday morning. This Wednesday, 11 am, they are coming. The Mayor to plant a tree in the Mayor's avenue, but also this year, our Member of Parliament is retiring and he's planting his tree too. So it's a double ceremony. As you probably know the MP, Sir Leonard Ford, is a cabinet minister...'

'Minister of Justice,' said Zar.

Ian gave the uppity Asian youngster a stern look and continued. 'So we'll get the Newham Recorder, maybe TV coverage. The whole park will be on show.'

'Are we invited?' said Rose.

'No,' said Ian. 'You are the back room boys,' adding, after a glance at Liz, 'and girls. I'll be your representative.'

'I'll be there,' said Liz. 'For the floral display.'

'So you will,' admitted Ian.

'There are always questions about the display,' she said, 'And I have to present bouquets to the Mayor and MP.'

'Yes, of course. Liz and myself will be there. Representatives of the park. We must be totally ship-shape. So let's get on the move. Here's the jobs to be done... Rose, you are on the leaf vac. Start with the main lawn.'

'I always do the leaf vaccing,' she complained in an appeal round the room. 'Can't I do the playground for once?'

'Don't argue with me, Rose. Leaf vac.'

Rose stood up with a pronounced sigh.

'Amy. Put out the tennis nets. Then playground for the rest of the day.'

'Do you want to swap, Amy?' said Rose.

'She does not,' retorted Ian, pointing to the door. 'You both know what you have to do. Off you go.'

The women started to go, Rose making clear her reluctance in her slumped posture.

'Zar. Bowling green. Get the swish, and clear the dew, then trim the banks.'

'It's a switch.'

Ian rapped his fingers on the table and stared at the young man.

'Are you trying to teach me something, Zar?'

'The correct term is switch, sir, used to remove dew and surface water from greens.'

'You know what I mean, smartarse. *Swish* it. Then give the bowling pavilion a sweep, inside and out. We might need it on the day.'

'OK.' Zar hesitated then said in a doubtful tone, 'I'm not sure if this is the right time, but about day release classes...'

'You're correct. It's not the right time.'

'When will be the right time?' Adding as an afterthought, 'Sir.'

'Never, if you don't get out and start swishing.'

Zar held up his hands in surrender, and rose.

'Bill. Clear the flower beds on the main lawn. Soon as they are cleared, dig the beds over and rake them, ready for spring planting. I'll send Zar over to assist when he's done.'

Bill nodded and stood up. He put on his cloth cap, and left Liz and Ian in the mess hut.

Ian waited for Bill to shut the door after him.

He said quietly, 'I wanted to talk to you alone, Liz.'

'I know what I have to do, Ian,' she said. 'Set up the

19

cascade. I've got to check the equipment and the plants...'

'Not about that.'

'What then?'

He hesitated, aware what he was most likely to get, but he had to plough on.

'About us.'

She stiffened. He continued, like a fly repelled first time against a window, and heading back.

'I know things didn't work out between us. I was hasty. My temper got the better of me. I have to realise when to let things drop. Give and take. Not hold grudges. Share. It has to be an equal relationship, compromise. Without compromise no relationship can work, Liz.' A few weeks ago, he'd written to a newspaper and was quoting the advice that had been given by the agony aunt. 'I'd like to give it another go.'

Her hand went to the side of her face as if she had toothache. She took a deep breath before speaking, gently but firmly.

'How many times do I have to tell you, Ian?'

'Is there someone else?'

She stood up. 'That's none of your business.' She took the few steps to the door. 'And if there's nothing work related...'

'Liz,' he said. 'I'll do whatever you want. A clean sweep. We start over. A new leaf.'

She half opened the door, and shook her head. She turned back, half in, half out.

'Ian, we are not right for each other. That's the way it is. I am sorry, I really am. But it's who you are and who I am. I'm not criticising you. Give it time, and we can perhaps be friends, but not with you trying to get us somewhere we could never be.' She held up her empty hands. 'I can't make you happy, Ian.'

He was breathing quickly, his stomach hollowed. He

didn't want to do this, but there was no other way. She had forced it on him.

'Close the door, Liz,' he said, his arms pressing his thighs. 'I've something important to say to you.'

'About us?' she said, holding the door edge, half outside.

'About you.'

She didn't move either way, the door bisecting her body.

'Whatever you've got to say, you'd better say quickly,' she said. 'I've a lot to do.'

'It's about your qualifications,' he said.

For a few seconds, she didn't move. Neither spoke. She bit her lip and closed the door.

'What about them?'

'On your application form for your current job, sent in three years ago, you wrote that you had a Higher Certificate in Horticulture Practice...' He was watching her closely. She was still, her mouth slightly open. 'And you haven't.'

'How do you know?' she said.

'I checked with the examining authority.'

'How did you know to check?'

'That's neither here nor there.'

She sank heavily into a chair. 'My gabby sister. She's dropped me in it.'

He held up a hand. 'Don't blame her. One evening last week, I was going in my house, she was going out, and I asked her where you were. She said you were at an evening class for your Higher Certificate. And I thought why, you've already got that. And so I checked. And found you hadn't.'

Liz sighed heavily. 'Three years I've been here. I can do the job, I do it well. Everyone agrees.' Her hands went to her scalp. 'I am taking the Higher Certificate in a few months...'

'That's not the point, Liz. You didn't have it three years ago. You lied on your application form.'

'OK, suppose I did. Spell it out. What does it mean?'

'When HR find out, they'll fire you. No excuses will

work. A lie is a lie. You'll be out on your ear.'

'Cashiered and disgraced,' she said with a long sigh. 'I'll have to move out of my cottage.' It had suddenly hit her. 'I'll get a lousy reference – and be lucky to get a job stacking shelves in a supermarket.' She appealed to her manager. 'If you expose me, Ian, I'll never get another job in this field... It would be my career over. You know how I love my cottage. You know I'm good at my job. Be reasonable, Ian.'

'Be reasonable to me then.'

She was quiet for a few seconds, before looking him in the eye. 'What do you want?'

'I want us to be engaged, Liz.'

She sank back in the chair and breathed out heavily. 'Right. I think I've got the picture. Though it's all a bit much for me right now. I'm overwhelmed. It's all somewhat sudden, hitting me all at once. Hell. It was going so well. Too well.' She scratched the side of her face. 'I need to go away and think about it, Ian.'

'I'll give you the morning.'

'And then what?' She flapped her hands rapidly. 'Don't tell me. I've heard too much already.' She took a deep breath. 'Right. Lunchtime. I know where it's at. More or less.' She stood up and strode rapidly to the door. 'I'll give you an answer at one o'clock. Promise me you won't do anything before.'

'I won't.'

'Thank you for small mercies.'

And she left him.

Chapter 5

Jack had separated the broken section from the good wall on either side, which left him a choice he hadn't yet resolved. If he wanted to do the job quickly, he should smash down the leaning piece with his sledgehammer and cart it away in clumps. But most of the bricks were sound, and he was reluctant to simply have them thrown away, to end up in landfill. But it would take him a fair bit longer, separating brick from brick, to get them in a reusable state, instead of just smashing them up and dumping the lot. Meanwhile, in the yard was a pile of new bricks all serviceable and present, except the bricks were yellow and new. And these were aged and red.

Two days meant using the new bricks. He'd earn more if he finished in two days. Do as you're told, mate. The mantra of the downtrodden working class. Except it would be a better job if he reused the old. Bob always told him he was a stubborn sod. But he hated waste. He'd only need a few of the new. They could be patterned in. All of which should be sorted out with the manager. Except he had a pretty good idea what the man would say.

Two days.

Damn it. It was only a small job. He'd do it his way. Once he was started, what could the man do? He still had a few hundred in hand from the shop he'd fitted out over the last two weeks. So he could survive even if he got his marching orders.

Risk it, and balls to the manager. There was a good chance he wouldn't spot what he was up to until he was well into it. Jack put the sledgehammer aside and took up the club hammer and the bolster chisel. He began at the top of the damaged section. First thing was to check the feasibility. If the mortar was hell to get off, depending on the mix they'd used, then forget it. But if it came off fairly easily, then plan salvage was on.

He carefully placed the wide chisel on the mortar joint and struck firmly with the hammer, moving round the brick until it pulled free. Once on a site, years ago, he'd seen an old hand getting off old mortar with the back of an axe. The old bricklayer had said it was better than a club hammer, less likely to break the brick. Jack had a hand axe in his tool box that didn't get a lot of use, and had thought of getting rid of it. Now it could earn its keep. He held the brick, the way he'd seen the old timer doing it, and chipped round with the back of the axe head, knocking off the mortar.

It worked, but he'd have to get a move on if he was to get anywhere near done in a reasonable time. Perhaps, if the manager saw a pile of old bricks, he might be persuaded. Move then. He worked on the top course, getting the double line of bricks free. Take down a course at a time, then work on getting the mortar off and his heap would be on the way.

Though there might be a fight on the horizon.

From the yard, he noted sudden activity, a buzz of conversation. A busier spot could hardly have been picked for him. A man in a flat cap exited, pushing a wheelbarrow with a spade and fork in it.

'Morning,' called Jack. 'You out to do some digging?'

'Clearing them flower beds,' said Bill. 'Bout time an' all, for all that grew over the summer. Waste of money those beds. Dogs run through 'em, kids kicking their balls in 'em. I saw a three year old picking the flowers and her mother just looking on. I said to her, stop your child please. She says he's not doing any harm...' He stopped and shook his head. 'Why do we bother to give people like that flowers? Tell me.'

'Not everyone is like that.'

'I saw a wedding group standing in the middle of the flower bed, tramping over everything, taking pictures. In the middle, trampling what they were photographing.'

Jack was going to say – not everyone is like that, but thought he'd just get another example of bad behaviour.

Instead he said, 'Why not concrete the lot over? That'd teach 'em.'

Bill blew a raspberry. 'Just end up as a rubbish tip. Human nature screws up everything.' He sighed. 'Can't stand here gabbing.' He screwed up his face. 'I wouldn't have a wall there at all.'

'Electric fence?' suggested Jack.

'Better than a wall. Gotta go Do something. No matter what.'

And Bill lifted his wheelbarrow and set off towards the lawn. Jack shook himself; the man left him in a graveyard of gloom. Everything is rotten in the world, everything failing, people are awful. Nothing can be done. Might as well cut your throat if there's not a nearby cliff to jump off.

He rapidly struck the mortar off a brick. Then a second. Working swiftly. Clear the head.

The young woman from earlier was coming out the yard pushing a machine that looked to him like a cross between a large mower and a very pregnant vacuum cleaner.

'What you got there?' he called.

'A leaf vac,' said Rose. 'I was on it every day last week. Makes a noise like a jet plane. I might as well be an office cleaner. To hell with it.'

'Nice to see you so cheerful. Must be something in the air. We still on for our dinner date, princess?' said Jack.

Her scowl transformed to a smile, as if she had changed identities from a drudge to a lady. She stepped away from

25

the machine, arms spread to show the width of her domain.

'With caviar and chocolates, wine and roses,' she said, waving a beguiling finger. 'And you never know what there might be for dessert.'

She tripped forward and gave Jack a peck on the cheek. Then quickly stepped back to be out of his reach.

'Must go.' She beckoned behind her and added with a hiss, 'The old prick might be watching.' And dropped back to her morosity. 'Bloody machine.' And headed off.

Jack rubbed the side of his face. A teaser, he was sure of it. How many other dinner dates was she setting up this morning?

A young Asian man had come onto the bowling green. He had a long thin flexible rod and began lashing it in long sweeps against the surface of the grass, throwing up sprays of dew. He saw Jack watching and gave him a wave, as he worked methodically, clearing the green in a line from gulley to gulley, then turning back and doing another strip. The cleared area was bright green, the dewy area a milky green sparkling in the sunlight, drops flying into the air as the lash struck.

Further up the drive, by the tennis courts, a small lorry had drawn up. Two men were taking out of the back large rolls of white canvas. Heavy bundles needing one on each end to get them out and lay them on the ground. They followed up with packs of poles. A marquee, Jack guessed. Who's getting married?

He rubbed his cheek where it had been kissed. And looked to where the woman was on the lawn, her machine ferociously sucking up leaves. Maybe, maybe not.

And he set back to work. Sometimes watching his hands as he struck the chisel and pulled out bricks. He enjoyed the sunshine but suggestive women sent his head spinning. He hadn't been thinking about sex at all until she came out of the yard and seemed to be handing it out on a tray like a free sample at a supermarket. Think of astronomy, the Square of Pegasus, finding the Andromeda Galaxy. Wasn't she chained to a rock and rescued by some Greek hero, he'd read in Astronomy Now. Sex even up there in the stars. Down here, Jack would have to rescue the woman from her machine. And then what?

The two men were sitting on one of the rolls of canvas, one of them smoking, the other pouring from a thermos into a cup. Too early for Jack's break. He needed a decent pile of bricks, if he were to have a chance at persuading the manager. Besides which he'd been invited to the greenhouse. A real invite, rather than a tease of a dinner date. Over an hour to that.

Then she came out of the yard, as if he'd magicked her up. She had taken her jacket off, revealing green overalls, her hair was tied back.

'Busy place this,' he called.

'Panic stations,' she said with a half laugh. 'We've got a big do on Wednesday with the Mayor and the local MP coming.'

'Too busy for me to visit you for tea?'

'Oh no. Please come. The first greenhouse.' She wiped her brow and shivered.

'You alright?'

'I've had a bit of a shock,' she said. 'About my job and my house... I live over there.' She pointed across the grass to the two cottages.

'Nice place. All that wide open sky.' He was thinking of his telescope, then admonished himself; she had troubles. 'Are they going to make you redundant?'

'It may well come to that,' she said.

'What, losing your job and your house together?'

She flapped a hand and sighed. 'Do you mind if we don't talk about it. I've only just heard – and I'm rather shaken up.'

'I don't have to come for tea,' he said carefully. 'If you've got problems you need to think out...'

'You'll think I'll be a misery guts?' She gave a half smile. 'I just might be.'

Jack wasn't altogether sure about the invitation. If she was preoccupied, what was the point? Except... He could show how considerate he was.

'I might be able to cheer you up...' But stopped himself, not so devious when it came to it. 'That was stupid of me. I haven't got a job and house to offer.' Then added, 'Not everything can be cheered up, can it?'

'No,' she said. There were lines etched at the corners of her eyes. 'Do come though. I'm sure you're good company. But you mustn't talk about you know what.'

'Taboo.' He shook his head. 'Though I am sorry about your news, even if I mustn't talk about it.'

'Not half as sorry as I am.' She sighed. 'It's my own fault really. I should have been prepared for this.' She shrugged. 'But there you are, going along merrily, and bang out of the blue...' She bit her bottom lip. 'There's me talking about what we shouldn't be talking about. Do come over. I'll give you the greenhouse tour.'

'I'll be along. Ten thirty.'

'I look forward to it.'

For a few seconds they gazed at each other, neither spoke, he was reluctant to let her go, she held him too, trembling slightly as if cold. Jack wanted to touch her cheek, but she was two metres away – and it would never do. Not in so public a place.

And she had other things on her mind.

'I don't know your name...' he said. 'I'm Jack. For short and who knows for how long.'

'I'm Liz. There's my greenhouse,' she pointed out, 'and I live over there in the first of those cottages. Who knows for how long.'

'And you like frosty mornings.'

'I do,' she said. 'Ice crystals shimmering on the grass as the sun comes up. I'd miss that.' She stopped, slightly embarrassed. 'What do you do, apart from knock down walls?'

'I look up at the stars.' His arm swept the heavens. 'The Milky Way is like a frosty morning. The stars like a ribbon of ice crystals.' He indicated across the lawn. 'There'd be a good place for my telescope, out there on the middle of the grass, one evening.'

'Could be arranged.'

Of course it could. Neither spoke. Both knew it could.

'Come at ten thirty,' she said. 'I've got some chocolate biscuits.'

'Scrumptious.'

'Must go now,' she said. 'The manager'll be out in a minute, and I've had too much of him already this morning.'

And with a wave, she was off.

Chapter 6

It was a pity that switching the bowling green was so speedy. Zar savoured the lash of it, the wide sweep of the glass fibre rod, the drops flying in the air, sparkling in the sunlight, dropping tingling cold on his neck and face. Best not tell Ian he liked it or he'd have him off it and sweeping paths.

He'd like to switch a golf course, walk the whole 18 holes on a misty autumn morning, switching each of the greens from 1 to 18 before the first golfers. Alone, without expectations from anyone.

It was why he liked working in the open air. Space, plants, distance from people. He'd spent a month in his uncle's accountancy office – and hated it. In a dark suit, stuck in front of a screen all day, his uncle trying to impress him with the good money qualified accountants earned, how he could get a big house and garden, have a wife and family. Be secure for the rest of his life, a respected member of the community.

He did not say – but uncle, I am gay. That wasn't a Muslim thing to say. Not to an uncle who was on the committee of the mosque. Or to anyone in his family when it came to that. Or to anyone in their circle. There was already talk of finding him a wife, but he was only twenty, plenty of time his father said. Pass your accountancy exams, Zar – and they'll all want you. You could take your pick.

And have a mortgage and work in an office for forty

years in a suit in front of a screen with figures, rows and rows of figures. Good times, bad times, the figures keep coming. Relentless columns of income, expenditure, cash flow, bank account, creditors and debtors; the world explained in pennies, pounds, dollars, and euros.

One bored morning in his uncle's office, he'd calculated how many numbers he might input in his working life. His uncle could see numbers on the screen so was happy Zar was working, but in fact he was calculating out how many seconds there were in forty years of working life, so that if it took a second to input a number how many numbers he would input in total, assuming seven hours a day, subtracting coffee breaks and meetings, holidays, and allowing time for chatting about football and whatnot. The figure he'd come up with was 189 million or so. For which he'd be well paid and could take his pick, when he'd passed his accountancy exams.

And be a respected member of the community.

But then again, when you get senior enough, your minions put the numbers in for you. You are responsible for them, but you don't do the drudgery. You pull in others to input the numbers in to the columns.

There was a nonsense in the world, a pointlessness, so clear to him in that office. So depressing. Columns of numbers. Years and years of them.

He'd once asked his uncle why all this bookkeeping was necessary. His uncle was taken aback at his naivety, but then explained that any business to succeed must be on a sound footing. And it was the firm's job to make sure its clients lived within their means.

For which you will get well paid.

And will input 189 million odd figures, or your minions will on your behalf. He felt as if he were one ant in a cell of an infinite ant hill. And all the banter of football, births, marriages, deaths, Eid, who's going on the Haj – was a sort of decoration, the ants convincing each other that they were happy. That it was all meaningful.

His uncle had gone as far as booking him on an accountancy course at college, one day a week plus two evenings, when Zar had told him this wasn't for him. Uncle was disappointed, so were his mother and father. His elder brother who worked for the council thought he was dumb. He said he himself would never get anywhere near earning the money an accountant could make.

Birdbrain.

Once free of the office, Zar knew he had to work outside. And got the job in the park. His family were horrified at the wages. He couldn't make them see that he needed to work outside, that office work crushed him. And that was without saying he was gay, that he didn't know what he was doing or where he was going, because they'd simply talk about money and marriage and getting a mortgage, and having children. The future they saw for him, an imitation of their own. And not his at all.

He'd finished switching. The creamy green had been lashed off, leaving the area a dazzling, sharper green. He wondered whether the effort really had any effect on diminishing the effects of fusarium and other fungal diseases. Was it just green keepers repeating the lore they'd learnt? Or were there experiments – with some greens switched and others not. And lots of numbers thrown into computers, showing switching removed 99.9% of all known fungi.

Reluctantly, he laid the switch on the bank and took up the long-handled edging shears. As far as he could see the bank hardly needed any edging, grass barely grew this time of year, and would stop dead in a few weeks. But the Mayor was coming and would spot a single blade of grass sticking above regulation height.

Back bent, a hand on each of the handles, he began

snipping, the cuts dropping into the gulley surrounding the bowling green. And thought about the bracket fungus he'd seen on the yew tree at the back of the shrubbery. That incredible yellow, a shock of a colour. He'd taken a picture of it on his phone and now thought he knew what it was. *Laetioporus sulphurous,* chicken of the woods, edible when young. He must get some, take it home. Get his mum to cook it.

At lunchtime usually, he wandered the park with one of his books. He knew all the trees and had recently become excited by the variety of fungi. Liz told him about the plants in her two greenhouses, how they were propagated. And he'd got himself a book on that too.

The two got on like rain in the desert, each enjoying the enthusiasm of the other. He might tell her he was gay. Maybe not.

He had no idea what he was going to do with his life, not accountancy, nothing in an office – that was for certain. He knew he loved plants and the outdoor life. And the best he could do here was get on day release, learn – and see what came up. Except Ian always said, don't bother me now, whenever he mentioned day release, as if payment for it came out of his own pocket. Zar could of course find an evening class himself, in fact might have to, but if the council would pay him to study one day a week then why not? Except for Ian, and his 'don't bother me now'.

He was racist, Zar was sure. Ignorant and proud of it.

He'd reached the section of bank near where the bricklayer was working. He was curious about what the man was doing with the axe, and so wandered closer to see.

'Ah, you're reclaiming the bricks,' he said.

'Well spotted,' said Jack, brick in hand, knocking surplus mortar off it with the back of the hand axe.

He put it on the pile of cleaned bricks and took up another with the old mortar clinging.

'Those bricks in the yard are all the wrong colour for this wall,' said Zar.

Jack screwed his nose up. 'Dead right, mate. You don't just order any old bricks. You take one to the merchant – and say 'how close can you get to this?''

'Or you reclaim the old.'

'Takes time,' said Jack. 'And I shouldn't be doing it, but I'm going to carry on till I get told otherwise.' He sighed. 'Builders have got into a lot of bad habits. We have to be pushed to change. We're too used to throwing everything out. Cheaper. It's what we've always done. Never mind all the materials and energy that's gone in to making it – dump it. That's no good, is it? Not in the long run.'

'We'll die out if we go on like that,' said Zar. 'Become extinct. Like the dinosaurs.' He bent down and said almost secretly, 'Do you know about evolution?'

Jack laughed. 'I'm a builder, not a professor. But I know,' and was almost quoting from one of his astronomy mags, 'how suns form from dust in space that amasses due to gravity, growing bigger and bigger, until at a certain size gravitational pressure sets nuclear reactions going, until you've got a huge, glowing atomic reactor like that one up there.' He pointed out the sun with his axe.

'And in four billion years it explodes to a red giant,' said Zar.

'Oh, so you know about stellar evolution.'

'I do,' said Zar. 'Not exactly Adam and Eve though, is it? The Big Bang and all that – and us developing from apes. Well, we are apes, except with big brains and opposing thumbs...' He stopped then added, 'I'm not supposed to believe that stuff; it's not in the Quran.' He sucked his lower lip, then added, 'And I'll tell you something else too. I'm gay.'

'That's all right by me. But not by your folks, I would reckon.'

'They don't know.'

'So why have you told me?'

'Because you know things, like evolution. And...' he shrugged, 'you'll be gone in a few days. And you don't know anyone in my family.'

'What would happen if you told your mum and dad?'

'They'd have a heart attack. Not literally. But lecture me about the family honour, how wrong being gay is, against the Quran and our culture. They'd take me to see the imam – and I'd get more of it, chapter and verse. They might try to send me to Pakistan.'

'You could leave home.'

He nodded. 'I'm going to, but I have to work things out. Everything I've done so far has been with my culture, school, college, mosque, all our family stuff. This park is the first time I've been out of it properly, with so many English people...' He stopped, and gave a short laugh. 'I know every tree in the park. They don't lecture you, or feed you crap.' He shook his head. 'I wonder what I'm doing here sometimes. I'd like to go on day release, get some qualifications, but Ian doesn't listen... He's scared I'll know more than he does. Though that wouldn't be much.' He pointed behind him. 'That bank doesn't need trimming.'

'It's why I work for myself,' said Jack. 'Not that that always saves you from crap.'

'Don't look,' interrupted Zar. 'Here comes Ian. Crap feeder in chief. I'd best get busy.'

Zar went back to the bowling green gulley, trying to look as if he'd just popped over for a second. Head down, he continued edging with the long-handled shears, hoping the manager hadn't noticed he'd been off the job.

Without looking up, Jack deftly chipped mortar off a brick. He'd got the knack now, a smart side smack with the blunt end of the axe. But it won't impress the manager, he thought. Far from it. I am about to get a bollocking. Out of the corner of his eye, he could make out the sombre figure, hands on hips, watching. Jack worked on, too aware of the manager's presence, like a grazing zebra trying not to notice a snarling lion. Waiting for the spring.

'What do you think you're doing, brickie?'

Jack stopped, and looked at the manager as if he'd just realised he was there. 'I'm cleaning off the bricks.' He put the one he was holding on to the pile of cleaned bricks. And laid down the axe; it would be too easy to throw.

'Who told you to do that?'

'The bricks in the yard are the wrong colour.'

The manager bent backwards, obviously affronted.

'You're not paid to judge the colour of bricks. You're paid to repair this wall using the bricks in the yard. I thought I had made that absolutely clear first thing.'

'Most of these are salvageable,' said Jack, indicating the buckled section of wall, knowing he'd lost, but at least he'd make his case. 'They'll match. It's an old wall. With some history. Put new bricks in, they'll stand out like a scar.'

The manager's face was cold. Jack knew the man couldn't back down. Having come in like a raging bull, calm discussion wasn't an option.

'Have you finished telling me what's what?' said the manager.

'Whatever I build now, you'll have to live with.'

'You're repeating yourself. Have you anything new to say?'

'I'm telling you what I think as a bricklayer.'

Actually he wasn't a bricklayer, but he could put a hand to it, like a number of other trades in the building game. He'd never call himself a bricklayer to a real brickie, but to this oil rag – he was.

'Using old bricks,' said the park manager emphasising the word old, picking up one from the pile, 'can you finish in two days?'

'No.'

The manager walked along the wall, licking his lips as if calculating the hours and minutes. But there was no disguising it. Granted, Jack was getting quicker at cleaning the bricks but each one took him too long. It would save maybe half a day, or more, just knocking the wall down – and using new bricks.

'Did I, or did I not, make it plain that the job had to be done in two days?'

'You did. But it's not as if I'm asking for extra cash.'

'Then two days it will be. No ifs, no buts. Just work. No one pays you to think. So dump those old bricks. And smash the rest of the wall up. Pronto. Take the debris to the dump, pick up the new bricks – and get laying.' He pushed his face close to Jack's as if daring him to punch. 'I don't know how many times I have to say this. You call yourself a professional?'

'I do.'

'Then give me what I want and stop mucking me about.'

'Right. You're the boss.'

'At last,' said the manager with a deep sigh, 'we're agreed on something.'

Jack was within an inch of walking off the job. Except the job would get done in the way the manager wanted whether he was here or not. And he'd end up not getting paid and maybe suffering a penalty. The battle was lost.

'I'll do what you want,' he said, straining to hold his temper. 'But I want it made clear that I don't think it's the best way...'

'You're a one-squawk parrot, Mr Jack of All Trades. I don't want to hear any more of you telling me what's what. I'm the one who says that. Get me?'

'What's going on here?' came a voice from a little way off.

Both turned to see a man walking up the drive from the

main gate, holding a couple of saplings. He was clean shaven, late middle-aged, and smartly dressed in a well-cut, grey suit, and an almost Alpine hat.

The manager straightened up nervously. 'We are discussing this wall, sir.'

The man put down the saplings, leaning them carefully against the wall, and wiped his hands together as he looked at the workings. Jack wondered who he was. Someone senior most certainly, from the way the manager was reacting.

'So this was the wall that the drunken tractor driver hit for six... Quite a bash.' The man felt along it with his hand.

'I'm the builder,' said Jack. 'And we were discussing whether to reuse the old brick, or the new brick from the yard. And I think we'd value another opinion.' Jack indicated the pile he'd cleaned up. 'I've salvaged this lot. And probably can salvage most of them.'

The man picked up a cleaned brick and looked it over.

'So they clean up easily enough?'

'I'm getting quicker. See,' said Jack. He took up a mortared brick. 'It comes off easy enough with a bit of smart bashing.' He demonstrated with the back of the axe head, chipping the mortar off the faces and the ends. 'There.' He held the brick out to the man.

'I'm impressed,' said the man. 'And I take your point. We should use as much of the old brick as we can. Sustainability. That's what everyone wants these days. Isn't that the truth?'

'The new bricks are the wrong colour anyway,' said Jack.

'That settles it,' said the man. 'Reuse the old.' He smiled. 'Recycling is the way forward.'

'Might I ask who you are, sir?' said Jack.

'Sorry, I should have introduced myself. I'm Ben Greene, Superintendent of Parks.'

'Pleased to meet you, sir. I do think sustainability is the

right policy. There's too much waste all round.'

'Absolutely. I couldn't agree more, young man.'

'Mr Greene,' said the manager, who'd been twitching as Jack and the Superintendent spoke.

'Yes, Ian?'

'If he reuses the old brick, with all the cleaning up – he can't finish before the ceremony on Wednesday.'

'Does that matter?'

'I thought we wanted everything ship-shape, the whole park tidy...'

'By all means tidy the park, Ian. But this is a working environment. There are always jobs in progress. Why should the Mayor and our Member of Parliament be shocked by a half-built wall, especially when being laid in old brick? I think the Mayor especially would appreciate it. He's quite a one for conservation, you know.'

'Then old brick it is,' said the manager, seeing the way of the wind. 'I'm glad we've cleared that up. I wasn't sure, so we were discussing what to do for the best.'

'Fine, fine.' The Superintendent picked up the two saplings. 'And maybe you could get your head round this conundrum. I've just picked these up from the nursery. They're the ones for the ceremony. Keep them in your yard, Ian.' He scratched his head. 'Except they don't look right to me. Mind you, I've forgotten more about trees than I ever knew. Comes of being so office bound. But I'm not sure they're oaks. What do you think, Ian?'

The two men inspected the saplings, fingering the twigs and buds carefully, like two jewellery experts handling a coronet, from the tip down to the roots bound in bulging hessian.

'Flowers are more my thing,' said the manager hesitantly, 'there are so many trees, all those varieties, – and when they haven't got leaves, well, to tell you the truth...'

'That youngster over there knows his trees,' said Jack

interrupting. They turned to him. 'He was telling me earlier. He knows all the trees in the park.'

'Bring him over,' said the Superintendent. 'We have to get this right.'

Jack stepped over the wall and up the bank. He waved both hands to Zar, who had his head down, edging. And called: 'Hey – over here. You're wanted, mate.'

Zar looked across, hesitated, and then began striding round the bowling green with the long arm shears in tow.

'We must make sure they're correct,' said the Superintendent. 'They have to match the others in the avenue. And with the MP coming too, we could well get TV coverage. It wouldn't do to plant the wrong sort.'

'It certainly wouldn't,' agreed Ian.

Zar had arrived. He stayed the other side of the wall, looking nervously at his manager and the newcomer.

'You wanted me, sir.'

'I hear you know your trees, young man,' said the Superintendent. 'So can you tell us what these two are?'

Zar stepped over the wall to get to the saplings. He looked at them closely, examining the twigs.

'*Quercus*...' he said tentatively. 'Probably *rubra*. *Quercus rubra*. Red oak. From North America, the Appalachians and the Great Lakes. Turns a beautiful red in autumn. *Quercus rubra* I'd say.'

'That's what they're meant to be,' said the Superintendent turning to his manager, then back to Zar. 'Are you dead sure?'

'Pretty sure. Crown terminal buds, longish. I've got a book in the mess room...'

'Go get it, lad. If you don't mind.'

'Yes, sir.'

Zar skipped across the drive and into the yard.

'Keen youngster,' said the Super. 'I like to see that. Got initiative. Knows his trees.'

40

'He wants to go on day release,' said Jack.

'Did you know about that, Ian?'

'I was going to talk to the lad about it,' said the manager.

'We won't be here forever, Ian. Just a couple of years left myself. We must train up the new generation. And when you spot keenness... Cultivate it.'

Zar came running out the yard waving his book.

'Here you are, sir.' He flicked through the pages and stopped. 'There. That's it. Look. *Quercus rubra.*'

The Superintendent took the book. The page had a photograph of the full tree and close ups of acorns, leaves and buds.

'It's a dead ringer,' he said. '*Quercus rubra*. Red oak. Glad that's settled. Thank you, young man.'

He handed back the tree book.

'About that day release,' said Ian. Zar turned to him. 'I was thinking you should go on it, seeing you are showing initiative. Reading books in your own time. What do you think, Mr Greene?'

'Sign him up. He wants to learn. He's pretty sharp already.'

Zar jumped up, arms raised. 'Brilliant. Oh, thank you so much, sir. I won't let you down.'

'I'm sure Ian will keep me informed of your progress, young man.' He looked at his watch. 'And now we'd best go to your office, Ian. We have to discuss the big day. The whole world coming.' He started across the drive in the direction of the yard, followed by the manager. Halfway, he turned. 'Thank you for your expertise, young man. And keep salvaging those bricks, brickie.'

They disappeared into the yard.

Jack looked at the wall and the brick in his hand. He shook his head. What a lot of sweat to get a simple job done.

'I'm on day release,' said Zar in disbelief.

Jack held out a hand. 'Congratulations.' They shook hands. 'I'm Jack.'

'Zar.' He spun around, arms high in the air, like a footballer who'd just slammed the ball in the net. 'Yippee! Something, at last, going right.'

Chapter 7

Rose was vaccing the main lawn, pushing the throbbing machine as if it were a plough going through heavy clay. The front end was like a mower but with a wider, sucking head. The leaves were drawn into a large bag, and beyond that was the handle to which Rose was reluctantly attached. On Ian's orders, she'd first cleaned up the area where the marquee was now being erected, but could hear none of the workers' banter over the blast, and was now crisscrossing the main lawn.

She hated the noise and vibration. The job made her feel like a menial. She was above this sort of work, having been told quite a few times that she should be a model. Just the other week, a photographer had stopped her in Stratford, taken her photo and said she had 'bone structure' and he'd get back to her. He hadn't, but you never know. And here she was, clodhopping. She'd die if any of her clubbing friends saw her. Although she'd told them she worked in the park, they imagined it was all flower arrangement or tying up dahlias in the herbaceous border. Not these dirty jobs. Not that any of them would recognize her in these overalls, boots and shapeless leather gloves.

It was death. This job, this time of year, this corpse strewn lawn. Rose had always known she was going to die young, tried not to think about it, and consequently thought about it a lot. She would be murdered or die of an overdose, some ill-prepared powder bought from a tosser in a club on a hot evening, and she'd drop to the dance floor like one of these dead leaves.

They'd done their bit, faithful factory fodder, making sugar for the tree over the summer. From sunlight – and what was it? Some gas in the air and some other thing she'd once been taught in biology. Photo-something or other. Liz would know, not that she'd ask her, Liz knew everything; even why these leaves had to be murdered every year when they'd skivvied away as long as the sun shone. And now dumped like garbage. As if the tree were a ruthless factory owner throwing out surplus workers. Except these pathetic things weren't just losing their jobs but their lives too. More like the trees were camp commandants given orders by Mother Nature to dispose of slave workers. Shoot them, gas them, strangle them. It doesn't matter how – terminate them.

She was part of the clean up squad. When the last dead leaf was vacced, she'd be made to dig her own grave, told to stand by it, a pistol would be put to her head – and she'd be shot, falling cleanly into her grave. Witness terminated; though they would have to shoot the person who'd shot her, then they in their turn would be shot, an ever increasing body count until the Führer alone stood triumphant on a mountain of bodies.

Death everywhere. Just over there was Bill pulling up the flowers in the bed, shaking the soil off and chucking them into his wheelbarrow like a plague waggoner. Every day the park was covered in layers of fresh corpses, to be vacced up, to make room for tomorrow's corpses.

And she was 30 today. How could she have got to this day? A tap had been dripping poison into her body from the very day she was born. In her 20s, she could deny it, but 30 and vaccing leaves. How could she deny the evidence? Every living thing dies.

She stopped her machine and picked up a leaf from a plane tree. It was huge, bigger than her two spread hands. Beautiful, green and yellow, with patches of rusty brown in the angular fingers. How could nature just throw this away?

Because Nature was a callous cow. Beauty didn't matter a fig to her. Cry, plead – she will not hear. Rather, lay waste, burn those praying in the citadel, take no prisoners. Cut every throat until the river runs red and bodies block the channels.

She read too much post-apocalyptic crap. After the catastrophe, the marauding gangs, and so forth; they were all the same. Why should she be one of the select? Today she was the grim reaper's slavey. As disposable as a soggy tissue.

Every living thing dies, she said again. The only way out is heaven – and she didn't believe in it. But she must; it was her only hope. The religious live forever; atheists die. Permanently.

Maybe she should try a church. The Church of the Live Forevers. All she had to do was persuade herself to believe. Eternity was more than a good reason. In the end, it didn't matter whether it was true or not, so long as you believed it. That made you happy. All she had to do was find a nice church. Not one of those heavy puritan churches that said no to everything, but one that let you get on with your life as you wanted to live it anyway She'd have to see what was on the internet.

She was vaccing the edge, where the lawn met the shrubbery. Rose stopped and felt the leaf bag. Five minutes maybe and it'd be full. She'd like to empty it now, get a break from the noise and death images, take her time at the dump, but Ian had seen her at the leaf mould pound, emptying a less than full bag last time, and given her a tongue lash. Five minutes of belch and roar to endure.

She'd tried out music and headphones on Friday. Useless in this racket. She'd have to get those really expensive noise cancelling ones. Except it seemed like a sort of cowardice, a denial. Like spraying a manure heap with lavender. It was still there under the smell.

This would be her hell, the one in waiting for her. Like what's-his-name with the big rock. She'd be given this massive vac, to suck in evildoers until the end of time. She'd empty the bag into a vast cauldron of boiling pitch, go back and find the path as full of sinners as it was before.

The machine was sucking just under a holly tree when she saw it. The leaves shot in to the machine, clearing a space, and there it was – a hand. She leaped back. Help! It was in her head, dead bodies – and there was one, or rather a bit of one, a hand and wrist. Rose turned off the machine. And bent down warily for a closer look. The hand was in a sleeve. So not just a cut off hand, a gangland job. It was attached to a body. What should she do?

She folded the hand back at the elbow so she couldn't see it. Dead bodies are dead. She could just carry on, pretend she hadn't seen it. And let some old woman with a dog snuffle it out. She turned on the vac and began sucking her way on, away from the holly and its secret.

And then stopped.

If she reported a dead body, she'd get a break. A good break, and a pat on the back. No one could tell her off for being a concerned, solid citizen and reporting an actual corpse in the park. And she'd have an exciting tale for a week. Guess what I found in the park? she'd tell her clubbers in the chill-out room. She'd leave out the leaf vaccing bit, but maybe not, they might find it suitably apocalyptic. Or she could make it sound like a blast. Being all on your own, with your thoughts, minding your own business, when a hand comes out of the leaves... Honest.

Better check first though. She turned off the vac and went back to the holly bush. Rose got down on her knees and looked under the canopy. And saw a grimy face looking back at her.

They stared at each other, it was difficult to say who was more surprised, the bleary, tousled head in the sleeping bag or the park worker who was thirty today. The head gave a half smile, almost toothless, breathing heavily.

Rose said, 'I don't care where you sleep, mister. It's all the same to me. But if you don't pull yourself in further someone will see you. And move you on. It's up to you. I don't care.'

The man put a dirty hand out to placate her, the nails bitten to the quick.

'I'm ill, lady. I can't get up. I need to get to hospital. Dicky ticker.'

Different situation. Something had to be done. When in doubt call Liz.

'OK,' she said. 'Don't worry. I'll get someone. You'll be alright.'

'Thanks, lady.'

She nodded. She could be a frightfully selfish cow. But here was someone thanking her. She took his hand and squeezed it.

'I'll just leave you for a few minutes and be right back. OK?'

'Thank you, lady.'

The man sank back as if the last few words had been effort enough. And he'd passed on responsibility to someone who wouldn't let him down. Rose let go of the holly branch and came out into the open air. Not a dead body. No story to tell her mates of murder and drugs wars. But someone alive, who couldn't afford to rent a room and was ill. Something she understood all too well in this town with sky high rents.

She headed for Liz's greenhouse.

Chapter 8

He was getting into a rhythm. Pick up a brick, chip off mortar, clip, clip, clip, each face, put it on the pile, take up another. Jack had taken out another two courses of bricks – and so had a longish task of brick cleaning. His hands seemed to be working almost without him. The left held the brick, the right the axe; almost like robots on an assembly line, programmed for one job. Clip, clip, clip, on the heap, pick up another. The heap was building up. Mind you, he wouldn't want to do this for too long, the wrist of his right hand, the one holding the axe, was getting sore. What did they call it? RSI. He'd get that alright if he did this day in, day out. There must be a machine that could do it. Or there should be. But too late to get it here. And too expensive, anyway.

He was cheaper.

But this was OK. Sleeves rolled up, the sun warm, chipping away. And that hassle, with new bricks versus the old, sorted out. Although the manager hated his guts. Twice he'd seen him go in and out of the yard. And he'd ignored Jack totally. Not that he minded, it meant he was left alone to get on with his work without the gimlet eye looking for someone to criticise. Probably some other poor sod was getting it in the neck for the battle Jack had won. Though he'd better make sure this was a first class job.

He glanced at his watch. Twenty minutes to tea break. Over in the greenhouse with Liz. Steamy biscuits. Oh yes. He tried not to think of what might happen after the last biscuit melted in the tea. Nothing most likely. She might be fixed up, a big bruising guy, a 10ᵗʰ Dan in some martial arts discipline involving flying kicks and punches that smashed planks in half. Or. There was the dream, the one he was a sucker for. His bedmate, the companion of his soul, the one and only... And he wondered if he was too awkward a bugger for that to ever really happen. Once he'd got off best behaviour, once he was seen for what he really was. A builder scraping a living, a drink away from a drunken sot; she'd run a mile.

Women aren't perfect. That had to be remembered. We are all dirty sinners, dressing up, washing and deodorising to give the lie to the lonely ape howling for love. Some of the guys at Alcohol Halt had it all down as original sin. The wicked trip of all humanity, with only one way to salvation.

The problem with dating, and such like, was that everyone was on best behaviour, making you think: I'm the only one pretending. Junk, pure junk, he knew. But he found at times it was hard to convince himself.

Shut up and clean the bricks. Enjoy the sunshine.

Don't damn a relationship before it begins.

And that other woman. He hadn't got her name yet. The one who was on the machine who'd kept teasing him about dinner tonight. He didn't know what to make of that. Down, boy. One at a time. Tea break. See how that goes, before you start thinking of the evening meal and its desserts.

This wall was a focus; most people came past here, to come in the park, or to leave, though there was another gate. This, the main one. And the park workers came in and out of the yard just opposite. The Superintendent had come back out, made a cheery remark about the lowering wall and the reclaimed bricks, the manager went out to bully his staff and in to do his paperwork presumably. That woman with the leaf machine had come in once. She didn't look half so attractive pushing that thing, hunched over and glowering.

49

She'd waved to him but hadn't mentioned dinner.

It was just a game, she'd already forgotten.

The marquee guys had driven past him and left the park, leaving their assemblage in the middle of the lawn. Two of its flaps were open – revealing the empty belly. Awaiting Liz's display, tables and tablecloths, canapés and the glasses and bottles to keep the nobs merry.

It could be lonely being a builder. Working on his own all day. Here, he had all the traffic, and wondered which he preferred. It depended on the traffic. Liz anytime, the manager, no thank you. The other woman? Maybe, perhaps. Depending.

His phone rang. He fished it out from deep in his overall pocket. Could be a customer. He had not much on after this job. Cross fingers. But no – it was his daughter.

'Hello, Mia.'

'Hello, Dad.'

'Shouldn't you be at school?'

'I am at school. I'm in the library, looking for a book on Mali cattle drovers... The librarian's in her office. And she can't see me behind the shelves anyway.'

'She might hear you.'

'I don't want to talk about the library, but about Tony.'

'Who's Tony?'

'Mum's boyfriend.'

'I didn't know she had one.'

'You're way behind, Dad. He's moved in. And he's a pig.'

'That was quick work. How's he a pig?'

'The way he eats, the way he talks, his smarmy smile. He's always touching Mum...'

What could he say about that? Hadn't he done the same? Except no kids were present at the time.

'It's a phase,' he said. 'He's just moved in. Love and all that. He'll get over it.'

'I hate being in a room with the two of them. The way

they smile at each other, touch knees under the table, hold hands while they're watching TV. They hate me being with them.'

'It's a phase,' he could only repeat. Though it was not a situation he'd been in; new lovers with a twelve year old sulking in the wings. What the hell do you do?

'I had to shut their door last night. The noise they were making.'

Jack chuckled. That would put a damper on their love making.

'You laughing, Dad?'

'Yes.'

'It's not funny. It's pathetic. I can't stand it there. The flat's too small for three. I've only got my room. Mum keeps having a go at me for being in it all the time. Tony bought me a tablet. I'm never going to use it.'

'He's only trying, Mia.'

'It's never going to work. He's a total creep. Oh, here comes the librarian. Talk to you later, Dad.'

She rang off. He put the phone back in his pocket and picked up the brick he'd been working on before the call. He felt sympathy for all parties. Her new beau wanting sex and love, adult things. Alison ditto. All perfectly natural. And poor Mia, feeling in the way, her mum with less time for her, Tony trying to buy her affection. He could imagine it in that claustrophobic flat in Brighton. He'd been there a number of times to pick up Mia. Fine for two people. Three OK – if they all get on well. But not with Mia in her room, sullen with one word answers. And Alison torn between lover and daughter. He could even feel sorry for his ex.

Not that sorry. Considering the time she'd given him. And to be fair, he'd given her. Until she put him out on the street with a suitcase. Awful time. Human beings are said to be social animals. So social that he was living on his own. In some ways happier, and some ways not so. Social, antisocial.

No wonder the rich have massive houses. Dilute the rows and body smells. We need space. We need to be together. How is it ever possible?

Poor Mia, with all this to and fro-ing the last few years. His drinking, mum and dad at war. And now, with dad gone, Alison's attempts at a new partner. But did she really have to move him in so quickly? Was she that in love? Or that desperate?

Not questions he could ever ask Alison. He had his own desperation to consider. And looked at his watch. Tea break. And his invitation to the greenhouse for tea and biscuits. He rubbed his hands; this could be good. Or just tea and stale biscuits. Don't assume, he told himself. Step by step. And other clichés. It takes two. And who knew if at the end of the tea break his fantasy might lie in tatters. She might be a Jehovah's Witness come to save his soul or a little Englander with nasty views on anyone not exactly like her.

And so forth and so on. Preparing for the worst while hoping for the best.

Jack packed his tools in his toolbox. Leave nothing out, a hard learnt lesson. Once, he'd been gone for five minutes, and lost a hammer, drill and spirit level. Another time, a brand new door had been taken off the roof rack of his van. All set to do the job, he'd just taken his tools upstairs, and when he came back out to pick up the door, there was nothing there but the bungee cords.

He put the tools in the wheelbarrow and wheeled it into the yard and into the shed, leaving the barrow in a corner out of the way. Should be safe enough there, with all the coming and going.

And then he headed for the greenhouse, and his assignation. Fancy word that. Wasn't it more for gangsters meeting in sleazy bars, than a polite tea in a greenhouse – with perhaps a combo playing snazzy jazz. No, it wasn't a club in Harlem full of tobacco smoke and illicit booze, but quite what it was he didn't know. A Smile-in, that might progress to a Hand-in. He couldn't help a silly grin at his hopefulness. But unsure what to expect, he'd brought his backpack, containing his lunch and thermos, just in case there was less on offer than tea and jam scones with cream on top.

He paused to admire the wall of the yard, OK, a delaying tactic. Be a little late. The eight-foot height of it brilliant with Virginia creeper, the leaves like flat fish, a sexy red. Did its roots burrow into the brickwork or was the plant somehow stuck on? He looked closely, following the branches with his fingers. And saw that the leaves came off of twigs which came off a thin sort of trunk that grew out of the earth at the foot of the wall. There were small pads that held the plant to the bricks. Damn clever. The brickwork was a support, not a substitute for soil. He could imagine, if he ever had a garden, quite getting into growing things. This plant without a single brain cell had come up with this ability to make use of a wall. How? And that red, a real shocker. It made him think of cabaret dancers with their slinky boas and ostrich feathers. Maybe in the jazz club in prohibition Harlem.

He was in quite a mood this morning, finding sex and wonder in everything.

Except at the greenhouse. The first one was locked. He tried the second. Locked too. He peered in the glass door, both were empty of people. He knocked on the door, just in case Liz was low down, under the shelving, or hidden in the foliage. But there was no response to his rapping.

He was flooded with disappointment. Ten thirty she'd said. It was a couple of minutes past. Well, there you go. That's the way of things. You think, you dream, poor sucker. And the door is shut tight.

It might have to be dinner with what's her name, which wasn't on offer anyway he'd decided.

There could be a good reason for Liz being out. Or maybe she'd forgotten. What was important to him might have been trivial to her. Though that wasn't what he'd felt. The intensity of that look between them; she was trembling. But he'd been wrong before. Assumed something was happening, and it was. But only to him.

Maybe something had come up, more important than tea with a builder. She was worried about losing her job and her house. Should he search for her? No, it was just a little invitation. Nothing special. It was he who was making too much of it. Fantasising and blowing up a look to heaven knows what. Really, really, he must grow up.

Turning away from the greenhouses, wondering where to have his tea break, he saw a group along the shrubbery, about fifty metres away. There was the manager, the woman pushing that big machine – the maybe-dinner sexpot, the old gardener, and there she was – Liz on the ground. What was going on there?

It was his tea break. This was a park. He was free to find out.

He walked towards them, over the damp grass, past the back of the marquee, about fifteen metres in on the green. He couldn't see the group too well, the machine partially obscuring his view. Something, or someone on the ground, it appeared.

Might he get a reprimand from the manager? Mind your own business, brickie, waving his self-righteous finger. So perhaps he should leave it and find out later… No, the manager would not be too willing to have another go at him. He'd stood up to him and won last time round. And this was his tea break after all.

Besides, there was Liz. There, not in her greenhouse where he should have been expected.

When he got to the group, he saw they were around a man in a sleeping bag splayed out on the grass, just beyond a holly tree. The sleeping bag was half unzipped, the man was fully clothed, a hand on his chest, eyes open. Obviously alive but not too well. Liz was on the ground by the man putting a pillow under his head.

'What's up?' said Jack to any one of those standing around, peering down at the prone invalid.

'Heart attack,' said Bill. 'Meths drinker. What'd you expect?'

'Eastern European, rather drink than rent a room,' said Ian shaking his head. 'A Pole, Estonian, Latvian, one of them.'

'I ain't Eastern European,' said the man through a constricted throat. 'From 'ertfordshire.'

'His pulse is weak,' said Liz, her fingers on his wrist. 'I hope the ambulance is here soon.'

'I'll leave you,' said Jack. 'There's more than enough here.'

Liz looked up at him and gave him a smile. That would have to do. The man needed her more than he did.

And he left the group.

Chapter 9

Now that Jack had gone, Liz wished Ian would go too. Just the two of them here with the sick man. The others had been told to get their tea. She was to stay with the man until the ambulance arrived. Ian wasn't needed, he'd said he was keeping her company in case. As if the man were a vampire and might leap up and go for her throat. She didn't need Ian but he was the manager of the park and held her fate in his hands. He hardly ever came into her greenhouses. They were her territory and he was intimidated that she knew so much more about the various hothouse plants than he did. But this was his ground, undeniably, out in the park; here he was her superior. His presence was a ticking clock, a continued reminder of their earlier conversation. Perhaps she should leave him here and go and get her tea, except she didn't want tea, having missed the one she'd planned with Jack. But she was the one with first-aid qualifications, though there was nothing she could do really. She'd got the man comfortable. He wasn't unconscious. But she couldn't do much for his heart.

Or her own, if it came to that.

All she could do was watch. Poor man. Say sympathetic things. Which was in truth why she stayed. She had compassion for the man, while Ian, although accepting the ambulance had to be called, regarded the man as a nuisance, getting in the way of the proper work of the park. A dosser, though not a foreigner which Ian would have preferred, being the unquestionable cause of all the country's problems. At such times, Ian seemed to have a flagpole up his back, the red, white and blue flapping over his head to the tune of Rule Britannia. Though she had to admit, he could be pragmatic. The ambulance had been called. And she'd heard, not altogether clearly, that Zar was going on day release. So maybe, she was too hard on Ian.

'The ambulance'll be here soon,' she said to the man. 'I'll just give your face a wash.'

'Yes,' said the man weakly, 'don't want to stink out the place.'

She took the flannel from the bowl of warm water by her side, squeezed it out and wiped gently round the man's face. The grime eased away. She wrung the flannel again and went back over.

'You're not bad looking under that lot,' she said.

'Gonna take me out to the pictures then?' said the man, ending in a fit of coughing.

'You're not going anywhere for a while,' she said. 'Don't talk, and give me one of your hands.'

The man held a hand out and she washed it with the flannel. The water in the bowl was dirty, maybe she was just moving the muck around, but it was easier than talking to Ian. Not after his ultimatum. Marry me or I'll get you thrown out on to the street. Well, she could leave, of course. Resign before he exposed her. And once she'd left might he not bother with the worst? Might she still get a reference?

Who knows? She had the feeling, though, he'd go for the jugular. And she'd lose her lovely house, and any chance of a job in her field. How could she talk to the man, in any civilised way? She either wanted to claw his eyes out or prostrate herself before him, beg to keep her life.

She mustn't simply give in. In the mess hut, she'd been aggressive and given him no room. In her own place, the right atmosphere, she might get a better deal out of him.

Some halfway house. Was that possible?

She heard Ian shuffling over her shoulder.

'Where's that damned ambulance?'

She'd thought once, she could change him. Gradually draw him down from his superior plinth. It must be possible. But then you don't have to sleep with someone for that. Well she had, and he was who he was. Put her error down to loneliness, to living in the park, associating him with it, the cottage, the space, wanting somehow to control it, own it almost, and with him, the two of them, somehow it would be hers too.

It had all been so ill thought out.

But now, she must be clear headed. Get the best she could out of this. Choose the place, make the occasion.

'Ian,' she said, putting the flannel back into the bowl. 'I've been thinking... Will you come to lunch at my place?'

'Of course,' he said, a little warily.

'I don't want to say anything now,' she said holding up a hand, 'as I'm not totally clear, but I will be by lunchtime.'

'I'll come,' he said. 'And I hope we can settle things.'

'So do I.'

Ian bent forward. 'Liz,' he said, 'we could do so much together, make this park ours. It'll all be different. I've changed a lot.'

'Lunchtime,' she said. 'This is not the place.'

'Of course.' Ian straightened himself as if he'd just been proposing, which perhaps he had been. He looked down at the prone man. 'He should be at the Salvation Army. Not in the park.'

She tipped the dirty water into the grass and wrung out the flannel.

'They won't have you with drink,' said the man croakily.

'We won't have you drunk or sober,' retorted Ian. He turned to Liz. 'I'm going to get a cup of tea. Lunchtime then.

I know you lay on a good spread. I'll send Amy out here with a cup of tea and a chair.'

'Thank you,' she said, 'Would you bring a glass of water for him?'

Ian nodded and glanced at his watch. 'The ambulance shouldn't be much longer.' He bent down to the man. 'It's more than you deserve, mate, but you're in good hands with Liz.'

He left them, crossing the lawn and disappearing behind the marquee, accepting the man was no competition.

She sighed with relief. That was done. Now she had to think what to say to him. To salvage something. Though, she was certain of one thing; she wasn't going to marry him.

'A fine mess we're in,' she said to her patient, and half chuckled. 'How did you get here?'

'Over the fence from Balaam Street,' he said, flapping a hand in its vague direction.

Which was an answer, but not to the question she was really asking. How did you get to the point where all you own are a sleeping bag and two carrier bags? Could this be her if she said no to Ian? Jobless, homeless. On the skids.

A tear slid down the edge of her nose. She wiped it away with a finger. It was for the man, not for herself. She would cope, somehow. She needed to accept the worst that could happen to her. Even so, she would not be here, laid out in the park. It might be a close call, but not now. Ten years ago perhaps. She could get a van, do private gardening. She had a way forward; all the better to face Ian. Not helpless, but with a possible path.

Say goodbye to the park.

She looked down at the man, the veins in the white of his eyes. She smoothed his brow. He smiled back at her. Someone's child, someone's brother. Jesus would say hers. My heavens, that was a lot to take on. A responsibility for others. Time perhaps that she should. Instead of just painting the world, shouldn't she be part of it? Change things a little. Instead of saying what a shame it's such a mess outside this park and her cosy cottage.

Even if she lost it.

She heard the siren. At last. The medics had come to take him away, to a ward of white coats and nurses' uniforms, to patch him up and send him back out to drink himself insensible.

'Somewhere warm and dry tonight,' croaked the man. 'That'll be good. Hot food in the hospital. Might spin it out a couple of weeks... Eh love?'

And she thought how long she might spin it out for. She could of course accept Ian and accept all that came with. And keep her house and job. But she knew she couldn't. And once she'd told him that, if Ian exposed her lie to HR, then she could be sacked on the spot. No notice. Instant dismissal. She might get a few weeks in the house. But elephantine thought of moving everything. Furniture, crockery, linen, clothes. And where to?

'You can't beat hot grub,' said the man. 'Three regular meals a day. In the warm. Getting chilly these nights.' He gave her a toothy smile. 'I hope it's Newham General, not Whipps Cross.'

'I'm sure it'll be Newham,' she said giving his hand a squeeze. 'It's only half a mile away. Warm and dry for you there. Good food. They'll look after you.'

'Just like a holiday,' said the man.

Chapter 10

Jack sat on the wall, a few feet from the section he was taking down, which was now just a few brick courses from ground level. His thermos and bag of sandwiches were beside him on the flat top. It was warm, he hadn't wanted to stay in the mess hut for his tea break, though he'd been invited to when he went in to wash his hands. He'd pleaded the sunshine, and that was true enough, but he'd rather be alone with his thoughts.

Liz was still a maybe. He'd clocked that much from the look she gave him, the smile by the side of the sick man, though she was too caught up in her Florence Nightingale ministrations for conversation. It somewhat disgusted him that he could consider sexual adventures on such occasions. But hormones are psychopaths Just as well no one could read his mind. His selfish forebrain, sprinkled with a deceitful flavouring of sympathy to make him appear civilised.

If she didn't happen, then he should invite the leafy woman over. Or would he be confirming the invite she'd already made for herself? Either way, he could press her to make a date of it or at least be straight with him. He could go and see her at lunch. Though she might be in the mess hut with everyone else and he'd have to entice her out somehow, with everyone watching. So what? He'd be away in the next few days. Let them say what they liked about him. She was racy, no doubt about that. But a manipulator too. Who was calling the kettle black? Working out his chances with either of the two women. But he'd seen Leafy on the phone a little while back, her machine switched off, in animated chat. Either fixing up something for this evening or teasing some other berk.

How can you trust anyone?

Commonsense told him Liz was the better of the two. They'd talked, not sparred. She was attractive and listened. Arty too. She'd hinted at a telescope session in the park. Could be arranged, she'd said. More than a hint. But the other, the leaf woman, was up front and asking for it. Or a hot tease.

Between musings, he'd kept half an eye on the paramedics. The ambulance had pulled into the park a few minutes ago. The vehicle had parked maybe thirty yards beyond Jack, by the side of the tennis courts. A man and a woman had jumped out of the cab, he would've shown them where to go, but Ian had come out of the yard and immediately taken over. He directed them across the grass with their stretcher, one or the other coming back every so often to get bits and pieces out of the ambulance. He couldn't see what was going on with the invalid because of the marquee in the way.

An old man was coming towards him, walking slowly with a briar cane. He was wearing a greyish suit and what they called a pork pie hat. Jack hadn't seen one of them for years. An odd item to perch on your head. It didn't seem very stable. The man had passed the ambulance and stopped for a little while by the tennis courts to watch what the paramedics were up to before continuing his stroll.

Jack thought about having a bite. He was peckish. Maybe half his sandwiches now with a second cup, save the other for lunch.

'Good morning,' said the old man when he reached Jack.

'Morning,' said Jack. 'What they doing down there?'

'Couldn't see much.' The old man shrugged. 'An injection

maybe and getting him on the stretcher... I live over there you know. That house. My son's the manager here. He said it's another of those Eastern Europeans.'

Jack could see the man's false teeth slipping. The old man pushed them in.

'We get a lot of them sleeping in here. They climb over the fence at night. We should have Alsatians wandering about. That'd keep 'em out.'

'He's English,' said Jack. 'From Hertfordshire.'

The man was disappointed, not knowing what to say about natives of Hertfordshire.

'Makes a change,' he said at last.

'How long you lived over there?' said Jack, hoping to change the subject.

'Five years. Since I retired. I was a foreman myself, sort of like my son. I got another son, he's a teacher, his marriage blown to bits. Lives up in Manchester.' He sniffed, looking at the wall Jack was working on. 'You're doing a good job cleaning them bricks.'

'Thank you,' he said, grateful to have got the man off his diatribe. 'I'm going to reuse them.'

'I was a brickie myself, before I got made up to foreman.' He wagged his finger, reminiscent of his son, 'I could hump twenty bricks on a hod, and run up three ladders with 'em.'

Jack didn't believe him, having heard this too many times on sites. A stupid boast anyway, with too many old builders ending up with back trouble.

'One in each hand is enough for me,' said Jack with a smile.

The man blew a raspberry. 'I'd've sacked you in five minutes.'

'I'd get the union on you.'

'Bleeding unions!' His stick was waving fiercely to battle off union tigers. 'Rainy day payments. Health and safety, this, that and the other. All a way of skiving off.'

'People die on building sites,' said Jack.

'People die everywhere. I'm going to die. You're going to die.'

'I don't have to die because scaffolding falls on me.'

'Codswallop. A load of softy tosh. You and your lot cause all the trouble.'

'Fine,' said Jack wearily. 'And if you don't mind, I'd like to have my tea in peace.'

From behind the marquee, the paramedics appeared, stretchering the ill man, followed by Ian and Liz.

'How much is that costing us?' exclaimed the old man. 'Ambulance, doctors, nurses, drugs... All coming out of our taxes.'

'I'm having my tea,' said Jack in annoyance. 'That man is ill. Why don't you go off and kick a tree? And leave me alone.'

'Filth,' exclaimed the old man and spat by Jack's foot. 'Union scum.'

'And Merry Christmas to you too, pal,' said Jack with a cheery wave.

The paramedics had laid their charge in the ambulance. One of them was putting a blanket over him, the other climbing out of the back. And then the doors were pulled shut from the inside. The paramedic outside, a woman in mauve overalls, ran round to the front and was quickly in the cab. The vehicle started up and began to back slowly up the drive beeping, on its way to the main gate. The old man pressed against the wall to give the ambulance room.

Once the vehicle had come past, Ian and Liz were approaching, watching its progress along the drive.

'What'd they reckon?' said Jack to Liz who'd stopped close by.

She shrugged. 'Heart attack. He'll probably need an operation. And then he'll be back out on the streets. And then what? Winter'll be here in a few weeks. No one should be on the streets.'

'Poor bloke,' said Jack, lacking the mental wherewithal to remedy the country's injustices.

The old man was talking to his son and waving his stick in Jack's direction. Jack wondered what the old man was telling him. Not likely to be complimentary, but then the manager already had his own views, so what did it matter?

'I'm sorry about our tea,' she said.

He turned to her and smiled, pleased to have someone more pleasant than the cantankerous old man to converse with.

'These things happen,' he said.

'I couldn't do much for him really,' she said, 'but I didn't want to leave him with Ian. Not that he'd have kicked his head in or anything. But he just hates anyone trespassing in his park.'

'So does his old man.'

'They take it personally,' she said. 'As if they own it.' She sighed. 'And now I'd better get some work done.'

'Might I come over with my telescope this evening?' She looked at him, eyes arched. 'You said earlier...'

She was thoughtful, biting her lip. Was she going to slam this one away?

'I've got an evening class this evening,' she said at last. 'You could come about nine. I'll make us a bite of supper...'

'And I'll show you Mars and the Andromeda Galaxy.'

Chapter 11

Rose wondered who else she might text. Or maybe go for that builder. He wasn't a bad looker and seemed keen enough. She didn't want another night in the bowling green pavilion. It got so cold in the early hours. She shivered to think of herself last night with all her clothes on and her knees huddled to her chest. There's the payoff for a cheap sleeping bag, OK for a midsummer night at Glastonbury but not much else.

She'd make a play at lunchtime. Firm up the invite. And if one of her texts came up, maybe drop him or maybe not. Why not give him a try? Couldn't be worse than some of the fumblers she'd had. OK when stoned, unbearable in the light of day. It was inviting them back to Liz's which got her kicked out. Her sister was as staid as a nun; five years older but you'd think Liz was her mother. Still, it had to be admitted the cottage was warm. Lovely and warm, no fares, and Liz always had food in the house, and didn't bug her for money, well – not that much. The hassles were about cleaning up and the racket at four in the morning, with men who came and went.

The problem was, useless men or otherwise, she was a night person. Could she help that? She could function on three hours' sleep. Day wasn't her time.

Back to the builder, she had yet to suss out the basics. Typical, her mother might say, if she ever gave her the chance. Anyone can flirt; that proved nothing. The guy might be married with three screaming kids. So check it out that he had a place on his own. She wasn't pushing for a screw in the back of his van, and then to be bundled out into the cold night air.

Jack of All Trades, she'd seen it on his van. That gave her a chuckle. She might just test it out.

There were maybe a dozen children present in the playground as she came in with the vac, all pre-school, with their mothers. She'd hate to be trapped with a sprog all day. Her idea of hell, stuck with a pushchair, fully attendant on a two year old, grasping and hollering. She shuddered. Even worse than a leaf vac.

A couple were gossiping as they pushed their toddlers on the swings, a regular haunt, she recognised them. A child of unknown sex was expertly climbing the net rope pyramid, watched by a mother who pleaded with him/her to be careful, Frankie.

Frankie had reached the top with Mummy pleading with him/her to come down. But Frankie was smart, and was sticking it out as she upped the offer: a bar of chocolate, sausages and beans for dinner, an ice cream. Frankie came quickly down.

Amy came out of the playground office, hardly an office really with its single chair and small table. She was a short, heavy woman who'd put on extra weight since being put on a regime of diabetic pills over the last year. All those steroids, she'd said, instead of making her into an Olympic athlete had made her a puffball. Though to her surprise, she'd discovered her husband preferred her big, which just went to show. Over her blonde, streaked hair, she wore a green woolly hat that she'd crocheted to go with her park's overalls. She saw Rose, gave her a wave and crossed to her.

'You are so lucky to be working in the playground,' said Rose, curling her claws in mock attack. 'How do you swing that on the old pig?'

67

'My charm, darling,' smirked Amy, swaggering with a hand on her hip.

'While I'm stuck with this leaf vac. I'm sure he does it on purpose. He wants me to go. And I might just. What's the point anyway? I'm going to be dead by the time I'm 35 – do you know that?'

'I don't know it. And neither do you.'

'I'm certain of it. As certain of that as of anything. I've nothing to live for. So why bother to get old? My sister loves her greenhouses. It's sickening. Gets up early to paint and plant her vegetables. Me? I don't care about a thing. That's why I'll be dead. My life is a pointless waste of breath and food.'

'You should get married, have a family...'

'Oh!' she grimaced, 'you're just like my mother. I can't stand kids.'

'You're just saying that, Rose. All women want kids really.'

'I hate them. I see a woman with a pushchair and I think, tip it in the canal. A woman with a pregnant bump and I want to scream at her: the last thing the world needs is another kid! Stick a coat hanger up yourself!'

'I am appalled at you, Rose,' exclaimed Amy leaning away from the tirade. 'That's so wicked. Where would families be if everyone thought like you? The other week, I was at the christening for my niece's first child. It was lovely. The baby girl in a white silk dress, water tipped over her head and given a name, Jamie, with her parents, aunties and uncles and all the grannies and granddads dressed to the nines...'

'Stop! All that sickly, drippy grinning stuff with the baby shitting its nappy – as if it's never been done before. Yuk! Another mouth to feed, another me, me, me, who'll want a house, a car and a job on this crowded tip of a planet...' Rose glared round the playground at the children and mothers. 'We should stop every one of them breeding for twenty years. A no child policy. And after that, it's one in ten allowed to have one baby only, by ballot... until we've got the numbers down to a billion. Then the rest of us could breathe without bumping into people, and choking on their effluent.'

'You're so selfish, Rose. I can't believe your attitude. You would deny anyone the joy of a family.'

'And you'd have the world packed so tight we'll be standing shoulder to shoulder, so that all we'll be able to do is screw, until we've squished ourselves into a great ball of lard.'

Amy threw her hands up. 'Then kill yourself, Rose. Do us all a great favour, don't wait till you're 35, and don't give me no more of this baby killing rubbish.'

Rose might have given her quite a bit more of her baby bashing tirade as she was enjoying taunting her, but a thin woman pushing a pushchair had come over. And Rose had to stop. The woman stopped by Amy.

'Is it you who does the Women Fly Women thing?' she said shyly.

'I do,' said Amy.

'I want in,' said the woman.

'Have you got the flight price?'

'I have,' said the woman and began to take some money out of her handbag.

'Let's go to the office,' said Amy and led the woman away from Rose to the playground office.

Rose watched. She had known for some time that Amy was up to something in the playground, some little money making scheme, but didn't know what. Amy was evasive when asked directly. But here she was in action and the woman eager to buy in. Rose knew she should be vaccing the playground, but she just had to know what was going on.

Except she couldn't see much. Amy was in the office, the

top half of the door was swung open obscuring her view so she could only see the bottom half of the woman with her pushchair and its occupant. Rose turned on her vac and began sweeping in their direction, more intent on what was going on in the hut than picking up leaves. She saw or thought she saw the rapid passing of notes, and the woman hurriedly putting a box into a shopping bag hanging on the handle of the pushchair.

When the woman had gone, Rose hoovered up to Amy and turned off the machine.

'What's Women Fly Women?' she said.

'Why? Do you want in?' Amy was sharp, her face concentrated, none of the usual easy giggles about her.

'How much do I need?'

'Two hundred.'

'I've got it.' Rose hadn't, but knew she wouldn't get any information if she didn't pretend. 'What do I get for it?'

Amy took her to the office and opened the top half of the door. There were a pile of white boxes, each about 20 centimetres square, taking up much of the floor space. Amy picked one up.

'This.'

'What is it?' said Rose.

Amy opened the carton. Inside were lots of ornate little bottles of an amber liquid. Amy pulled one out and gave it to Rose.

'Smell it.'

Rose twisted off the gold top and gingerly smelt the liquid. 'Perfume.' She sniffed again. 'Quite nice.' She put the cap back on. 'Is that all I get for 200 quid?'

Amy took the bottle from her and put it on the office desk.

'There's 20 bottles in this carton. You sell each one for a tenner...'

'That just gets me my money back,' Rose shrugged. 'All sweat and no profit.'

Amy tapped her nose conspiratorially. 'But you don't lose any. And that makes you a passenger.'

'But I've badgered all my friends, just to get my original two hundred.'

'The next step,' said Amy, 'is to sign three of them up. You get a tenner for each one you bring in.'

Rose shrugged. '30 quid for all that hassle. Not even minimum wage.'

Amy ignored her and went on. 'Then in three months you get a £1000 pay out.'

Rose was startled. 'How does that work?'

'It's all the profit up the line. It's why that woman was so eager to sign up. Her mate just got £1000.' Amy smirked at Rose. 'It's winners all round. Women Fly Women.'

'How much are you making on it?'

'That'd be telling. I'm a pilot, so of course I make more.'

'You a pilot? Where's your plane?'

Amy sighed. 'It's just what I'm called. When you buy the box of scent you become a passenger. Then when you bring in three others, you become a crew member. And I'm the next rung up, a pilot.'

'Who's over you?'

'The captain.'

'Then who?'

'The marshal and that's the top.'

Rose was scratching her head, trying to work it all out. 'Who's your captain?'

'You're not even in yet and asking me all these questions.'

'Two hundred quid you want – and I can't ask how it works?'

'Do you want to make a thousand or not?'

'Of course I do.'

Amy laughed. 'And you told me there's nothing you want.' She rubbed her fingers together. 'Money, that attracts you. You want to be rich.'

'Well, it's better to be rich than poor. But you don't understand, Amy. There's nothing I want to do with my life. Being rich would give me nice clothes and a decent place to live – but I know I'd be bored, because it's all pointless.'

'Oh, you give me the pip! A woman at your age, with your looks, shouldn't have any trouble. Find yourself a man.'

'And then get stuck cooking and cleaning for him and wiping babies' bottoms.'

Amy pointed across the playground. 'Ian's heading this way. I think you'd better look active. And if you want to be in Women Fly Women then get me the flight price – and you're off.'

The two women split as Ian came into the playground. Rapidly Rose had the vac sucking, as Amy strolled about the playground smiling at the users.

PART TWO:
THE MURDER

Chapter 12

Bill stopped for a cigarette, a thin rollup, pre-prepared in his tobacco tin. At the tea break he'd made himself three to last till lunch. If he couldn't give up, he liked to claim he had enough willpower to limit himself to three prison slims. And so what if they killed you. Living did that anyway.

Zar was forking out the border of alyssums on the flower bed they were both working on, and loading them into a wheelbarrow. Bill had done almost half the snapdragons that filled the centre. The bed looked at its worst, half cleared and trampled, half full of keeling plants, like despairing orphans in a witch's orphanage.

'When d'you start your day release?' asked Bill between puffs.

'Next Monday,' said Zar.

'So who's going to be doing your work here?'

'You,' said Zar with a laugh. 'You won't mind that, will you?'

'I never went on day release,' said Bill rasping his lips. 'I learnt on the job. There's nothing in those books.'

'There's got to be something in them,' insisted Zar, 'all those words and pictures, on all those pages. Got to be something, Bill.'

'Nothing that's useful.' He stomped the ground. 'Out here, on the ground is where you learn. Tell me something useful you got from a book.'

'What's an F1 hybrid?' asked Zar.

'Well, it's a type of hybrid...'

'That's in the name. Anyone could work that out. But what type of hybrid is it,' pressed Zar.

'And how's that useful to me? Why should I waste my time learning it?'

'You don't have to. I'll waste my time learning it for you, Bill. To save you the bother.'

Bill flicked away his dog end. 'You'll end up so whooshy clever, you won't be able to do the spring bedding, so up in the air clever you won't be here to prune a rose, or trench dig a flower bed. And those without their heads in a book will have to do it for you, and on half your office-wallah money.'

Zar forked the last of the alyssums into the barrow.

'Did you know there were death stalks in the shrubbery, Bill?'

'What's a death stalk when it's at home?'

'Poisonous mushrooms. Why don't you read it up? There must be someone you want to kill.' And without waiting for a reply, he took the handles of the wheelbarrow, and set off across the grass to the yard.

There was no point arguing with Bill. You could never win. The best thing to do was take the mickey out of him. Undercut him. Though he was a good gardener, but you wouldn't want to be his apprentice.

Zar came into the yard, past the two piles of bricks, the new and the reclaimed bricks the builder was gradually taking into the yard. At the dump end was Rose with her vac. She was sluggishly emptying the bag of leaves.

'Liz says it's your birthday,' he said.

'I wish she wouldn't tell people,' she said crossly. 'It's nothing to be proud of. Being 30. Just that bit nearer death.'

'You're in the prime of life, Rose.'

She indicated the leaf dump. 'Is this really the prime, Zar?'

'Who knows what the future's going to bring?'

'Nothing.'

'Then forget the future and enjoy the present.'

'Oh God, Zar, you sound like one of those new age hippies.'

'I was only thinking of buying some cakes to celebrate your birthday and my going on day release.'

Rose smiled at him sadly. 'Oh, it's a pity you're so young, Zar.'

'What, not old and worn out like you?'

She punched him on the shoulder. 'I was going to say because you're the nicest person in this park, but I've changed my mind. Bill is.'

They both laughed.

'Do you want to come out and get some cakes with me?' he said.

'Yes.' She sucked her lower lip thoughtfully. 'Chocolate éclairs or Danish slices? You win. I'm a convert to your religion. Take me to the temple of cake, oh master.'

'One more load, then we'll head off.'

Chapter 13

Ian left his office. He straightened his tie. The leaf vac had been parked untidily by the dump, taking up too much room. He moved it to a better position, out of the way. So easy, why don't people do it? He'd tell Rose off. Or maybe not. She was Liz's sister, might be his sister-in-law. He'd need to think that one out. How relationships change. Though Rose could be so sloppy.

He was nervous. This lunch. How might it go? Would you invite someone to lunch to give them the push? Didn't seem likely. But could be a way of getting the best out of him, short of marriage. He must take it step by step, see exactly what she was offering, and never forget that he held the ace. And she must know that he would play it.

The whole point of a deterrent.

In the yard, he noted the builder had piled his reclaimed brick by the new brick pile. Neat enough. He didn't want another argy bargy with him. Provided he did his work, though he had seen Liz talking to him earlier. About what? That was the thing with women, how much could you trust them?

That was part of what had broken them up. She went out a lot, to various classes, her painting courses. She talked to people for too long – and he got jealous. He couldn't help it. He saw the way they looked at her. And she was his. He knew what men were like.

He came out of the yard. There was the builder sitting on the wall eating his lunch like he owned the place. To hell with him and his old bricks. He'd be gone soon enough. Cocky so and so, legs spread like he was ready for it. If Ian had a pitch fork, he'd teach him to be ready.

Cool it. This was no way to be. Jealous of a brickie. He was ten times better. This was his park. He had the ace.

Ian turned away from the bricklayer and walked down the drive. Bowling green fine, though the verandah of the pavilion could do with a sweep. Get Zar on it. Tennis courts clear of leaves, but the net was sagging. Get Amy to tighten it. A couple of male pensioners were playing on one of the courts, a lot of talking, not much hitting. The other court was empty.

Ian crossed onto the lawn and looked in the marquee. Liz's cascade was half out, the frame of it, a sort of staircase thing that would have plants trailing down the edges and water flowing down the middle. She'd had an interrupted morning with that dosser, so excusable how much she'd done, what with her greenhouse work. Perhaps she needed some assistance.

Wednesday had to be pukka. No mistakes, the park looking good, everyone on best behaviour. He would be judged by it and it had to be right.

Ian crossed to the playground but didn't go in. Clear of leaves, all but the paddling pool. That needed a clearing and hose down. Really, it could do with a cover, or it just collected rubbish. Money, it was all about money. Budgeting drove him crackers.

He turned into the Mayor's Avenue. The cottages were at the end. There were two rows of oak trees, set in from the drive, six on one side, five on the other; each planted by a mayor of the borough, but this Wednesday the retiring Member of Parliament would add his as well. Two holes had to be made ready, one on either side, totally circular and neat, a post in the centre of each. Tomorrow he'd set Bill and Zar on it.

Ian looked in the rose garden. It hadn't been vacced. Really, vaccing should be no more than a morning's work. How she dragged it out! He'd seen her jawing to Zar and Amy... If he wasn't watching, she'd jaw all day and do nothing else.

But she was his putative sister in law. If things went as he hoped. His stomach was all a skitter. This could go either way. Lunch could mean she accepted the inevitable, saw it was all for the best. She would grow to love him as he became part of her life. As they went places together, foreign holidays and so forth.

She was a vegetarian. Another difficulty last time, his meat eating. A meal wasn't a meal without a chop, a piece of steak, bacon, a couple of burgers even. He'd have to compromise there, though how much? That was the difficulty. She would have to compromise too. He couldn't expect her to become a meat-eater; he'd tried that last time and it just ended in too many rows. She was a vegetarian, he would accept that. One hundred per cent. But he was a meat-eater. There was room for both in the world.

Dead heading. After the rose garden had been vacced, Rose could do that.

He'd stopped, halfway up the drive. He didn't know what he was walking into. Was she really in any position to say no to him? And he wouldn't stand for any prevaricating. If it was on, it was on. And no messing him about.

He took a deep breath and strode out smartly. She might be looking out of the window, he must appear confident and in charge. He held the big trump. And she knew it.

He opened the gate of her cottage and walked down the short path. She was in the kitchen and waved to him through the window. So no need to ring. He stood at the door, breathing regularly, his shoes smartly together as if he were courting.

She opened the door and gave him a nervous smile.

'Come in, Ian.'

He wiped his feet on the mat and she led him into the kitchen where food was spread on the table.

'You have been busy,' he said.

'I left a little early,' she said, 'as this was rather important.'

She held out a chair for him and he sat down. She took her place opposite. It was a small table, just large enough for two. And she had prepared a plate of food for them both with pie and sauce, lettuce, spring onions, tomatoes and a rice salad.

'This looks awfully nice. How did you prepare it so quickly?'

'The salad I had anyway, and the pie I just added to and microwaved. And sauce is only a few minute job. A mushroom, walnut and tahini quick fry.'

'I'll take your word for it.' He tentatively tried the pie. 'It's very tasty.'

'Don't sound so surprised.'

'I know you're a good cook, Liz.'

He was on careful ground. No threats. She poured them both a glass of white wine. He noted her hand was shaking. What could that mean? She raised her glass.

'Cheers.'

'Cheers.' He raised his to hers and they clinked.

It could go either way, he thought, the meal a sort of consolation prize. But he mustn't bull into it, that would be asking for trouble. He saw she was nervously eating, trying to smile, not too successfully. She'd changed into a dress, a summery affair, a paisley design, shapely. She was beautiful out of her overalls, though even in them, saggy things, she had a feminine presence.

The pie was good, he wasn't just saying it. It almost tasted meaty. The sauce lovely. He didn't want to talk shop with her, the Mayor coming and all that. Nor yet get down to their real business, much as he wanted to know what she'd decided. Chat. Not something he was good at, but try.

'That's a lovely dress,' he said.

'I thought overalls wouldn't do,' she said.

'Is the salad from your garden?'

'The tomatoes are, as well as the spring onions and the spinach in the pie. That's the last of my lettuce.'

'Home grown food tastes so much better,' he said. 'The tomatoes have flavour. Some of the supermarket ones, well they look like tomatoes, but they lack sweetness.'

'The big vegetable growers simply go for big croppers,' she said. 'They look good, like a tomato or carrot, but taste pulpy. Whereas in your own garden, flavour is number one. A tomato that tastes like a tomato.'

'Exactly.'

This was going well, fairly easy conversation. He took a sip of wine. They could eat together, so important for any future. He didn't mind at all there was no meat in the lunch. He could compromise. And surely she could.

'More pie?' she said.

'Yes, please.'

She gave him a slice and poured sauce on top from the jug, her hand a little shaky which endeared her to him. She needed his protection.

'The trick to a good meal,' she said, 'is the colours. It's like a painting really. If it looks attractive, contrasting colours, then you want to eat it.'

'This is very good.'

She beamed at him. At last. Well, it was time then. The big question had to be broached.

'Have you thought about my proposal?' he said carefully, as nervous as if he were about to go on stage.

'I have,' she said. 'And there's a few things to clear up before I give my answer.'

'Go ahead.' He took a forkful of pie, hardly aware he was

doing it, simply needing to be doing something.

'Suppose we got married,' she said, 'and it didn't work. What then?'

He cut the pie on his plate into manageable pieces, aware his hands weren't steady. Important question, and in the right direction.

'You'd have to give it a fair go, Liz, before calling it a day,' he said. 'Let's say after five years. If it isn't working, then we could separate.'

He watched her keenly. She nodded. Good. He worked to even his breathing.

'And you wouldn't expose me?' she said.

'I wouldn't.'

'Even if we divorced?'

'No. Even if we decide to divorce. We will have given it a fair try. Five years. I can't ask more of you than that.'

'More salad, Ian? More pie?' She held up the dish; her hand was shaking again.

'I will have some more, if you don't mind. It's delicious.'

He lifted his plate, she put a generous portion on, and then poured sauce over the top.

'Lovely,' he said, taking a bit. 'I hope I can work after all this. Only a town hall meeting with the brass this afternoon, and they'll have been out for a big lunch themselves.'

'Where would we live?' she said.

'My place is slightly bigger than yours.'

He had already considered this aspect, and thought it a pity they couldn't have both the houses. Knock them through. But it wouldn't be allowed.

'What about your father?' she said.

'I can't kick him out. Can I?'

He took a sip of wine. She refilled his glass and then her own. For a little while both contemplated this matter. He could see, by the way she was wiping her brow, how important this was to her. Totally understandable.

'He can be difficult,' she said. 'He might get between us. Being there, always.'

'Never easy,' he said, 'living with an in-law.' He had thought about this one. A newly married couple want the place to themselves. They have a life to work out. His father wasn't an easy man to live with, he had to admit that. Three in the living room, three at meal times. It would be a source of arguments.

'A dominant in-law,' she said, 'would come between us.'

There was no getting round it. But it was clear to him. He wanted her, far more than he wanted his father.

'I'll find sheltered housing for him,' he said, surprising himself with the degree of his compromise.

'Before we marry?'

'Yes.'

My god. It was happening. She was coming towards him so quickly, as they cleared away the obstacles one by one.

'And my working?' she said. 'I want to carry on.'

'I'm happy with that,' he said, almost adding 'my dear', but not yet. He must not make it look like he knew it was happening. 'We would make a good team. Run the best park in the borough.'

'And I can trust you, on your honour, to keep to what you are now offering?'

'You can, my dear.'

He'd said it. This was the very moment, the one they had been building up to. His fork halfway to his mouth awaited.

'Then I accept your offer, Ian. I'll be your wife.'

He dropped the fork to his plate and his hands went to his head. He cried out in joy.

'Oh my dear, my darling, Liz...' She beamed across the table at him. 'I am so happy.' And he hadn't had to mention the employment contract at all. That could have been such a spoiler to this celebration. He raised his glass.

'To us.'

'To us.'

They clinked glasses and drank. He couldn't stop looking at her. She was to be his. His wife. Liz, so beautiful. She had agreed. He had heard her, clear and free of coercion. And without any unpleasantness. He must be worthy of her. He had his part to play.

'When?' he queried.

'Let's give us time to get everything organised,' she said. 'We want a decent sized wedding... Say six months?'

'That's fine.' He was nodding like a dog in a car window. He'd never been so happy. 'When can we announce it?'

'When you've bought me a ring.'

She held out her ring finger, awaiting his diamond.

'I'll get it in the next few days.' Of course he would. 'You promise to wear it?'

'Certainly I will. With pride.'

He poured wine into both their glasses. And raised his.

'To the engagement of Ian and Liz.'

'To our engagement.'

They clinked glasses and drank. He gazed at the face gazing back at him. She looked a little afraid. Perfectly understandable. It was a big step to take.

'More pie, Ian?'

'Just a little. It is delicious, my dear.'

Chapter 14

Jack was on the wall eating his lunch. He'd gone to the van to get his fleece and to the mess hut to refill his thermos. There were only two of them in there. The rotund woman and the old moaner. She was happy for him to take tea and milk, but the grouch on his own may well have begrudged it. She'd invited Jack to stay, but he'd pleaded fresh air. Often he'd found mess huts stuffy, and in small ones, especially, you were stuck with the dominant conversation which so easily dropped into casual racism. And then he felt compelled to respond, and cowardly if he didn't. And if there was an aggressive comeback, his head would be taken over for the next few hours.

So, peace in the autumn sunshine.

He'd read his Daily Mirror. War, disease, and footballers behaving badly. So goes the planet. His sandwiches were on the stale side. He ate them anyway; it was that or go to a café – an expense he was reluctant to make. It was a bad habit eating out at lunchtime. A couple of sandwiches made at home were a quarter of the price.

He'd best do some shopping on the way home.

But all in all, things were looking up. She'd agreed to him coming over with his telescope. About nine. And then supper. Jack assessed the sky. There was some cirrus cloud about but plenty of clear blue. He hoped it stayed that way or what would he say to her, if it clouded over? Cross fingers. By the marquee was a good place for the telescope. In fact, shelter if it was windy.

And then supper. He rubbed his hands together.

Twice he had spoken to her, neither time had she said much but each time he'd picked up on her sensitivity. She was more than a good-looker, admittedly he'd take sex when it was offered by an attractive woman, but she had more. A soul mate. But if you don't believe in a soul, then what was it? It reminded him of AA, the Higher Power that you should submit to in the Twelve Steps. Call it a doorknob, they told the non-religious. Call a soul mate a doorknob, call love a doorknob.

All words. Twisted and devalued.

Was that his problem? No faith. Not believing in doorknobs. And why in the end any relationship he had would shatter into disbelieving bits.

In the meantime, make the best of it. The sun was shining, the wall was coming down, and stargazing and supper were on the evening timetable. Hope on, and stay the course. He had a couple of hundred or so in the bank, another job starting next week. Just a few days' work, but something else might turn up. You never know. Wasn't that what kept him going?

Uncertainty.

Jack toasted his fortune in tea. Anything could happen. It probably wouldn't, but you never know.

At what point in your life do you give up? Realise this is it, till you drop down dead. And, of course, if you believe that then it is all the more likely. You won't even buy a lottery ticket.

Zar and that woman were coming towards him from the main gate. Sexy even in her baggy overalls, but then she was one of those who'd be alluring in anything. The dinner-date-maybe woman. Zar was swinging a full carrier bag.

They stopped by him.

'Been shopping?' said Jack.

'Cakes for tea,' he said holding up the bag. 'To celebrate Rose's birthday and my day release.'

Rose, he said to himself, at last, a name for a body.

'Shall we invite him?' said Zar to Rose.

'What?' she said, hands on hips in a mocking stance, 'a builder with cement under his fingernails?'

'That's tomorrow,' said Jack. 'Today I'm just covered in brick dust.'

'Then I'll lay you down in the yard,' she said, 'and run you over with the leaf vac. Then you can come.'

'I'll put the cakes in the fridge,' said Zar. 'See you later.'

He left them.

Rose sat on the wall, partly over the gap.

'Budge up,' she said.

He moved along a couple of feet and she moved next to him until they were touching.

'I hope you're not corrupting that young man,' he said.

She gave a short laugh. 'Is that what you think of me?'

He nodded. 'A very corrupting person.'

'Well, you needn't worry about Zar,' she said, adding in a lower voice, 'I think he's gay.'

'What makes you think that?'

She shrugged. 'He's not forever looking me up and down, like some people.' She nudged him. 'Know what I mean?'

'You do have a nice up and down,' he said.

'Before we go any further, I have a few questions for you.'

'An interview, Ms Up and Down?'

'You could say so.'

He looked at his hands and overalls. 'I'm not dressed for it.'

'I'll take you as you are. Question one.' She paused to get his attention. 'Are you married?'

'Divorced, two years ago. I have a 12 year old daughter

who lives with her mum in Brighton.'

'8 out of 10. A pass. Next question. Very important this one.' She turned and looked him in the eye. 'Do you have your own place? I mean, do you live on your own.'

He laughed; this was a sizing up for certain ends, but okay, let's see where it leads.

'I have a small flat, one bedroom. And I live on my own.'

'Full marks. Good. Next question. Have you a girlfriend? I mean fixed. Not the odd date now and again with any old scrubber. Are you itemised?'

'I am free,' he said.

'Another one with full marks. Nine out of ten overall. That's a merit. And a merit deserves...' She rubbed her hands together as if warming them. 'Dinner this evening. Your place.'

He felt somewhat cornered, not unpleasantly. She was a force.

'I'm going out tonight,' he said reluctantly.

'Can you cancel it?'

'No.' He just couldn't. Not even if... He just couldn't.

'I suppose that's in your favour,' she said. 'Though I'd definitely cancel if I had a better offer. But there you go. First date?'

'Yes.'

'Her place?'

'Yes.'

He was a sucker for her directness. Straight in, no messing. She knew what she had.

'Okay,' she said. 'I'll do a deal, Mister Bricklayer.'

'Jack.'

'Fine, Jack. I'm glad we are on first name terms. Where was I? Oh yes, the deal. I'm currently between houses. Or, let's come clean; I'm homeless. My sister kicked me out on Saturday. I slept in the bowling green pavilion last night. And I froze.' She clutched her arms round herself and shuddered to give the feeling. 'I don't want that again. So let me come back with you after work. And if you score with your date, good luck to you. If you don't, then you'll have someone to come home to.' She put a hand on his thigh. 'What d'you say, Jack?'

'Interesting deal,' he said.

'Is that a yes or a no, or a give me a week to think about it?'

He should say no. Commonsense said that. He didn't know her. She might smash the place up, rob him...

'Yes,' he said. 'A deal.'

'Shake on it.'

They shook hands for rather a long time. Anywhere else and Jack would have... He looked around for somewhere suitable.

She broke away, and jumped off the wall.

'I hope your date goes badly.' She straightened her overalls. 'Cakes at three. Don't forget.'

And headed into the compound.

Chapter 15

Liz was down the far end of the greenhouse when Zar entered. It was an overwhelming feast coming into her jungle. The heat hit you at once along with the luxuriant green filling much of the space. And then the flowers came at you, here and there, as you ventured further in. A climbing begonia today, spiralling round its post, throwing out deep red florets as it made its way to the glass roof.

She was almost hidden in ferns, potting up. There was a mound of compost on the bench, which she was putting into a very large pot. To one side was a pot-bound Bird of Paradise. She stopped working when she saw Zar, wiping her hands on her plastic apron.

'I'm looking for Ian,' he said. 'Do you know where he is?'

'He's at the town hall till after three. I'm in charge until he gets back. What's the problem?'

'Well,' he began, 'I had a wander round the park at lunch time. A twenty minute stroll, looking at the trees. You know?'

She nodded. 'Good for you. I like to have a wander myself.'

'This is not about trees though. They're alright,' he half laughed. 'But I found something else I thought I'd better report.'

'What's that, Zar?'

'Death stalk mushrooms, growing at the base of a couple of beech trees.' He stopped. 'Do you know about death stalks?'

'A little,' she said. 'Very poisonous I hear. Where did you find them?'

'They're growing in the big shrubbery, I haven't seen them anywhere else – but they might be elsewhere.'

'I'm glad you've told me,' she said, rubbing the side of her face, making marks from the soil. 'I'm wondering the best thing to do.' She expired deeply, contemplating.

'I spotted them yesterday but I wasn't sure, so last night I went online to check,' said Zar. 'And yes, they're death stalks. If you eat them, it can be eight or more hours before any symptoms appear. Then the victim vomits and has terrible stomach cramps... But by then it's too late to do anything.'

She put a hand on his arm. 'Enough of that. You're giving me the shivers.' She bit her knuckle. 'Let me think, Zar.' She started to bite her thumbnail, tasted the soil in it and took it out of her mouth, and wiped her hands on her apron. 'Right. We don't want to panic everyone. So I want you to keep this to yourself. Especially with the ceremony on Wednesday. It would never do to have a hoo-ha with all the bigwigs here...' Adding on reflection, 'Or even without them. A child might...'

'I could gather up the ones I've seen,' interrupted Zar, 'then see if I can find any more.'

'That would be the best thing to do,' she mused, 'except we need to give you a reason for looking everywhere.'

'I could be doing a tree inventory,' said Zar excitedly. 'Official.'

'Oh, what a great idea,' exclaimed Liz. 'In fact, we could have one for the ceremony, so there'd be some point to it. Come over here.' And she ushered Zar to her desk area. She gave her hands another wipe and took a blank sheet of A4 and a pencil. 'Let's do a plan of the park.' She began drawing rapidly on the paper, the lines flowing as she spoke. 'There's the bowling green, next to it the tennis courts, then the playground, and across the drive to the rose garden, down the Mayor's Avenue to the two cottages, shrubberies here, here and here, the main lawn, the two glasshouses, and yard...'

'That's really good, Liz.'

'A first sketch,' she said, adding touches to her rough. 'Let's give you a clipboard.' She pulled one out and put the sketch into it, and handed it to Zar. 'There. You look thoroughly official. Now go round with your tree book, put all the trees in the park on the plan and label them.'

'And pick up any death stalks I see.'

'Exactly. Don't tell anyone. This is a tree inventory.'

'I could wear my backpack,' he said conspiratorially, 'have my tree book there, and hide any mushrooms in it.'

'That's the idea. You fill in that rough sketch. And I'll make it into an A1 park plan for the ceremony, with watercolours for the various areas. I could do it tomorrow night... Back it onto card and we could put it in the marquee on an easel. Give you credit for the inventory.'

Zar clapped his hands. 'Great.' He looked over her sketch on his clipboard. 'I'd better get going.'

'Don't tell anyone the real reason. You know what a gossip factory this place is. No panic. Trees, that's the excuse. Give the mushrooms to me and I'll burn them in my back garden.'

'Will do.' He was about to set off, then turned to her. 'Oh yes, you have to come to the mess hut at three. There's cakes for Rose's birthday and for me getting on day release. I know sometimes you don't come at tea breaks.'

'I'll be there, Zar. Promise. I'm really pleased you've got on day release. You deserve it. Now, off you go, before anyone else notices the you know what. Or children pick them, and then there'll be an awful fuss. You get to them first.'

Chapter 16

Rose was vaccing the rose garden. She minded it less here, being out of sight of the compound, and she could see anyone coming. Well, Ian. So as long as she kept the machine on, he would assume she was working. And, well, she might be, and she might not.

Did it matter? The leaves she didn't get today, she'd get tomorrow. There was a tedium in this work. Keeping a park tidy. If it was down to her then she'd leave it to nature, let her go her own way. But, of course, this was a city. The park would fill with rubbishy things, dumped by rubbishy people.

The rose garden was here to give the park a bit of class. A level above the usual municipal dog walk. And as such, the litter had to be continually cleaned up. She'd done more than her share of that. How come Amy always got off it? It wasn't fair.

Over there. Queen of the playground. Look, taking money off a woman. If that's four today, then Amy's cut is £80 – and the day's not over yet. Rose couldn't make out how it worked, Women Fly Women. Where the money went, how it came back. Not that she could get in on it; she didn't have the £200 to buy in. And even if she had, she'd need it to find a flat, what with deposits and agent's fees.

Tonight, at least she had something.

Pity he had a date. But there you go, a warm room couldn't be complained about, especially when she thought of last night. So cold in the bowling green pavilion. She must get somewhere permanent, but it was such a chore, and such seedy rooms for such astronomical prices. Even in Newham. Well, everyone came here now because it was cheap. Except it wasn't. Nothing was. And as for Stratford... Well, the Olympics and Westfield had made that strictly no-go. She'd love to get into the Olympic village, but Newham had twenty thousand on its waiting list. And it would do her no good going on it unless she had six kids, half a kidney and was in a wheelchair.

Private landlords simply fleeced those who couldn't afford to buy. And some of the squalid rooms she'd seen, you wouldn't put a dog in them.

Forget it for now. Too depressing, the whole rip-off scene. Tonight she had a room. Let tomorrow look after itself. Better do something.

There were only a few blooms left on the roses, dotted here and there, most of the foliage fallen. The blooms were the centenarians, hanging on in there like ultra wrinklies in an old people's home, everyone dying around them, and on they go to more birthdays, garnering up congratulations for simply living so long, forgetting everything in the present, but remembering so clearly all that happened a hundred years ago.

But in a few weeks, the last blooms would go, forgotten like all the rest. Don't kid yourself, she flicked a bloom. We come, we go and we are walked over. She'd made a song list for her funeral. That kept you in mind a little longer, some bouncy music, plus a good spread. She'd like an amusing epitaph on her gravestone, something people would stop and point out. As she vacced she considered these last words. Important, as she didn't have long.

'She played fast and loose. And in the end lost it.' Not bad. How about: 'Do not disturb. Having a long lie in.'

That amused her, like a message on a hotel room door. Except it wouldn't be allowed. She'd have to write it in Latin or Serbo-Croat. But then what would be the point of that, if most people couldn't read it? Maybe just burn and go. Leave nothing but a few ashes to be thrown in the gutter.

Zar caught her attention. He was in the shrubbery with a clipboard. What was he up to? He gave her a wave. She waved back. A nice kid. Bought her some lunch and paid for the cakes. She really shouldn't be so spendy. That came of living with Liz who could be relied on to pay for everything when Rose fell short, as she mostly did. Clubbing was costly. You needed the gear, plus cash for drinks and the dope...if you couldn't get them bought for you. Not forgetting the ticket.

Zar was at the back of the long shrubbery. The key was in his pocket for the bowling green pavilion which he'd been due to sweep out, but had been interrupted by the change of priorities. He'd get round to it later this afternoon most likely.

Or not. He shrugged. So what? This was so much better. He'd stopped by an ash, most of its leaves scattered about its foot, the buds sooty black. Unlikely to be any death stalks here. Mostly around beech and oak, the mushroom book said. But he liked the ash, the bark close ridged as if you could strike a light on it from its gunpowder buds. He rubbed his finger up and down, enjoying the crumbly texture. He couldn't believe it; he was getting paid to do this. Do a tree inventory. Any day of the week. And while you're at it, see if you can find any death stalks. Take as long as you need.

Nice one, Zar. Doing what he wanted to do, as work. Better bag this one. Look busy. He drew a circle on Liz's sketch and wrote by it: *Fraxinus excelsior*, and in brackets, Ash.

Best not take liberties. He owed it to Liz; she was trusting him. But the fact that he knew about trees and mushrooms was because he'd gone over the park with a book or two. Nature enthralled him, the variety of growing things, how they connected. Like the oak using the underground mycelium of the death stalk to make nitrogen. Or was it the other way round? But then it had to be both. Symbiosis. He'd have to check it out.

He crossed to a nearby beech. This one was legit. Death stalks grew around the roots of such trees. But not up in the air where he was looking. Such a muscular tree. Quite sexual, like a man's leg or a powerful arm. It was almost perverted looking at it.

Were other people turned on by trees? They did hug them, so maybe. Besides, it was harmless enough. He wasn't about to drop his trousers and stick his knob in a knot hole.

He strolled round the wide trunk, stepping carefully over the thick ropy roots. Ah! There was one poking out of the leaf mould. He knelt down to scrape the leaves away, and smoothed the soil away from its base with his fingers to show the cup-like volva that the stalk emerged from. No mistaking what it was. The volva was the clincher. Funny word. Like vulva, women's fannies. You could say fannies were like a cup, he supposed. Not his thing anyway. He was more turned on by the beech limbs. Though Rose had been trying it on at lunchtime, fluttering her eyelids at him in the café. He actually had to tell her to stop and she was quite offended for two minutes. Until the food came and she forgot.

He liked her, but she could be pretty heavy, when she wasn't trying to pull. She was so up and down.

Or like Volvo. Weird when you think about it. A Swedish automobile reminiscent of a poisonous mushroom, reminiscent of a fanny. You wonder what was in the car maker's head. Unconscious most likely, but sex, they say, is in everyone's head, all the time.

He dug his trowel under the mushroom and levered it out. What a beauty! Yellow cap, a hint of green, the gills underneath as soft as a flower petal.

He took the carrier bag out of his backpack and put the death stalk in, to join those already there. Then thrust the bag deep down in his backpack. Back to his alibi. He drew a circle on the plan, and by it wrote: *Fagus sylvatica* (beech).

Chapter 17

It was getting near Jack's tea break. Mustn't leave his tools out. Best to get these bricks in too, though he'd noted some barriers in the tool shed. He could put them round his workings. This being a park, he had to be more careful than he normally might be.

He filled his barrow with reclaimed brick, and laid on top his tools. And wheeled off into the yard. Past the tool shed, to the area by the dump where he'd already begun stacking his bricks. And added these to the pile. He left the barrow and tools there, to be picked up after the break. Then went to the tool shed and took out two wooden barriers. They were awkward to carry, and he reflected they would be easier on the wheelbarrow, but it wasn't far to go.

As he humped them across, he thought: this is the way to get back trouble. Too much trouble to use the wheelbarrow. It would take thirty seconds of his so valuable time.

Back at the wall, Jack placed them to protect the gap in the wall, now down to the last couple of courses. There was a pile of bricks he'd yet to knock the mortar off. Could he leave them out? It was a hassle to get the wheelbarrow, just to bring them out again after the break to work on them.

Behind the wall, he thought. And opened one of the barriers, and placed the bricks behind a good section of wall. Then put the barrier back. They should be safe there; they weren't visible and kids were still in school.

All this tidying up for a fifteen minute tea break.

As he was going in the yard, he saw Zar crossing the lawn heading his way, and Rose coming down the drive pushing her leaf vac. Liz was locking her greenhouses. It was as if a siren had gone off. Tea break! Eeeeeh! Bill had joined Zar on his way in. That just left the big lady, what was her name, anyway, her, but she wasn't coming.

Jack went in the mess hut. The urn in the corner was steaming away; he might have made the tea, but not being sure where everything was, and just a guest anyway, thought it best to leave it to the regulars. He washed his hands at the butler sink and took a seat on a side bench as the others came in. They quickly washed their hands in a huddle round the sink.

'Who invited him?' said Bill indicating Jack.

'Me and Rose,' said Zar.

'The place is hardly big enough for us lot.'

'The more people, the warmer,' said Liz with a broad smile.

Zar took up the tea pot, and set to making tea. Rose went to the china cupboard and removed two large plates and half a dozen smaller ones. She then went to the fridge and took out two cardboard boxes of cakes. She was plainly enjoying being the hostess. From one box, she slid out a cream and jam sponge cake, and from the other, a chocolate cake.

'Just for looking at,' she said to her audience. 'Like me.'

'Congratulations to both of you,' said Liz.

'Nothing special for me, another birthday,' said Rose dismissively. 'I just had to keep feeding myself.' She reflected on what she'd said. 'Well, all considering, that takes some doing, day in day out, what with all the other things you can spend your money on.'

'Can't you just accept a happy birthday?' said Zar.

'Nope. Though I'll have some cake. Consolation for the fact that today I am 30 years nearer to my death.'

'Were you like that when you were 30, Bill?' said Zar.

'I was working in a stately home,' he said. 'They worked you hard there, I can tell you. No skiving off with the leaf vac, and going round looking at trees.'

'I'm doing an inventory,' insisted Zar, putting out a row of mugs by the large tea pot.

'And how's that going to keep the park tidy?' retorted Bill.

Liz leaned in to Jack. 'How's the wall going?'

'I hope to have it down by the end of today,' he said. 'Start laying bricks tomorrow.' He indicated the room. 'There's one of you missing.'

'Amy,' said Liz. 'She doesn't come over for afternoon tea. The kids are coming out of school soon, so she stays in the playground. Makes herself tea in the hut. Save Amy some cake, Rose.'

'I'll take it over later,' said Rose. She had cut each cake into eight slices. 'That's two each. One of jam sponge, one of chocolate.' With a slice she set to, putting two on each plate and passing them out to the salivating group.

Ian entered, obviously pleased with himself from the broad grin on his face.

'This all looks very jolly,' he said. 'What are we celebrating?'

'My death,' said Rose.

'Her 30th birthday,' corrected Liz.

'Same thing,' said Rose. 'It's all a matter of perspective.'

'And me getting on day release,' said Zar.

'Well, I'd like to congratulate both of you,' said Ian. '30 is a milestone. A time of maturity.'

'Oh dear,' said Rose.

'A decade when we are more sure of ourselves, when we consolidate...' he went on.

'No more,' said Rose, putting her hands up to protect herself. 'I can't take it.'

Jack was unsure whether this was put on or not. Maybe half and half.

But Ian had taken the hint. 'And well done to Zar. You've impressed everyone in this park with your enthusiasm. Your thirst for knowledge. May I on behalf of everyone wish you well on your day release.'

'Hear! Hear!' chipped in Liz.

'It's a day of good news all round,' said Ian, beaming like a vicar looking in at the village fete.

Chapter 18

Zar had been around the park again, through all the shrubberies, back and forth. He'd put every tree in the plan and found a couple more death stalks, and thought there couldn't be any more. The problem was, though, they came up overnight. Most of the fungus was underground, feeding off the tree roots. The mushroom was just the fruiting body, and they'd keep popping up, so long as the mycelium was feeding. The beginning of the month had been wet and now with this warmth, perfect for growth. Cold would halt its munching. Heavy frosts would see the end of mushrooms, until the spring.

Liz had collared him and asked him to get her some liquidambar leaves while he was on his wanderings. She wanted some for her display. And why not? Hardly a chore. There were three of the small liquidambar trees at one corner of the lawn, the five fingered pointed leaves a fierce blood colour, quite shocking. The middle point was bigger than the others, penile, he couldn't help thinking, the effect added to by the prongy, dangling balls that were its fruit.

Sex was in everything. Male and female trees, in flowers. It enabled diversity, gave evolution more options.

But was one hell of a hassle.

At home, Zar was looking at too much gay porn on his laptop. He must stop. Soon as he heard someone on the stairs, he'd switch to a site on trees he also had open, or wild flowers or botany. It was pointless, all this pretending, he had to leave home. Nothing was possible there. He was simply postponing the day, becoming more desperate.

He'd tentatively tried online dating, but had become quite shocked by the openness and demands. He'd found a Muslim gay site, the tales there much like his own. Most of the guys hid behind avatars, as he did. He was Fraxinus, the genus name for the ash tree. All the secrecy the writers needed, family rows when they dared come out. A few were accepted, provided they shut up and didn't tell the relatives. It was all so furtive. A couple of the guys had lesbian girlfriends, but then all the farcical shenanigans when they had parents pushing for the wedding. A few, though, were out. They made it plain; come out or be crushed.

Easy to say. True as it might be. Fear of living on his own held him back. Though he knew he had to get his own place. He had timidly tried a few weeks ago. Gone to look at a room offered by an Asian family. They were pleasant, and so wanted him to take the room that they reduced the rent, thinking him a nice Muslim boy. He'd be one of the family!

He shuddered at the memory. How stupid it would have been to move in. Simply living the lie somewhere else.

Rooms were expensive though, wherever you looked. Even round here. Perhaps a flat share. But with whom? They would have to be people who accepted him as he was. And vice versa, of course. The world scared him. Drugs, violence, racism. Judgement by people who never reflected on their judgement. Though he must take the plunge. Go online, see what was about.

What a chore! He and Rose had been talking about it over lunch. It took so much time, and what on earth did you get for all the money you paid out?

But it must be done. His life must begin. There were gay clubs. A pity, though, they all seemed to involve alcohol. Wasn't one sin at a time enough? Or as the imam said, one led to another, down the slippery slope, until you were thoroughly damned.

Well, he was anyway. In thought. And ready for it in deed. Besides, if he was going to be openly gay, it wouldn't matter to his family if he did it with a fruit juice in hand or a whisky. Gayness was the bugbear.

Then there was the park to consider. What would happen if he came out? It wasn't illegal. He couldn't be sacked for telling them. As it was, he suspected that being Asian was bad enough for Bill and Ian. But then one thing at a time. Leave home. Make up a reason to placate the family. Though he could hardly think of an acceptable one.

Deal with the park later, when he was out of the clutches of the community. Stronger. With new friends.

The bucket was full of red leaves. A good haul. He set off for the marquee where Liz was working on her cascade. He'd like to tell her. But you never knew, she might gossip, she might not, but why chance it? He'd told that builder. And wished he hadn't.

But that was done. And the man would be gone in a couple of days.

Chapter 19

She was in the rose garden, dead heading and weeding. Ian had been surprisingly gracious when she pleaded to be off the vac for the rest of the day. A birthday treat perhaps but it was unlike him to bother with such sentimentality. There are plenty out there without jobs, he'd normally say.

At last, off the monster.

The dead heading was easy enough. Any pathetic rose, or rather has-been rose, she pulled off and threw in the bucket. She was the grim reaper. Not actually, they were dead or good as by the time she got to them. She was simply collecting the bodies. More like a funeral director.

Weeding she was less confident on. Which were weeds and which weren't. Liz had told her that a weed was any plant you didn't want. Which wasn't a lot of help, as quite a few weeds she liked. There was one, a pretty little thing, Jack-by-the-Hedge, small white flowers smelling of garlic. A weed, said Liz. Why? she'd asked. Because it was in a flowerbed for snapdragons and alyssum.

That's Nazi, she'd declared. Racial cleansing. Liz had agreed but didn't seem as upset as she was. Fascism was OK in the garden. But then Rose was on the side of the weeds; she knew she didn't belong herself. One day they would ethnically cleanse her. She was sure of it.

In a way, it was stupid. Plants didn't have feelings. You needed a brain for that. Plants were dumb, vegetable things. Growing because they had to. Living because they were. As senseless as the leaf vac.

It didn't stop her feeling sorry for the weeds.

Once she'd watched Bill with his hoe. Thoroughly ruthless, like a concentration camp guard. Mow them down! Hacking through them, chucking them in the wheelbarrow without a care. Never mind they'd put all that energy into growing, into making flowers and seeds in the hope... Well, they didn't really hope, but she hoped for them. In the hope of living on through future generations.

Chop, went Bill's hoe.

She was a crappy gardener. You can't wince at every weed you pull up. Well, you can, because she did. So maybe the leaf vac was right for her. Sweep up the bodies, don't kill them. Mother Nature did that. And Rose had no way of stopping her.

The bucket was full. Mostly with weeds. And they must be weeds as Liz had said: in the rose garden, if it isn't a rose it's a weed. Besides which, the day was almost done.

She popped into the playground.

Amy was doing a round with her litter picker and sack. She was quite deft. The picker had a handle you squeezed, connected to a rod which closed the jaws at the bottom over a sweet paper or crisp packet.

'Nice birthday cake,' she said on seeing Rose.

'Zar bought it,' she said. 'I'm broke.' And then remembered she had earlier told Amy about being interested in buying into Women Fly Women, and so added, 'I mean none on me. Enough in the bank, not in my pocket.' She knew she was trying too hard. And why, anyway?

'I've got five new passengers today,' beamed Amy, patting her belt. 'Five! That's a record. I usually do three. Four on the odd occasion, but that's my first five.'

'And you make twenty on each?' recalled Rose.

'Brilliant day.' She looked about, then said quietly, 'Three crew members got their pay outs last week, that's why the passengers are queuing up.'

107

Rose pointed out Amy's bulging belt. 'There must be a thousand pounds in there.'

Amy put a finger to her lips. 'Shh!'

'Isn't it risky going around like that?'

Amy shrugged. 'I'll pass it on to the captain soon enough.'

'And who's that?'

Amy waved a finger. 'No, no. You won't get that out of me. Rules are rules.'

'Is it anyone I know?'

'No comment.'

'Does that mean yes or no?'

'No comment.'

Rose hissed, 'I've a good mind to hit you on the head and rob you.'

'I'm bigger than you.'

'I've got longer nails.' But she realised she'd get no more out of Amy, and added, 'I'm off to the yard. By the time I've emptied this and washed up, it'll be knocking off time.'

She left the playground, knowing Amy would be working half an hour longer, and maybe make it to six passengers, before she closed up.

Chapter 20

Jack wheeled the barrow into the yard, his wrists aching. He stopped the barrow for a moment and jiggled his hands and wrists as if to shake them off. He rubbed them over each other. This was the final load and he hadn't needed to work so hard. But he'd made it a sort of race to reclaim the last brick by the end of the day. Commonsense said he could just as well complete them in the morning, but he'd jettisoned that in his feverish hammering off of mortar as if he'd be shot if there was a single brick left undone. And even gone on fifteen minutes over time.

Idiot.

He could feel the blood running through his wrists to his fingers as if still carrying the workload. It wasn't sensible working at that rate, though part of him wanted to complete the work in two days just to show the foreman that he could do it, and in the right way. So unnecessary. He need prove nothing to that man. And it was not as if he had a new job to begin on Wednesday. His next start was Monday, a week away.

He picked up the barrow, and headed on to the heap of bricks he'd been building near the dump at the end of the yard. There, he unburdened the barrow, placing the final bricks on the pile. Done. He massaged his wrists once more and twirled them about, stretching the fingers to prove to himself there was no damage done. Then he took up the barrow and pushed it into the tool shed, where it would stay overnight. In the barrow he put the tools he'd been working with, bolster chisel, club hammer and hand axe, along with his hard hat and goggles. The shed was locked up overnight; they'd be safe.

Jack went into the mess hut and washed his hands in the butler sink. Enjoying the warm, soapy water, letting the water run a while, his hands dangling. Then wiped them on a paper towel and left.

A day's work done.

Outside the yard, he looked at the wall he'd been working on. Going well, once the argy bargy of the morning had been sorted out. The damaged section was demolished, the bricks reclaimed. The wooden barriers covered the gap; tomorrow's work was to fill it. Bricklaying.

Should he go to the greenhouse, to remind Liz he was coming back at nine with his telescope? He took a few paces in that direction and then stopped. She knew anyway. It made him look like an overeager schoolboy. They'd confirmed it at tea break. Leave it. He had her phone number.

Just remember, it was an astronomy evening. Anything else that happened would happen if it happened.

He headed for the park gate.

Go home, shower, eat, read a bit, watch some TV maybe and then come back with the telescope. He looked up at the sky. Pretty clear, lots of blue stretches. Could be a good night for stargazing. Might be cold. Woolly hat and fleece. Mars was at its closest for some time this month. He was hoping for a good view of the red planet, and hopefully a photo.

Once outside the gate, he saw her at once. He'd completely forgotten, being so taken over by his mortar race. She was leaning against the van, one leg bent against the front tyre. With her overalls off, her figure showed to advantage. The complications exploded like measles in a children's nursery. All he'd done was say yes. And might yet regret it.

'I've been waiting over ten minutes,' she said crossly.

He smiled at her. It was hard to believe her cheek. He hardly knew her. Who was doing who the favour. But then he had to admit, his own motives weren't simply altruistic.

'I had to put everything away,' he said.

She gave him a sidelong glance. 'Did you say goodbye to my sister?'

'Your sister?'

'Liz,' she said, wide eyed. 'Didn't you know?'

'I didn't,' he said, feeling somewhat trapped.

'She was chatting you up at tea break.'

'Hardly,' he said, opening the van door. 'Let's go.'

Complications.

Chapter 21

Zar was on the bus home to Ilford. It was busy downstairs with a few standing but he'd managed to get a seat. Good job he had a bus pass, as he'd spent all that money on cakes and bought himself and Rose a meal in the café. He only had a few quid left; he'd have to bring in a lunch tomorrow. His mother usually had leftovers from the evening meal that would do.

A book on wild flowers was open on his lap, but he wasn't looking at it, but thinking about the day he'd had. For the first time, he'd told someone face to face that he was gay. That made him squirm, but he needed to get used to it so that he didn't.

But it was hard to take disapproval. He'd never been good at it. At school, at home. He must toughen up if he was to get anywhere.

Today had been good though. He'd enjoyed doing the tree inventory. That had annoyed Bill, to see him wandering about with a clipboard. He'd called him a jumped up gaffer. And why should Zar mind that? He'd put all the trees on Liz's plan, the exciting ones like the Atlantic cedar, the tree of heaven, the liquidambars, the tulip tree, the Indian bean, as well as the more usual beech, oak, ash, hawthorn, maple and the Japanese cherries. Liz had suggested there could be a children's tree trail in the summer.

And finding the death stalks. Much better informing Liz than Ian. She said, don't tell anyone. No panic. They looked so harmless, so ordinary, no wonder they caused so much trouble. He'd handed all he'd found over to Liz who said she was going to burn them tonight. He wondered how they got in the park in the first place as surely they can't be usual in town parks. But spores float on the wind and there were woods not too far away. Maybe he should check the woods out.

And day release had happened. That had come out of the blue. He'd thought Ian was simply going to block him forever. But incredibly, it was Ian who said it was on. When the Superintendent of Parks was there, and Zar had confirmed the trees he'd brought in were red oaks. Worth the cakes that he shared with Rose twice over. He was going somewhere at last, quite where he couldn't say, but plants and horticulture were drawing him in. It was exciting, and so new, all the growing things. In gardens, woods, even the trees down the streets.

He'd never seen any of it before he'd got this job. That is, he'd never looked. No one in his family knew much about plants. It was a happy accident that he'd got a job in the parks. And started looking. Beginning with the tree book, identifying every specimen in the park, and then on to wild flowers. Weeds mostly. The park should have a wild flower area. He'd talk to Liz about it. And about the possibilities for his own study, what it could lead on to. Day release was only a beginning. Starting on Monday. So stirring. He wondered who his fellow students would be. How much they knew already. Zar had missed a few weeks of the term and would have to catch up. He might need to buy a few books and really work at it.

At last, something to tell his parents. The job wasn't a stopgap. Tell Mum first. Dad wouldn't be back until later. His father was hardly speaking to him. He'd wanted Zar to be an accountant and when that fell through, or rather when Zar had walked out, his father was so disappointed in him that he'd given up on him. Expected him to be a perennial letdown. Well, he'd tell him that today he'd taken the first step towards a career. That was the word that mattered to his dad, career.

The next bus stop was his, Barking Station. He put his book away and stood up, working his way through the passengers to the door of the bus. It was bursting in him, to stand on a seat and announce to all the passengers about his career. His future. The woman in the hijab with the pushchair, he wanted to tell her not to force her child into a preset mould.

But then maybe all parents did, without knowing it.

It had not been his ambition to be an accountant. Ever. It had been his father's for him, perhaps to make up for his own frustration in the shop. We want our kids to fulfil our dreams.

He got off the bus and walked round the corner to Ilford Lane. He strode out quickly, along Barking Park, the mosque on the other side of the road. Oh, he wanted to get home and tell them!

Before it got dark, early these days, while waiting for dinner, he'd prune the roses in the back garden. Reveal his new skills. He knew how to prune and had borrowed some secateurs from the park tool shed. Some of the roses at home had not been pruned for years, or so lightly pruned that they were thick and woody. They needed renewal. Liz could tell him how to take cuttings, or whatever you did, to propagate roses. He should look that up when he got home. There'd be stuff on it on the internet. Try and keep off the porn tonight.

He turned off Ilford Lane into his street, eyeing the plane trees that were planted every 30 metres or so along the pavement. They'd been so hammered with pruning in the spring. In full leaf the bruising was hidden, but now when the leaves were falling, the arthritic knuckles were revealed. Did they have to cut them back so hard?

There was so much to know.

First a cup of tea with his mother and tell her the good news. Then prune the roses in the garden to show what he could do. And over dinner, inform his father the steps he was taking and where they might lead him.

To Kew maybe. That would be the place. All those amazing plants, all those world experts.

He opened the front door and his mother immediately came out of the kitchen.

'Come in here,' she said.

Her face was so stern, he wondered what tragedy he was going to be told. Had someone died? He stepped into the kitchen and there on the table, it was revealed.

'What are these magazines?' she said.

Gay magazines he'd bought. He'd been disappointed in them, although some of the pictures turned him on.

'I found them,' he said.

'They are disgusting. Sinful. Depraved.' She poked him in the chest. 'Sit down.' He sat by the table. There was not going to be tea and a good news discussion. He'd have to fight to get out of this one.

His mother stood over him, she obviously had much more to say.

'After I found these under your mattress,' she said, 'we had a look at your laptop...'

'Who's we?'

'Me and Leila.'

His sister. Trust her to work out his password.

'It's private,' he said, knowing it was too late to protest the invasion. Once they were in, there were no secrets.

'I had to scrub my hands after all that filth,' his mother exclaimed. 'Pornography beyond belief, gay dating sites and emails you've been sending to perverts.'

'I'm gay,' he said for the second time today. 'I was looking for help.'

'From perverts and paedophiles!' she yelled. 'You need to

see a doctor. The Quran forbids this corruption.'

'And allows slavery,' he interjected.

'In Pakistan you would be stoned to death,' she went on.

'And in Saudi Arabia I would be beheaded.'

'Yes,' said his mother. 'With your family's blessing. You must know you cannot be gay and a Muslim, Zar. Your father will take you to the imam. How can you have such desires?'

'Being gay is not a choice,' he said.

'Don't give me your rubbish. It is the devil in you, choosing wickedness, bringing shame on the whole family.' Her hands shook frantically as if he were a plague of flies. 'Go to your room. You disgust me. Your father will be here in half an hour. How did I ever come to have such a son!'

She was boiling with fury, intermingled with tears. He stood up, and held her arms as he attempted to explain that he had his own life.

'It's the 21st century, Mum. We have moved on from this medieval agenda. I don't live in a Pakistani village.'

'Let go of me!' She struggled and pulled away. 'You cannot be gay and my son. This is a Muslim house. A place of respect and honour. Go to your room and wait for your father.'

He might have said more, there was so much welling in him, but saw the futility in her face and body. She could not listen. It was all as he'd feared. He was the enemy, bringing shame like a dreadful disease into the family. They would cure him or cut him out.

Zar turned on his heels and left the kitchen. He took the stairs two at a time, with her yelling behind him.

'The Quran forbids it. I will not have a pervert in my home!'

He slammed the bedroom door on her. And pressed his back against it, though he knew she would not come up. The next harangue would come from his father. Whether he would beat him or whether it would be cold anger – Zar was not going to stay for it. He'd learned from the websites of forced visits to doctors, imams, of sham marriages, of young men and women being packed off to Pakistan. And lectures on lectures about shame and Muslim values.

Zar began packing a rucksack.

Chapter 22

Jack sorted out the food that he had from the cupboard and fridge. Not the greatest of choices. Two sausages, two eggs, a can of beans, four slices of stale bread, a little bit of cheese and that was it. He'd meant to do some shopping on the way home, but Rose's arrival had thrown him. It would have to do. He had supper coming later at Liz's. This just needed to fill a gap between times.

He put the sausages under the grill. Then cracked the eggs into a bowl, added a little milk, scrambled the mixture with a fork and added bits of cheese and pepper. Toast on, kettle on, he set the omelette frying.

Rose was having a shower. There was no clean towel so she'd have to manage with the one he had. And as he was having a shower later, he'd have to manage with the wet one she left him. He must buy more towels or at least wash what he had more often.

He put the beans on. This was his all day breakfast. Quick to cook but not particularly healthy. Lacking any greens. He had a couple of days off this week, following this job. He'd stock up on tinned greens, peas and broad beans, that sort of stuff. Get some potatoes for baking, good this time of year, and sprouts. It just took a bit of thinking ahead, something domestically he was not that good at.

Alison had run that side. A very organised woman. He'd done what he was told, until his drinking got the better of him – and he'd done nothing at all. In fact, it had undone any good habits. The people he'd met at AH, he noted, were a slobby bunch. That's what happened once alcohol took over with its vomit and diarrhoea. Squalor became the default.

Once they'd divorced, Alison had forced him to make an effort. Or Mia wasn't coming over. So he'd bought a second hand washing machine and plumbed it in. Even used it sometimes. He had a vacuum cleaner, and did know how to use it, but it was a chore changing the bag and it seemed to get buried in the cupboard. Besides which, dust settled only very slowly.

He set the food out on the table in the living room with the teapot and mugs. Rose came out of the bathroom in his dressing gown. She was barelegged, and from the bundle of clothing she was holding, obviously naked under the gown. She sat down at the table. Jack had already started eating. She commenced.

'You wouldn't have a hair dryer?' she said.

'Never use one.'

'Then I'll have to do without. I really needed that shower. After leaf vaccing all day, and the dust where I was last night.'

'The bowling pavilion hotel,' he recalled.

'I wouldn't recommend it,' she said with a short laugh. She took a bite of toast and a bit of sausage. 'So who's your date then?'

'No one you know,' he said, head down.

'How do you know who I know?' She wiped the egg yolk with toast. 'You could still cancel it. It's not too late.'

'Wouldn't that be rude?'

'You apologise profusely,' she said, 'and say what an awful headache you have. Brick dust. Or what is really good is the runs. No one wants you to come then.'

'It doesn't help courting,' he acknowledged.

'There's a quaint term,' she said peering at him, 'but then

there is something old fashioned about you.'

'I don't know whether to be pleased or angry.'

She shrugged. 'I suppose it's the van. Man with a van. And the clodhopping boots.'

'My working gear,' he said. 'Not made for a disco.'

She pondered a moment and snapped her fingers. 'It's my sister. Your date.'

He concentrated on wrapping the toast round a sausage.

'And what if it is?' he said at last. 'Do you mind?'

She screwed her lips. 'I do actually. Liz kicked me out on Saturday. And then gets in first with a man I fancy. I would not have thought that of her.' She ate some sausage and took a bite of toast. 'She's a nifty cook. And a good painter. You don't deserve her.'

Jack laughed. 'Too good for me?'

'I'm more your class.'

'I don't trust you,' he said.

'I don't trust you.' She shrugged. 'Sex is like that. Who can you trust?'

'Not even your sister.'

'Especially not your sister.'

After their meal, Jack went for his shower. Rose said she'd wash up. As the hot water ran he contemplated what was happening. A bird in a bush... He could go to the park, set up the telescope, see Mars and maybe Andromeda. Have some supper and that could be that. It never was an invitation to screw, but a more high minded invitation to look at the heavens.

He soaped himself under the arms and in the groin. He pointed his face into the jets and soaped his hair.

It had been a genuine invitation to see the stars. Meaning what? That he would set his telescope up and look skywards. But then after... Like a dinner date. You hoped it wouldn't stop there. And sometimes it did, with maybe a kiss on the doorstep.

He could phone Liz. Tell her the telescope was broken. She might invite him anyway for supper. Then he'd have an interesting choice. But supper might just mean supper, of course. He could then say he was mid mending the telescope and wanted to finish it. Not leave it in pieces in his sitting room. His hands were greasy.

And so on.

And simply stay here, and take what was plainly on offer.

He disgusted himself. How could he have a long term relationship with anyone when he was so dishonest? You had to be open, you had to share. You couldn't be forever calculating how to get your leg over.

He'd change tomorrow, the day after. Depending.

Sex was like alcohol. The way it worked on you, took you over, pushing everything else aside. All aspirations, promises. You craved. You lied and schemed. Fill my glass. Fill my bed.

Just a phone call. He couldn't do it in front of Rose. But why not? She'd suggested he cancel. It would make them conspirators. She'd have one over her sister. Might make her sexier.

The towel was disgusting; she'd just left it on the bathroom floor. It was a dirty damp rag, but all he had. He bunched it up and rubbed off the wettest bits, here, under there. And finished himself off with his soiled vest.

Jack dressed. He rubbed his chin. And had a quick run around with his electric razor. A little aftershave to salve the tenderness and add to his allure. He looked in the mirror. Who would want that lying bastard?

Another lying bastard.

He came out of the bathroom. Rose was asleep on the sofa. She had a pillow from his bed under her head and his duvet over her. She looked so cosy, so innocent. So set for the night.

Half an hour later, Jack left with his telescope.

Chapter 23

The sheet of card covered most of the kitchen table. On it she'd drawn a plan of the park, and, from her rough sketch filled in by Zar, she began putting in small circles for trees. Not the names yet. With her water colour palette, she touched in the shrubbery, the grass, the bowling green, to give it some life and vibrancy. She'd leave it when she'd finished colouring; tomorrow, she'd ink in the tree names and areas of the park.

The finished work would go on an easel in the marquee for Wednesday. It would be an extra to her cascade, something for visitors to look at as they chatted. She was glad to have this project on hand. It had been convenient to give Zar a reason for going round the park searching out the death stalks – but now it had utility. A busyness. So necessary. It had been a day too long. Ever since Ian's blackmail in the mess hut... What an age ago that was! Watching, doing her work, keeping sane. And still waiting, hour upon hour, until the poison took effect.

He thought that she'd committed herself to him. So unbelievably pleasant to everyone this afternoon, she'd almost regretted her action. But not quite. He was still Ian. He had forced her to promise to be his. To love, honour and obey. To have and to hold. For five years at least. To sleep with him, submit to his demands, cook and clean for him...

The last she'd seen of Ian was about five thirty; he was fine, beaming like a birthday boy with all his presents. No sign of anything eating away inside.

Suppose it didn't work? In that case, her plan B was to leave. Give her notice. Go. He might then do his dirty work, knowing he'd get nothing out of it, but damning her work prospects. So be it. She'd leave and make the best of it, whatever that was, wherever that was.

If plan A didn't work.

The builder was coming over with his telescope later. She'd skipped her class, knowing she wouldn't take anything in. Much better doing this tree plan. And then outside with Jack. Have someone to talk to, stars to look at. Astronomy, which she confused with astrology, which she didn't really believe in anyway. Why should the stars give a damn about us? But if it were so, their power, their influence, must be directed here, tonight. It hardly mattered what she did; it would be zoomed into what was happening to her and to him, an inevitability ray.

That didn't make any sense. If things were inevitable, she couldn't do anything other than what she was going to do anyway. Which she didn't believe.

So scrub that thought. Scrub any deep thinking. Her head was a-tumble. Just paint.

She'd promised the builder supper. Well, there was plenty left over from lunch. Did she want him to stay the night?

Yes and no. Company, uncomplicated, someone to talk to, to hold her as time passed. No – she might weep, talk too much, give herself away as events unfolded. Time so stretched out when you were waiting. With nothing to fill you but the event you wanted and dreaded.

And then? Once it happened.

Nothing perhaps. Or a funeral. Or an investigation.

Zar knew too much. Would talk innocently about the work she'd given him. She would be questioned. And be believed or not believed.

In time. Hours and hours later. In the meantime, nothing

could distract her. No music, no book, no chatter. Perhaps it would be better if she suffered alone, if the builder had not been invited. Then, at least, she would not betray herself.

She could claim a headache. Not so far from the truth. A terrible migraine. She would be oh so apologetic, but really she couldn't... Did he mind?

Her bell rang.

It couldn't be Jack. Too early, and he didn't know the gate code. Though Ian might have given it to him as he had to come and go. She went to the door and looked through the spy hole. It was Ian. The man she'd promised herself to. Still standing upright. There was no point not answering the door; she was obviously in, with the light on in her hallway, kitchen and sitting room.

She opened the front door.

He beamed at her like a shy suitor.

'Might I come in?' he said.

She thought a moment and then said, 'Let's go for a stroll, Ian. It's mild out and I've a bit of a headache. Fresh air might clear it.'

'Oh dear,' he said. 'I've a bit of a tummy ache myself.' He rubbed the area. 'I don't know what it is.'

'Worry about the ceremony,' she suggested.

'Probably.'

She took her outdoor jacket off the hook and slipped it on. She felt for her keys, always necessary now she lived on her own again. Though she had a spare set under a brick, just in case.

She closed the door behind her, and ushered Ian along the path and out of her garden gate. She joined him on the drive and took his hand. He squeezed hers. They were enclosed in darkness.

'Can we walk a little slower?' he said. 'I feel a bit twingey. It comes and goes. A sort of stabbing.'

'No rush,' she said. 'We'll go at your pace.'

They slowed. She couldn't see his face but through his hand felt him wince every so often.

'I am a worrier, Liz. Do you think I'm getting an ulcer?'

'It's said to be a stress thing,' she said. 'Just walk slowly and remember, everything is in hand. And I am your backstop.'

'Thank you, Liz.' He stopped and rubbed his stomach. 'I would love to walk with you, but it's no good. Not tonight. I think I should go home. I don't feel well at all.'

'Let's get you back then. Tuck you up with a hot water bottle.'

'Oh! That was a kick.' He stopped walking, and hunched over clutching his stomach with both hands. He was breathing quickly, the two of them still on the drive. 'It's as if I've swallowed glass. Can we stop a while?'

'Of course, Ian.'

She stood a little way from him. He was a dark shadow against the deep purple sky. A bat flipped past like a constricting handkerchief a little over their heads. They were on the main drive by the playground, the swings and roundabout silent and dead, barely visible in the gloom.

'I enjoyed today,' he said, the words coming slowly as if he were frozen. 'Our lunch especially. And the cake at tea was a jolly thing. Everyone coming together.' He suddenly recoiled and grabbed her arm in a tight grip. 'My stomach is turning like a washing machine.' He winced again.

'Would you like to sit down, Ian?'

'That might be a good idea. Thank you, Liz.'

She led him slowly to a nearby bench where they sat side by side. He rubbed his stomach with both of his hands, his breathing rapid and thick.

'Ooh! Where did that come from? It's like I swallowed a brick.' He rocked backwards and forwards. 'I don't know what's the matter with me, Liz.'

'Acid indigestion,' she said. 'It can be very painful.'

'No, no, more like...' And he kicked one leg out, then the other. 'Bloody cramps. It's like metal bolts up my legs... Oh my God!' His arms were thrashing.

All at once his head shot forward and he vomited, a forceful gush that flooded out in a splash. Bent over, he continued heaving.

'There's something the matter inside,' he moaned. 'This is awful.' He retched again. 'Help me, Liz.'

'Stay where you are,' she said. 'This is serious. You don't want to be moving. I'll get an ambulance,' she said. 'Could be appendicitis. I'll phone from the house. Don't worry. I'll be back as soon as I can.'

She left him and walked quickly to her cottage. She let herself in, closing the door on the park and the man on the bench. She leaned her forehead against the cold glass. It was happening. She must not intervene.

She did not phone. She did not go back.

Chapter 24

Jack took the telescope mount out of the back of his van. He put it down on the pavement. And took out the telescope itself which was wrapped in a blanket for protection from the tools and oddments in the back of his vehicle. He laid it carefully on the pavement. It was quite an operation, as this 8 inch Newtonian weighed fifteen kilograms. Not made for carrying about. Something he should have considered before he'd bought it. He didn't have a back garden, so was always travelling to sites away from city lights. A favourite of his and Mia's was up a hill by Epping Forest. Once, it had clouded over even as they were climbing up to the viewing point, arriving at the top with all that weight, simply to have to carry it down again.

Tonight, though, was reasonably clear. Some cloud, but plenty of sky between. Mars, he'd already spotted, and hopefully the Andromeda Galaxy would be out of cloud. In his backpack, he had his camera; he'd try for some photos, plus a head torch to help set up. It was easy to drop things on dark nights.

Jack locked the van and thought of Rose out like a log on the sofa. Just as well he was here. No complications. He'd enjoy a session under the night sky – with no lies to tell.

He took the mount, then the telescope to the locked gate. And phoned Liz.

When she answered, he said, 'It's me, Jack. I'm at the gate with my gear.'

'I'll let you in.'

The gate buzzed. He held it open with his shoulder and brought the gear in. The gate snapped shut behind him. The mount was over his shoulder, the telescope he carried in his arms like a mother with an overweight baby. Jack had decided earlier where to set up. Just outside the marquee. It offered wind protection and shelter if needs be. They'd be looking south at the ecliptic, the line that sun and planets took from east to west, which was unobstructed in the park.

Past the wall he'd been working on today, barely visible in the gloom. In the faint glow of streetlights, the park trees were like black cut outs against inky sky, pinpricked with stars, amidst cloudy islands.

The plan was to set up, then go and collect Liz.

He crossed onto the lawn and could make out the outline of the marquee. Somewhat forbidding in the dark. An owl hooted. Underfoot the ground was soft, dew settling. In the two cottages, the lights were on, fortunately with the curtains closed, so not too polluting.

Jack put down the mount. And then the scope, carefully on the blanket to keep the moisture off. He took out the head torch from his backpack and set it onto his forehead to light his setting up. He hoped Ian knew he was here – or he might, on seeing the beam, come out yelling, Get out of my park! or whatever.

Under the headlight, he assembled the telescope and mount. And switched off the torch, being careful on the battery. Also, it was best practice to get your eyes dark adjusted before viewing. Should he take a quick look before getting Liz? Make sure he could find things. The confident astronomer.

He looked into the heavens. There was the Square of Pegasus, three of the four corner stars clear and bright, one in cloud. He followed the left hand corner star, alpha Andromeda, along a couple of stars and then up. That's where the Andromeda Galaxy should be. In non light-polluted areas you could just make it out with the naked eye. At two and a half million light years away, it was the most distant object visible without magnification.

No, he wouldn't start yet. He'd bring Liz out. Share the discovery together.

He left the assembled telescope and walked towards the cottage. He'd ask her to make up a thermos of coffee. Maybe bring out a couple of folding chairs. It was good to have a house close by.

It was then he heard the groaning. Jack stopped, unsure what it was. An animal? He listened. A low moan. And tried to catch where it was coming from. Somewhere in the direction of the playground. He set off that way, switching on his head torch. And in the beam saw someone on the ground, rocking.

When he'd got to him, Jack saw it was Ian, the park manager. He was lying on the grass, plainly in agony. Jack knelt down to him. The manager's eyes were screwed tight as he writhed.

'What is it, mate?'

The only reply was a repeated moan with hands clutching his stomach.

Jack loosened Ian's tie and undid his collar buttons. There was little else he could do. He took out his phone and dialled Liz.

'Liz. It's Jack. I've just found Ian out here, near the playground. He's very sick.'

'I'll be right out.'

While waiting for her, Jack considered what to do. He could phone an ambulance or take him to hospital himself. The man was writhing and groaning, plainly something was very wrong. There was Liz in his beam, coming out of her gate at a run, her coat open.

'What's happened?' she said when she'd got to him.

'He's in a bad way,' said Jack, deciding even as he spoke. 'I'm going to take him to hospital.'

Chapter 25

At Newham General, he was reprimanded for not calling an ambulance. He suffered it, while Ian was rushed into intensive care. He gave the information that he knew for records. Name, address. He couldn't give much more beyond knowing the next of kin was his father who lived at the same address. As for the father's name, Mr Swift was the best he could offer.

And that was that for him. He'd got the man to hospital. Got a dressing down for his pains. There was nothing else he could do here. He'd passed on the patient to the experts, and was a free man.

Outside by his van, he phoned Liz.

'I don't know what they're doing,' he said. 'They rushed him off for emergency treatment. That's all I can tell you. You'd better tell his father where he is.'

'I will,' she said. 'Though I'm not sure whether to do it now. It's rather late.'

Jack looked at his watch. It was almost eleven.

'You might as well leave him sleeping,' he said. 'There's nothing he can do except worry.'

'I'll tell him first thing in the morning,' she said.

'There's no point me coming to you now,' said Jack, half hoping she'd disagree.

'No,' she said. 'It's late. I am sorry. It's blown out our stargazing and supper.'

'Another time,' he said. 'Will you move my telescope into the marquee? Just in case it rains. I'll see to it when I get to work in the morning.'

'I'll do it right now,' she said.

And with their farewells, that was that. As far as a date goes, a non event. Jack set off home. It was a night that had got lost somewhere. No Mars, no Andromeda Galaxy, no supper. Nothing nice at all, as Mia might have said when she was four. Only then recalling, there might be something after all. Rose. And presumably, well rested. So the night might be salvageable.

Stargazing with Liz had not even begun. Neither his fault nor hers, but that of a very sick man who could hardly be blamed. He and Liz had hardly spoken tonight beyond dealing with the invalid. Hardly an occasion for intimacy. Pity. But there you are. Events. There might be other starry nights.

As he drove up Greengate Street, he wondered what was up with Ian. His knowledge of medical conditions wasn't great. Heart, brain, guts, take your pick or all three together. We are machines, we break down. Leave it to the mechanics.

He could do with some warmth. A little reassurance. All this running around for other people's benefit. Enough.

The traffic was light, and he was back home in Forest Gate in less than ten minutes. Back to where he'd been three hours ago, with the younger sister asleep on his sofa, as he'd crept out. She'd said if it didn't work out, then... And yes, it hadn't. Not even a kiss on the doorstep. So...

He crept into a silent flat. Rose was not on the sofa, though the debris of her bed was. A screwed up duvet, the pillow with an impression of her head. She was not in his bedroom either. Nor in the kitchen, where the washing up had not been done. There was a note on the sitting room table:

'Nothing on TV. Tired of waiting for you. Borrowed £30. Gone Clubbing. Rose PS might be back.'

Jack looked in his drawer where he kept spare cash. It was cleaned out. He was past caring. He went into the kitchen and put the kettle on. And while waiting for it to boil, he washed up.

Chapter 26

Zar was in his sleeping bag fully clothed. His torch was fading, so he turned it off, and nibbled at the chocolate he'd bought, washing it down with bottled water. He had contemplated going to a hotel for the night. Except it wouldn't be for just a night. He had left home. There was no going back. It would be humiliating. He'd have to agree to whatever conditions they set, once the verbal bashing was over.

Impossible.

There were three texts on his phone. One from his sister, two from his parents. He wasn't going to read them. He'd heard too much from his mother, her view was plain. And Leila had given his mother his password. How, he wasn't sure. Had he given it to his sister, had she worked it out? Not that it mattered. Just that she'd given it to Mum. And it had to be willingly, as she could have said, I don't know it. And how would his mother know otherwise?

His father would be up to speed. His mother would have given him every detail. She'd show him the magazines... Fortunately she couldn't show the laptop as Zar had it, but would rattle off her disgust at what she'd seen. Leila would fill in the gaps.

Earlier, he'd gone into a hotel near Ilford Station and enquired the price for a single room. £60. At that rate his savings would last him barely five days. And he needed to eat too. And all sorts else, as he wasn't going back home. Clothes and so forth, he'd have to buy. Charity shops, which his mother always shunned, they'd be his best bet.

His one piece of luck was finding the bowling pavilion key still in his pocket. Hardly good luck, considering the proportion of bad. He knew the park gate code, Liz had given it to him. He'd once had to open up when Ian was away overnight and Liz had been sick. Though he could have climbed in the park easily enough – where the fence met a brick pillar.

Coming in, he'd seen torchlight near the playground. Zar had hidden behind the marquee to get as close as he dared, to find out what was going on. Some way off, there was Liz with a torch and she was over someone on the ground, injured it seemed. And then a van came in the gate and along the drive. The builder's van.

It drew up to where Liz and the injured person were. And he couldn't see what was going on as the van was in the way. But he could guess what was happening, Jack would be taking whoever it was away, most likely to hospital.

It was only once the van had gone, taken away the sick person, Liz gone back in torchlight to her cottage and all was quiet in the park, that he'd headed for the pavilion. Once inside, he'd settled for under the counter. It was out of any drafts, and not obvious, should anyone come in. Though he hoped to be up and out before that might happen.

Tomorrow, he'd have to get a room somewhere.

But it had happened. His family knew. Although it was forced on him, he was out. Left to himself, he may well have prevaricated forever. A life of excuses and lies. But no need, that was the good side. He was free. Homeless. But free.

He needed to shake his parents and Leila out of his head. Impossible. Had they contacted his brother? So what, if they had. Assume they had. Told the worldwide Muslim network, the United Nations, and broadcast it on the BBC. He was a degenerate. Not quite an apostate, though it hardly mattered. He might as well be tarred and feathered with that too. A total bogeyman. All that was needed was a fatwa from an Iranian mullah and he'd have to spend his life in hiding.

Zar was wide awake. He wanted to be asleep, be out to the world, but his head was a beehive buzzing with his angry parents and his predicament. Above all, he knew, he must hang on to his job.

Get a room. And work out how to live.

Chapter 27

Jack's phone rang. He wasn't yet asleep, so picked it up straight away. There were any number of possibilities for a late night call. Well, two. But it wasn't either of them.

'What are you doing calling me so late, Mia? It's twelve thirty.'

'There's a terrible row going on, Dad. Can you hear it?'

He pressed the phone hard to his ear.

'I can hear some yelling. What's happening?'

'He called her a bitch, she called him a complete prick.'

'Nice.'

'And a lot worse. I'm not sure I should tell you... They're throwing things now. She's saying he's a two-faced bastard. Can you hear?'

'I can't.'

'I'm surprised. It's very loud.'

'Do you know what it's about, Mia?'

'It's a bit difficult to understand, but I think he's got someone else... Someone called Emily. Mum just called him a two timing fucker. Sorry about the word.'

'It's alright when you're quoting.'

'I think Mum had a look at his phone...'

'Oh, that's despicable.'

'Didn't she have a right to?' queried Mia.

'Well, I suppose it's better than two-timing...' he said, contemplating his recent thoughts, if not actions.

'She's yelling: out, out, out! Get out of my house this minute... Ooh, it's getting exciting. There's things being thrown about. I should hide in a cupboard. The bedroom door's slammed.' She hushed her voice, 'He's in the hallway and shouting some really awful things, the c-word. She's yelling about the police... There's thumping and banging, and running down the stairs. He's at the bottom. Oh Dad, he called her a useless whore. And she said he was a prick brain... Oh! The front door has slammed. I think he's gone. Wow! She kicked him out.'

Jack thought of his own ejection. Not quite so dramatic, but she'd pushed him out on the pavement with a suitcase. With nowhere to go. Over two years ago.

'Do you think he's gone to Emily's?' she said.

'No, she's probably in bed with her husband.' Then aware of what he was saying to a twelve year old, added, 'Only joking.'

'Maybe she'd slam the door in his face. For two-timing. Hello, Mum.'

Faintly, he could hear Alison. 'Who are you talking to on the phone, Mia?'

'Dad.'

'Hello, Jack,' said Alison, who'd taken the phone. 'Been getting a running commentary?'

'Very exciting,' said Jack. 'Keeping our daughter and me awake.'

'The bastard's had two of us on the hook,' said Alison. 'And lying every time he opened his mouth.'

'That's men for you,' said Jack.

'I should know better by now. Though you never had anyone on the side,' she said. 'Or did you?'

'I didn't.'

'Are you on your own?'

'Fraid so.'

'It has its advantages, Jack, I can tell you. Now me and Mia are going to have a hot chocolate, and go to sleep.'

'Night, Dad,' called Mia.

'Goodnight, Mia. Sleep well, Alison.'

'I will, Jack. I've got the whole duvet to myself. Goodnight.'

They rang off.

Jack lay there, contemplating the Brighton scenario. He couldn't feel sorry for Tony. Mia didn't like him, so he didn't either. But he wondered about Tony's life. Was it just two he had? Or more? And the stress of it. The lying, having to keep all the stories straight, pretend business trips and so forth. There's a clear lesson, if you have two at once, you are likely to come to grief.

Chance'd be a fine thing.

Chapter 28

Zar thought of going for a walk round the park, or a run even. Six laps, race himself to exhaustion. Anything, so he could switch off. Oblivion. Wake up in the morning. Then work. He'd even volunteer for the leaf vac. Blast his head off.

Sleep was doomed.

The chocolate was gone. He remembered there was some leftover cake in the mess hut fridge; he'd have it for breakfast. He checked his phone. Six texts. Five from his parents, one from Leila. He would not read them. Why even keep them? What on earth did he think they were saying? *Please come home, Zar. We don't care what you are. We love you no matter what you do to other men. Say whatever you want in chat rooms. Go to gay clubs with our blessing. We love you. Just come home.*

He deleted the texts, one by one. Exalting in their death, their hold on him. He should get a new phone, then they couldn't get at him this way. A cheap one would do. A new number for a new life.

In five years, he might return home with his lover, when he was the Director of Kew Gardens. That might have to be ten years, maybe fifteen, say twenty then. With his chauffeur driven car and Nobel Prize.

Stupid, stupid. Sleeping on floorboards under a counter, dreaming of Nobel Prizes. As if he could buy his parents' love. Enough honours and even they would clasp him to their bosom.

Who exactly was forgiving whom?

The door of the pavilion opened. There were footsteps and voices. Zar sat up under the counter, alert. Was this a break in? He looked at his watch. Two forty five. What was going on? He pulled his knees up to his chest and listened. Bad as things were, he had no wish to be murdered.

A man with a deep, booming voice. He couldn't understand what he was saying, though it was English. And that was Rose. He'd recognise that laugh anywhere. He felt relief. He wasn't about to get cut up into bits. And recalled that Rose had told him at lunch yesterday that Liz had kicked her out. She obviously had the same idea as he had for a temporary refuge.

Though who was with her?

'This is real cool, Rose,' intoned the deep male voice. 'The stars have led us here.'

'I led us here,' said Rose. 'The stars have nothing to do with it.'

The lights came on.

'Switch them off, Man,' said Rose. 'We'll be seen.'

'We are an island of light,' said Man. 'We are the centre of the universe.'

'You're stoned, Man. How many dingbats did you take?'

'Everything communicates through me. I am the exchange. Every wire and email comes through my mind. I am the heart and soul. There is no heaven but through me.'

'And I am tired of listening to you,' said Rose wearily. 'I hardly slept last night. Got a lie down earlier but not enough... And I've work in the morning.' Then adding with a sigh, 'It is morning. I've got to work in five hours, Man. Stop playing with the light, will you. Someone is bound to see if you keep flicking it on and off like that.'

'I am the source. I am the target.'

'Leave it out, Man.'

It was dumb bringing Man Mountain here. She hadn't

meant to, but he had the taxi fare – and she'd thought he was just dropping her off, but he had other ideas. Quite what they were in his state, she couldn't fathom. The centre of the universe wasn't interested in sex. Just as well, the size of him. He'd squash her to a leaf.

Don't think of leaves. Anything but.

'I hold the light,' he chanted. 'It beams through my fingers with my permission. I give it to you, Rose. I give it to everyone on Earth. You are children of my light. I give you authorisation. Use it in your houses. Light up your little lives.'

'Wouldn't you like to sleep, Man?'

'If I sleep, the lights go out in the universe. The world freezes over. I must stay awake for the sake of everyone. I must give heat, the daughter of light. I am the exchange.'

'You've said that twice, Man.

She was seated in a chair, eyes barely staying open. Man was flicking the lights on and off to show his power. The monkey-brain. She was exhausted. Clubbing had not been the greatest of ideas. Especially when there was a warm bed she could be in right now. With a warm body next to her. She wouldn't have gone if she hadn't found the thirty quid. Something that she'd have to explain in the morning. It was morning.

'Through me the world becomes. Through me energy is manifest. I give orders to the quarks. I am all quantum levels.'

'You are a big, very stoned man, flipping a switch,' she said wearily.

He was so hyper, she'd never get to sleep with him here, spouting his nonsense while dingbats sizzled his brain. She had to get rid of him. Get him elsewhere, anywhere.

So, how?

'Your stars are calling you, Man,' she said, trying for

141

sincerity as she took his arm. 'Out there, up in the cosmos. They need you. They are pleading for your love. Come on, Man. Come to your darling stars.'

She drew him towards the door.

'My droplets, my sprays,' he intoned, looking skywards. 'I have not abandoned you. You are my love. I will envelop you in the fullness of my being.'

She drew him out the door and on to the verandah. The pavilion door closed.

Zar listened as their voices faded. More stars, darling things, calling Man's love... Until Zar could hear them no longer. The light was still on in the pavilion. He should turn it off, or there was a good chance he'd be discovered. What cretin had she brought with her? All that twaddle about light and the universe. Where were they going now?

Away, he hoped. To a distant galaxy, far far away.

Never mind the star seekers. Get the light off. In case Ian or Liz looked out of their cottage windows, or passing cops, for that matter, spotted the light... He drew off the sleeping bag and crawled from under the counter. He was fully dressed, apart from his shoes and jacket. He needed the loo. Another minute of light would do no harm. He crossed the pavilion hall and went in the gents. He would have had to get up for this, anyway, fairly soon.

Having done a pee, he automatically flushed the toilet. And regretted it. This wasn't his house. He was not supposed to be here. Remember?

Lights on, flushing water, all he needed was a megaphone.

Zar washed his hands and face. The water was cold but soothing. He thought of the situation back home. Were his parents sleeping? Or still ranting about the shame? His phone vibrated in his pocket. Another text had come in.

He wiped himself on a paper towel. Best turn the lights off now. Shut himself away. Privacy.

As he came out of the toilet, Rose was coming in the door.

'Zar! What are you doing here?'

'I've left home,' he said.

'Good for you,' she exclaimed. 'And company for me. Let's turn the light off or Man Mountain will be back. I left him in the marquee communing with the grass. He's taken his shoes off. I don't really understand why, but something about recharging Mother Nature.'

She turned off the light. He was standing in darkness, but knew his way to the counter. He could just make out Rose at the door.

'I'm locking up,' she said. 'Man Mountain will be alright. He's got the whole universe.'

He heard the door click.

'Isn't that BFG? Man Mountain,' he said.

'No,' she said, 'Big Friendly Giant is Roald Dahl. Man Mountain's from Gulliver's Travels. That's what they called him in Lilliput. At least, I think so. Anyway, I don't want to talk literature. I want to go to sleep. Where are you sleeping?'

'Under the counter.'

'Can I join you?'

'I'm gay,' he said.

'Then we're both safe. Look, I don't want to make love, just a little warm company. I've got a sleeping bag in the cupboard. Dare I switch the light on to get it?'

'I've a torch.'

'You are the light, the centre of my universe, Zar. Go get it.'

'I'm glad you came, Rose. I'm so miserable.'

'If I could see you, I'd give you a cuddle. Now go and get your torch.'

Chapter 29

Liz had not slept at all. Tried for several hours and then given up. Her head was too full of Ian. What might be happening to him in the hospital. Eating into his organs, like soldier ants roaming and gnawing.

Was intensive care rescuing him or was he beyond their assistance? If she hadn't invited Jack over, then Ian would have laid out in the park all night. And that surely would be too late for any recovery.

But she had invited the builder. And he had discovered him. And like a good knight, Jack had taken him to hospital. Much better if he hadn't come, much better if she hadn't needed company. Which she didn't get, daren't have considering the state she was in.

He would've seen. He would've guessed.

She was in this alone.

About three in the morning, Liz had got up and worked on Trees in the Park, painting and writing in the names of the species and areas of the park. For a period she was able to forget, and then it slammed back at her like a ball rebounding from a squash court.

She was a lousy murderer. She would never do it again. But doubted that would soft soap any jury. She wandered about her house, sitting here and there. Next door Ian's father would be asleep, utterly unaware of what was happening to his son. Outside the park was completely dark. An owl hooted. Tears came. But none for Ian. Not at all. They were for herself.

For the day ahead.

At 7.15, she had a coffee. She couldn't take food. Just the caffeine hit. She needed to act human. She washed. There were dark rings round her eyes, but she looked surprisingly well. Incredible what could be hidden behind a wash, clean clothes, brushed hair and a little make up.

All she had to do was walk straight.

She looked out of the window and yawned. It was drizzling. Never the best of days in the park. And there was a lot to do, with her in charge. Let it happen.

At the door, she put on her Wellington boots and waterproof coat. Did she need an umbrella? No, the rain would wake her up.

She went out.

The sky was battleship grey. Treetops swishing in the breeze, fallen leaves plastered on the drive like jigsaw pieces awaiting a puzzler. And clusters of them on the lawn, collected up for company. It was raining steadily, the droplets jumping into the puddles in suicide leaps.

Liz walked down the Mayor's Avenue, head up to face the rain, like a pilgrim doing a penance. At the junction of the main drive, opposite the playground, she turned left in the direction of the back gate. Once there, she opened up, swinging the iron gate back. It had the same code as the main gate. Really, it should be changed as too many people knew it now. She almost said to herself, when Ian gets back. Which he might or he might not.

When Ian was on holiday, she opened up the park; on all other days he felt it his duty to do it. To show ownership.

Liz headed for the main gate. Past the playground, past the tennis courts. Leaves had settled again, like slippery flat fish. There were puddles in the ochre of the courts. We should get some more in and level it. Talk to Ian...

She must drop this default.

Someone was coming out of the marquee. A huge bundle of a man. Very tall and rotund. In some sort of party clothes, as if it were all happening in the tent.

'What are you doing here?' she called, though she hardly cared.

The man looked at her as if she were a strange being. He scratched his head.

'I don't know.'

She crossed to him. The big man wore a shirt of red horizontal bars on which were cartoon musical notes dancing. His pantaloons came just below the knees; they were blue check, with noughts and crosses games in some of them. He was barefooted.

'I can't find my shoes,' he bewailed.

'How did you get in the park?'

He shrugged. 'I don't know.' He pointed back at the marquee. 'I woke up in there. I'm freezing. I can't find my shoes.'

She led him into the marquee.

Her cascade had been knocked down. She had a look at the blocks. No real damage. Just toppled. Then she saw the telescope in a corner of the tent. The telescope and mount were lying on their side on the ground. That was a more serious matter. Last night, she'd left it in here upright.

She went over to it, and bent down for a close look. On the grass were mirrored splinters of glass. It was clear what had happened. The hulk had knocked it over. And broken something.

'Found my shoes,' he exclaimed.

She turned, and saw him sitting on the wet grass, putting them on.

Take me somewhere else, she thought, wondering who was liable for the broken telescope. The big man, her, the park. Oh dear. She had enough on her plate this morning.

What did it matter.

Chapter 30

'I saw Liz taking Man Mountain to the main gate,' said Rose. 'I hope she got some sense out of him.'

'Where did you find him?'

'At the last café in the universe... I pulled in with my rocket ship and found him trapping aliens in his laser beams.' She stopped and smiled. 'At a club. I've seen him before. He's always stoned. I think he's a banker.'

They were both under the counter, washed after a fashion, dressed, gear stowed away.

'I'd murder for a coffee,' she sighed. 'Liz makes the loveliest Italian. I must go over there and get some clean clothes and persuade her to let me use the washing machine.'

'Why did she kick you out?'

She gave a short laugh. 'I have a habit of bringing people back. You might have noticed. And I'm not the tidiest person in the world... Liz is very organised. I'm a little too wild for her. I wish I wasn't. No I don't. Yes I do. You see – that's me all along. Don't know what I want.'

'My telephone.' He took it out of his pocket. 'My parents texting again. I delete them.'

'Can I read this one?'

He handed her the phone. 'Tell me whether it's good or bad.'

She clicked and sucked her bottom lip as she read. 'Bad,' she said. 'You have been taken over by the devil, they haven't got a son, never would they believe the filth...'

'Stop.' He put a hand over her mouth. 'I don't want to know.'

'Right.' She switched off the phone. Then turned over the back, took off the plate and removed the SIM card. She held up the little square. 'Get a new one.'

'There's twenty quid on it.'

'Ah.' She put it back in and put the plate back on. 'Run it out, then get a new one.' She gave him the phone.

'I was glad you came last night. I was feeling terrible.'

'Poor Zar.'

'I'm alright now. I've got the day ahead. Then after work, must find a room. Might have to take the day off tomorrow. What do you think?'

'Try newsagents' windows.' She sighed. 'Though you'll end up in some poky little room in a family house. Or some buy-to-let rip off.' She threw her hands wide. 'They are the worst, I tell you. Buy-to-let landlords. One I had in Manor Park. Retired. I was his pension, he told me. So he resented being asked for repairs. In fact on the second one, he gave me notice.'

'Not noisy guests?'

'He didn't live there. And the other flats in the house were students, so I had competition for noise.'

'I must find a place,' he said. 'Somewhere, anywhere.'

'Time for us to join the living,' she said. 'I have a route. We leave by the back window, then along the hedge. Best go one at a time...'

'You first.'

'Can you sub me a lunch?'

'I have to get some money out anyway. Alright. Get going.'

Chapter 31

Having opened up the park, Liz's next port of call was to Mr Swift to give him the news about his son. She headed for Ian's house but on the way saw Mr Swift wandering about near the playground. He was in his suit and tie as if about to go to work, an umbrella fending off the rain. She invited him to her place for a coffee.

'Ian's in hospital,' she said, once they were seated.

'What's happened to him, where?' asked Mr Swift anxiously.

She didn't want to mention the builder finding him, though why shouldn't she... No, her life was her life. What there was of it.

'I found him collapsed out there on the grass about 9 o'clock last night. Vomiting, cramps, I don't know what it was, but he was obviously very ill.' She realised she'd have to mention Jack, or get into a tangle of lies. 'The builder took him to Newham General.'

'What was he doing here?'

'My guest,' she said, hoping she'd not have to elaborate. And really there wasn't much more to say. 'He ran him to hospital in his van. And they took him straight into intensive care.'

'I couldn't find Ian this morning,' said Mr Swift. 'I'm an early riser, always up by seven. I thought he was taking his time opening up the park. He's always back for a cuppa together before work. So I went out to have a look.' He stopped, and added in some alarm. 'Heart, do you think?'

'I don't know.'

Most likely liver, she'd read up on death stalk, or kidneys. She hadn't thought of the effect on Mr Swift. Of what would happen to him if Ian died. When. Too involved in herself, to think beyond herself. But what was done was done. She'd have to ride it out.

'He's keen on you,' said the old man with a smirk. 'He bought a ring yesterday. He showed it to me. He was going to give it to you last night.'

So that's why he'd called. The ring moment, interrupted by vomiting.

'I never knew,' she said, knowing too much.

A flash of complications overwhelmed her. If Ian died, Mr Swift would have to leave his cottage. It was a tied house, dependent on Ian working for the Parks Department. She'd never meant to make the old man homeless. Yesterday she wasn't thinking clearly. Ian had sprung his threat on her. It would have been simpler, better all round, if she'd given notice and gone. Begun again somewhere else. But we are where we are. She was a host of homilies.

'I am so sorry,' she said, and she was sincerely. 'It's hard for you.'

'What should I do?' said Mr Swift.

'Can you make yourself breakfast?' she said.

He stiffened as if she was implying he was helpless. 'I do it every morning. Cornflakes, toast and marmalade. Listen to the radio. Do you know I'm learning the ukulele?'

'I didn't.'

'We've a band at the pensioners' club. Thirty of us learning music hall songs. We play and we sing. This morning we get together for a practice.' He stopped, aware he was off topic. 'What should I do about Ian? Do you think he'll be alright?'

'I hope so.'

'He won't die, will he?'

'He won't die,' she said.

She felt like a vicar patting a pensioner's hand. But sincerely, she didn't want him to die. Not today. When it wasn't the end of the world, when she was aware she could have said no to Ian. And left. This is what happens when you panic. You trip over your own feet.

'He took me in after his mother, Elsie, died. I was a bit lost then,' said Mr Swift, adding, 'I got so low. I was thinking, how can I manage. Then he took me in. Saved my life, in a manner of speaking.'

And if he dies, where will you be then? she thought but didn't say.

She looked at her watch. 'You go home and have your breakfast, Mr Swift. And I'll arrange a lift for you to the hospital.'

'Thank you, my dear. Ian was right to choose you.' Then added thoughtfully, 'But would you have had him?'

'You're quite embarrassing me, Mr Swift.'

'I didn't mean to do that. And it's none of my business anyway. Though you had that builder over, so maybe you've got your own ideas.'

Too many, she thought. Impractical at that.

With a few words of parting, she accompanied him to his door. It was raining hard, the wind blowing in sheets along the drive. He had his umbrella up. She suffered the weather in the few steps to his cottage.

'You could do worse, you know, than my boy,' he said with a wink as he let himself in.

She had done worse. She knew that as she strode across the lawn through the downpour to the mess hut.

Chapter 32

Jack sat back in his van in no hurry, drinking tea from his thermos. He'd parked close to the gates, so as not to have far to ferry his tools. The rain was sluicing down the windscreen and rattling on the roof. No work could be done till it stopped.

He should report in though. Show willing. And his telescope mustn't be left out. In fact, now was a good time to collect it. He couldn't do anything else, and it shouldn't be left, not with the public about. True, not many, but best be safe. It should be in the van locked up.

Finish his cup of tea first. He yawned, though he'd slept fairly well after Mia had phoned. But it had been a frustrating evening. No viewing, no supper, and no female company. One had gone clubbing, the other spoilt by Ian's sickness. Once at the hospital, the medics had whisked him off to intensive care; the speed was impressive, if somewhat scary. Their almost military rigour.

He wondered if there was any news.

And then, his fallback had left him with the washing up and thirty quid short. He laughed at his dashed hopes, coming into an empty flat. She had a cheek, Rose. And he had a vision of her naked in his dressing gown while she ate. Where did she end up last night?

Quite a body. But you don't just get a body. A person was included, with their foibles and hang-ups. He thought of Alison, her throwing-out of Tony. Sex wasn't enough there. Not in the end. Where did he end up?

Sleeping in his own bed, alone?

He screwed the cup on his thermos, and put it in his backpack. Jack opened the van door to be hit by the splash of a passing car. He cursed after it. It was belting down. Jack got out quickly and went to the back of his van. Crawling about inside, he gathered his bricklaying gear: trowel, bucket, shovel, line and spirit level. The wheelbarrow had been left in the tool shed overnight.

He was about to lock up, when he recalled the telescope – and shifted bits and pieces to make room for it. Then made his dash to the park. Down the drive, bucket rattling, shovel and level in the other hand. And into the yard, and a beeline for the tool shed.

His hair was wringing in that short distance. He shook it like a sheepdog just out of a pond. If it didn't clear up, this could be a day of nothing. He left everything he'd brought in the wheelbarrow, ready to begin as soon as he could.

He was standing at the door of the tool shed, when Liz came out of Ian's office.

'Morning,' he called to her. 'Got your water wings?'

'Oh, Jack.' She stopped undecided, the rain dripping off her hair, running down her face. 'Something's happened to your telescope, I'm afraid.'

'What?'

'Wait a moment.' She dived back in the office and came back out a few moments later with a large golfing umbrella. 'I'll show you.'

She crossed over and they both sheltered under it. Mostly it worked, though Jack had to lean in, their shoulders bouncing against each other as they walked swiftly. As they came out to the drive Zar and Rose were running in, their hoods up. They quickly yelled 'Morning,' and some comment on the rain as they dashed past into the yard.

'What's happened to the telescope?' said Jack as they scampered on.

'I'm not sure,' she said. 'But something's broken.'

'Oh, great.'

The park was a pale curtain of rain. Mist crept about the shrubbery and children's playground. Jack was half protected by the umbrella, his exposed hand cold and wet. The lawn was squelchy, his boots the cleanest they'd been since new.

In the marquee, he immediately spotted the telescope in one corner. And sped across to examine it. He knew at once what had happened from the shattered glass. It was a punch in the guts.

'The mirror's broken,' he said, down on his knees, looking at the bits as if he might be able to piece them together.

'Is it serious?' she said.

'Yes.' He was already calculating what, if anything, could be done. 'There was an 8 inch convex mirror in there.' He slapped the telescope body. 'It collects the light from the stars and planets, whatever you're looking at. It's the most vital bit of the telescope.'

'Is it replaceable?'

'I don't know,' he said turning up his hands. 'Never had to do it before. What a wreck!' He looked at the scope and mount. 'It's like a car without an engine. You can salvage the bits, but it's not a car anymore.'

'I'll replace it,' she said.

'Why?'

'I put it in here.'

'I told you to.' He stood up, wiping off tiny splinters of glass from his hands. 'It's my stupid fault. I should have put it in my van before I went to the hospital. This is what comes of cutting corners.'

'I put it in here upright,' she said. 'I tested that it was standing secure. But I should have laid it down on the grass. Anyway, I was opening up this morning, when a big hulk of a guy came out of the marquee. He didn't know where he was, how he got here. Drugs, I think. He knocked over my cascade.' She indicated the blocks in disarray. 'And this too. I am so sorry, Jack.'

'Damn it all,' he exclaimed. 'It's not your fault. All mine. One hundred percent. I should have put it in my van. Because that's what happens when you don't. 600 pounds of telescope down the drain.'

'Maybe it can be repaired.'

'I'll investigate tonight. See if I can buy a mirror for it somewhere. I can't imagine it'll be less than one fifty. If I can even get it done.'

Rain was pelting on the canvas, dripping down in a few areas, where canvas sheet met sheet, and puddling on the grass. There was a blast of thunder and, a few seconds later, its echo.

'Is there anything I can do at all, Jack?'

'Don't think so,' he said, shaking his head. 'It's happened.' He flicked a hand, 'It's only money.' He gave a short laugh, thinking of the few hundred cushion he had. He didn't have a spare one fifty. Or whatever. Pox.

'Do you want to leave it at my place?' she said.

'I've got to get it back home,' he said. 'I'll have to take it apart and ferry it to the van. It has to end up at my flat.'

'Bring the van in,' she said. 'I'm in charge today.'

'I will,' he said. 'Thanks.'

'And one more thing. It's a cheek asking, considering what's happened. But can you take Mr Swift to the hospital to find out about Ian?'

Jack considered her request for a few seconds. He'd had a row with the old bastard yesterday. Then again his son was in hospital and very ill.

'OK. I can't do anything else, this weather,' he said. 'I might as well do something useful.'

Chapter 33

All the park workers were in the mess hut drinking tea when Liz came in. Zar and Rose were finishing the remnant of yesterday's cake.

'Tea, Liz?' said Amy.

'Please.' She sat down and waited for her tea. There was quite a bit to do, and not that much of it could be done. She'd scratched herself some notes. Amy put a mug of tea in front of her. 'Thank you, Amy.' She looked about her. 'Everyone here?'

'Except Ian,' said Bill.

'Let's begin with that then,' she said. 'Ian's in hospital. He was taken ill last night and had to be rushed to casualty.'

'By ambulance?' said Bill.

'No,' she said. 'Jack, the builder, took him.'

'What was he doing here?'

Here we go again, she thought, her private life paraded. 'He was my guest,' she said. 'Or he might have been, if he hadn't found Ian vomiting his guts out, out there by the playground. About nine o'clock.'

'Do they know what's wrong?' said Amy. 'How long he'll be in for?'

'Don't know to both questions,' she said. 'Jack has kindly offered to take Mr Swift to the hospital – and we'll know more when they're back. In the meantime, I'm in charge, probably for the next couple of days. Any questions?' She looked around at them all, giving them time to take it all in.

'He was fine when we left last night,' said Bill.

'I've never seen him so cheerful,' said Amy.

'Obviously very sudden,' said Liz. 'Jack took Ian in, as I've said, and they rushed him to intensive care.'

'That builder is getting his oar in everywhere,' said Bill.

'What do you mean by that, Bill?'

Bill blew a raspberry. 'He's just a contract worker. Here today, gone tomorrow. And here he is, in the park after dark and now taking the boss's father to hospital.'

'Do you want to take him, Bill?'

'I've only got my bike.'

'Then shut up.' She watched him grind his teeth. She'd never liked Bill and knew it was mutual. Everyone was watching her, waiting. Had she been too harsh? Too late. 'It's indoor work this morning, until the weather eases off. The playground and courts stay shut. Bill, Amy and Rose, you can tidy the tool shed. It's getting a bit of a tip anyway. Sharpen the baggin hooks. Zar, you can help me in the greenhouse and marquee.' She looked at her watch. 'A few minutes to finish your tea, and then off you go.'

She wanted to rush out of the mess hut but felt she should stay to see them all cut to work. She was the temporary boss now, and, if Ian died, the permanent one. She wasn't sure she liked it. The antagonism, the need to face down hostility, every day.

One day at a time.

She felt very alone. But she'd done it. Put herself here. It had never been her intention to make herself the boss. Everything was changing too quickly for her to catch up.

Chapter 34

Jack's first van stop was on the drive parallel with the marquee. It was raining hard as he crossed the lawn to pick up the mount. In the marquee, he detached it from the telescope and braved the weather to dash across to the van. He put it in the back and returned to the marquee for the telescope. He wrapped it in the blanket, though it hardly mattered now. Habit. When could he afford to get it repaired? It hurt. He'd loved that scope. Out in the evening scouring the skies. It would sadden Mia too. She was often out with him when she was over, looking at the moon, the planets and into deep space.

It had happened. No one had died. Once at the van, he put in the scope, shook his head at the damage, some other day's worry. And closed up the back and got in the front. He sat back, wiping his wet hands on his trousers. So he'd slept alone, there are a lot worse things. Today was another day, he might try to visit Liz in her greenhouse later. And who knows?

He drove to the cottages.

He rang the bell of number 1. There was movement inside and Mr Swift answered the door.

'What d'you want?'

'I've come to take you to hospital.'

'I'm not going with you.'

Jack could easily have walked away at that moment. He was doing the old man a favour. This wasn't in his contract.

'It's pouring with rain,' said Jack. 'I know we had a bit of a row yesterday...but your son's in hospital. And you need to be there with him.'

'I do,' admitted Mr Swift.

'You don't have to talk to me Consider me your taxi.'

Mr Swift looked at him fiercely. 'You won't come none of your union nonsense?'

Jack couldn't prevent a short laugh. 'Let's say that's a topic we stay off of.'

'Unions have ruined this country.'

Jack held up a hand. 'Don't start, if you want a lift.'

'You don't agree with me?'

'I don't.'

Mr Swift seemed about to put his fists up. Jack had his hood on but was getting severely wet, the rain soaking into his trousers.

'You coming or not?'

'I'll get my coat,' said the old man.

Jack got into the van and waited for him.

They drove off, neither wanting to start a conversation. The traffic was busy at the Greengate junction with the Barking Road, the windscreen wiper overworked. The sort of weather where you consider every driver a menace. And wonder what you are doing out in it yourself.

'You having a thing with her next door?' asked the old man at one point.

'Nope.'

'Then how come you were there last night?'

Jack laughed. 'I might have got to the point of having a thing but your son put a stop to it. Any more questions on the subject?'

'The two of you seem to be getting on well.'

'And I'd like us to get on better,' said Jack, 'but things happen.'

'You know my son's keen on her?'

159

'No, I didn't know that,' he said, adding after a second's thought, 'Is she keen on him, though?'

'I don't know,' said Mr Swift. 'He's brought a ring. So he's dead serious.'

Meaning I'm not, thought Jack.

'He was going to give it to her last night,' went on the old man.

'I hope he's alright,' said Jack, noncommittal. There was no point getting into a wrangle over an affair that had never started.

'I'll be missing my ukulele session this morning,' said Mr Swift.

'A secret talent,' exclaimed Jack, happy to get off the topic of Liz. 'How many chords do you know?'

'Six,' said the old man. 'And I bet they'll be learning a new one. I'll have to find out what it is and catch up on my own. It's a band. We're learning *Down By The Sally Gardens*. Do you know it?'

'Can't say I do?'

The old man began singing:

It was down by the Sally Gardens, my love and I did meet.
She crossed the Sally Gardens, with little snow-white feet.
She bid me to take life easy, as the leaves grow on the tree,
But I was young and foolish, and with her I did not agree.

'You've got a good voice,' said Jack. And thought, not bad at all, considering his age. He held the tune well. 'It's a sad song,' he added.

'About life and love,' said the old man.

'Then I'd better hear some more,' said Jack. 'Sing the rest of it.'

The old man smiled, obviously pleased to be asked. He sang on.

In a field down by the river, my love and I did stand
And upon my leaning shoulder, she laid her snow-white hand.
She bid me to take life easy, as the grass grows on the weirs,
But I was young and foolish, and now I am full of tears.

Down by the Sally Gardens, my love and I did meet.
She crossed the Sally Gardens, with little snow-white feet.
She bid me to take life easy, as the leaves blow on the tree,
But I was young and foolish, and with her I did not agree.

Jack reflected, there was more to the old boy than he'd first thought. Avoid snap judgements. And don't talk about unions.

They parked in the hospital grounds. Jack was annoyed at the parking fee, but kept it to himself. Mr Swift was his guest, so to speak, and had enough troubles. Besides which, he could hold a tune which was more than Jack could do himself.

Jack and Mr Swift went to the reception. There, he asked about Ian Swift who'd been taken into intensive care last night. The receptionist phoned through. She had a short conversation, and asked Jack and Mr Swift to sit down, a doctor was coming for them.

They took two seats in the front row of the waiting area. There were about a dozen rows of seats, about half full, men, women, all ages and races Jack wondered how many were seriously ill, how many trivial. He knew himself that he'd have to be at death's door before seeing a doctor, and knew, too, that wasn't necessarily a good thing.

He shivered. An intimation of mortality. Then felt a duty to his charge.

'You used to be a bricklayer, didn't you, Mr Swift?'

'And so I was, before they made me foreman.'

'You can give me a hand then.' He'd said it without thinking.

161

The old man looked at him. 'You serious?'

'Only if you want to. I'll do all the donkey work. Make up the mortar. Then we both lay the bricks.'

The old man considered it, his tongue lolling in his cheek. 'I quite fancy that. Mind you, these hands are not as good as they were.'

'If you can manage a ukulele, I'm sure you can handle a brick.'

Mr Swift put his hand out. 'Put it there, chum.'

They shook hands, just as a young Asian woman in a white coat came over.

'Mr Swift?' she enquired.

'That's me.'

'I'm Dr Khan. If you'd like to come this way,' she said. 'Some privacy. And I'll tell you what's going on.'

She led them along the corridor and into a small room with three chairs and a desk. They seated themselves. Jack and Mr Swift waited for the young doctor to begin. Jack sensed from her face it wasn't good.

She said, 'I'm afraid I have bad news for you, Mr Swift. Your son came in last night. We put him straight into intensive care. We did all we could, I assure you, Mr Swift. But he died half an hour ago.'

'Dead?' said the old man. 'You say Ian is dead?'

'I am so sorry to be the bearer of this news,' she said. 'But yes, I'm afraid he's dead.'

The room was silenced by the impact of this. Jack could see the young woman was uncomfortable. She hadn't done this often.

'Do you know what he died of?' said Jack.

The doctor shrugged. 'Some sort of poison affecting his liver and kidneys, it would appear. That's all we can say at the moment. There will be an autopsy, which should make it clear.'

'Where is he?' asked Mr Swift.

'He's been taken to the mortuary. Do you want to see him?'

'Yes, I do. If you don't mind.'

'Not at all. I'll take you there.'

Along the long corridor, Jack took the old man's arm as they walked, following the white-coated doctor. They ambled, Mr Swift was slumped onto his walking stick, as if he'd aged five years in as many minutes.

'I am sorry, Mr Swift,' said Jack. 'It was obvious he was in a bad way last night. I just hoped they'd be able to rescue him.'

The old man turned to him. 'Everyone's gone. Elsie, Ian.' He gave a long sigh. 'It's just me by myself now.'

Chapter 35

Liz and Zar had reassembled the cascade. The wooden blocks needed two to lift them in place to make up the unit, which consisted of steps of non-uniform size, down which water would run in simulation of a waterfall. Alongside the cascading water would be various plants, depending on the season, as Liz set it up about four times a year around the borough for various occasions.

Both were in their park overalls, wearing Wellington boots. The rain rattled on the top canvas and the sides shook like sails in a gale. The roof was sagging on one side where a puddle was collecting above, drips coming through the joins.

They had a wheelbarrow of compost. Liz and Zar were putting it in the cavities down the sides of the cascade, for plants to apparently grow out of, though in reality they'd remain in their pots which would be hidden by the compost, giving the effect of prolific greenery growing alongside a waterfall.

'I don't know how that man got in the park,' said Liz. She had a smear of compost on her cheek and forehead. 'He was enormous. Round as a compost bin, almost as high as this roof. I couldn't imagine him climbing over the park fence. When I asked him, he looked utterly bewildered, didn't know where he was, as if he'd suddenly appeared from another planet.'

'He must've barrelled into the cascade,' said Zar.

'That hardly matters,' she said, 'but the worst of it was

Jack's telescope. When he took Ian to hospital, I put it in here to protect it, for heaven's sake.'

'That's a real shame,' said Zar.

'Jack's upset. And I feel responsible. I should have laid it on the ground. Not left it to be knocked over.'

'You weren't to know that man was around.'

'No,' said Liz with a sigh, 'but you just can't assume. And next time, I won't.' She went to the marquee entrance and looked across the lawn. 'Oh, this rain. The beds have to be dug over and flowers in by tomorrow.'

'What if it rains all day today?'

She shrugged. 'Then nothing will get done. There'll be puddles everywhere. And I'll have to explain to the Mayor and MP, and whoever they bring with them, that the rain gods have cursed us.'

'It'll be just you at the ceremony. Not Ian. With him in hospital.'

'I doubt they'll wheel his bed along.' She shook her head. 'I'm sure the bigwigs just come for the food and drink. A catering company brings it all over tomorrow morning. It's such a palaver for one hour. Then off they all go, to the pub for all I know. Or their next do.'

What was she to say to the guests about Ian? As little as possible. Ian is ill; he's sorry he can't be here, and so forth. Then stand by the cascade and the Tree Plan and try to keep to park topics. Show them the greenhouses...

'I've been thinking about Ian,' said Zar.

'Thinking what?' she said, thrown from her own thoughts.

'You know the death stalks you had me pull out. Do you suppose he might've accidentally picked them? Thought they were edible.'

'I suppose it's possible,' she said carefully.

'But then Mr Swift would have had them too,' said Zar dismissively. 'So not very likely.'

165

'Not very likely,' she agreed.

She could so easily have yelled – shut up! Which would only have alerted him. She just hoped Ian was alive and recovering – and they'd never find out who or what caused his sickness. Put it down to some mysterious bug. She wiped her eyes with the back of her hand. She couldn't go on like this.

'Carry on with the compost, will you, Zar?' she said, turning away. 'I'm going to the office.'

And she ran out into the rain.

Her tears were smothered in the raindrops. Zar was smart. She'd kept him with her so he wouldn't talk to anyone else, but then he talked to her. About those damned mushrooms.

Ian was in intensive care with drips and doctors, and she was here, doing her job as if it were simply another autumn day, the leaves falling and the rain having its day. The day was so slow, as if Ian's hospital bed were moving imperceptibly down a mountain glacier while she waited at the foot to know what was happening to him.

She was in the office when Jack arrived. When she'd first come in, she'd done nothing. It was a hideaway. Then wiping her eyes, she must appear normal and not simply wait for news. She must busy herself or time would never pass. And so she looked up telescope mirrors, thinking she might surprise Jack with a present. But was quite bamboozled by the technical language. It had killed twenty minutes but not been a useful quest.

'How was it?' she said as he entered.

A question normal people asked. Her heart racing, guessing the outcome from his dour face. Not wanting to be told.

'He's dead,' he said.

'Oh no!' Her hands slapped to her cheeks. 'How can that be?'

'He died half an hour before we arrived,' said Jack. 'The doctor took us to the mortuary. There he was, still in hospital pyjamas, as if he were asleep.'

She uncovered her face, a tear slid down her cheek, that she caught on a finger.

'How did Mr Swift take it?'

'He was quiet on the way back. Worried about what's going to happen to him.'

'Oh dear,' she said. 'It's always the living that suffer.' And felt she should ask, as anyone would ask. 'Did they say what it was?'

'Some sort of poisoning. They don't know what. There'll be an autopsy.'

'Oh,' she said, overcome with exhaustion, 'I just want to close the park. Send everyone home. Bring down the shutters on today.'

'You're the boss now.'

'I don't want to be anyone's boss,' she said dabbing her eyes with a tissue.

'You'll do it better than he did.'

'He was my neighbour,' she said. 'I'd hear his television faintly through the wall. He helped me put up my bean poles.' Speak no ill of the dead. Everyone knew that. She handed out further memories like old photos. 'I gave him tomatoes, he gave me broccoli... I pruned his roses while I was pruning mine. I looked after his rabbit when he was away. We had a drink together on Christmas morning...'

It had happened. The event she'd put in train when she gave him lunch yesterday afternoon. Did anyone know they'd eaten together? Zar must keep quiet about the mushrooms in the park. Her thoughts flowed under his words like a second sound track.

'You can't help wondering,' said Jack. 'Or maybe it's the way I think, but could it have been deliberate, the poisoning?'

'What do you mean?' she said, knowing absolutely what he meant.

'Suicide or even murder,' he said.

She flapped a hand in dismissal. 'I can't believe it. This is not gangland drugs turf. It's a park. These things don't happen. Not here.'

'Put it down to my sick mind. Too many crime movies.'

She was trembling. She wanted him out of her space but didn't know how to get rid of him. Ian was dead. Did she seem too upset? Not upset enough... or in the right way? Why wouldn't the builder leave? Was he watching her?

'You've a smudge on your cheek and forehead,' he said. He took the tissue out of her hand and wiped them off. 'That's better.'

'Thank you, Jack. Now I'm suitable for the troops.' She managed a half smile, her stomach tumbling like a drier. 'How's the weather doing?' Always a safe topic.

'It's stopped raining,' he said looking out the window. 'Well, well. Might get some work done today. Blue patches are opening up.'

She looked at her watch. 'It's almost lunchtime. I'm going home. I can make something for Mr Swift.'

'He looks rather lost,' said Jack. 'I said he could help me with the bricklaying this afternoon.'

'That's good of you.'

Go, she thought. She needed to compose herself. Take in this new world. Not chit chat. Or what might she say? And then it occurred to her, she could at least restrain speculation in the mess hut over lunch.

'Don't tell anyone about Ian,' she said. 'We'll have a meeting after lunch and I can tell them formally. Better than piecemeal.'

'OK,' said Jack. 'I'll leave it to the boss. I'm off to eat.'

And he left.

Just like that. As if nothing much had happened. He

came, gave the news. He went. She sat numbly in Ian's chair. Hers now. With a whole half day to get through. Home first, shut the door on the world for an hour, weep her eyes dry. Make sense of it, if sense there was. And return to the new regime.

Chapter 36

As Jack left the park office, Rose came out of the tool shed. Her hair was awry, her face grimy. As she saw him she frowned; a second earlier and she might have ducked back into the shed. 'I'm sorry about your telescope,' she said.

'Some giant was wandering round the park,' he said. 'Knocking things over.'

'Really,' she said, not catching his eye. 'Quite a fairy tale.' She bit her forefinger, then added, 'I will give you back the thirty quid I borrowed.'

'Nicked,' he said.

'Just borrowed,' she retorted. 'I saw it laying around.'

'In a drawer?'

'Well, that's not exactly in a safe,' she said.

'Oh, so it's my fault then. I get it. I shouldn't leave money around my flat. At least, not if I invite you over.'

Hands on hips, she said, 'You going to call the police on me?'

'No. But I want it back.'

'OK. You'll get it.' Her nose screwed up. 'Alright, I shouldn't have done it, but I was so bored.' Then she added with a placatory grin, 'I did mean to come back last night. But you know what it's like at a club...'

'I don't, actually.'

She shrugged. 'Come throwing out time, you just do what everyone else is doing. You follow whoever is going on to somewhere else.'

It occurred to him; there was Rose tagging along in the

early hours with the oddbods chucked out of the club. Maybe...

'Did you stay in the pavilion last night?' he said.

'Yes,' she smiled. 'My new address. Spartan, but somewhere to crash. Besides, it was so late... Zar was there too.'

'Quite a guest house,' he said. 'Might there have been a big man you brought along from a club?'

'Of course not.'

Jack stared at her for any hint, she stared back, daring him to challenge her.

He held a finger up. 'Wait.' And stepped into the tool shed. In the gloom, Zar and Bill were hanging up tools on hooks. 'Zar!' he called. The young man turned. 'Just a word, Zar.'

Zar nodded and came to the entrance.

'What's up?'

'Did Rose come on her own to the pavilion last night? Or was she with someone?'

Zar looked at Rose. Her face was stony. He turned back to Jack.

'She was on her own,' he said.

Jack was exasperated, he'd seen no communication. Rose was grinning smugly. Were they lying? He couldn't tell. Did it matter? Yes. His telescope was in bits.

'What were you doing in the pavilion anyway?' he said to Zar.

'My parents kicked me out...' he began, then corrected himself, 'Or rather, I left before they kicked me out.'

'I'm sorry.'

Zar shrugged. 'It was going to happen. Just happened a little sooner than I'd planned... Sorry about your telescope.'

'I should pass the hat round,' he said bitterly. 'Not that I'd get a bent penny from you,' he added, prodding Rose on the shoulder.

'Lay off,' she said resentfully, pushing his hand away.

Jack looked at his watch. 'I'm going to wash up for lunch.'

'Jack,' she called as he began crossing the yard. He turned. 'It wasn't my fault.'

'OK,' he said, waving a hand in the air. 'It was the wind that done it.'

Chapter 37

He ate his lunch on the wall, placing a plastic sack underneath him, to keep the damp off. He'd unrolled his shirt sleeves and put his denim jacket on. He was too grumpy for the mess hut, wanting no more sympathy for his telescope. Besides which, Liz had told him not to tell anyone Ian was dead. So best that he keep his own company, and read the Mirror.

He thought of Rose. Lively and attractive, too lively, promising everything to everyone, but that only works for so long. Her sister had kicked her out, had enough of her. He didn't trust her either. But then again, what was he up to himself? She'd been the understudy, knowing the audience would be disappointed when she came on. Could he really complain when she wasn't in his bed, waiting?

Hardly. But yes, there was resentment. The 30 quid didn't matter. Not much anyway. The telescope, yes, but she wasn't part of that. Or at least, she didn't do it herself. Some drugged up giant, who she may well have pulled in from the clubbing scene.

Forget Rose.

It had to be Liz. A star session tonight? Last night's hadn't happened. And his telescope was kaput, but he had his binoculars – and the skies were clearing. He could suggest another go. Though she did seem overwrought. Understandable, suddenly being manager, Ian's death, and on top of it all the fuss about tomorrow's ceremony. She hadn't exactly been chummy in the office. Maybe it was his attitude and she'd picked up on it. The busted telescope, the rain, a trip to the mortuary...

He cared a lot less about Ian than she did. Well, she was his neighbour, he'd been here less than two days and the man had hardly said a pleasant word to him. No wonder he couldn't grieve.

He'd been so proud of his 8 inch Newtonian. But it was a heap of junk. Get used to it. Unless he could find a dealer who supplied telescopic mirrors. At a price he could afford. They didn't give them away.

Lunch over, he walked over to the cottages to pick up Mr Swift. And found him ready for work, in his overalls and boots. He had a spirit level, a string line and a bricklayer's trowel.

'I see you've got the gear,' he said, looking him up and down.

'It's been sitting around a while,' said the old man. 'Let's see what I still remember.'

Liz waved to them from her kitchen window. Jack waved back. She blew him a kiss. And Jack wondered. Sometimes it was better not to talk.

'How was your lunch?' said Jack.

'Liz made me up a salad with some very nice pie. I don't know what was in it. Some vegetarian thing. Surprisingly good. Tasted almost like meat. And we talked about Ian. She's more upset than she'll admit.' He shook his head. 'Ian went to lunch there yesterday. They were getting close. And now...' He flapped a hand weakly.

Ian for lunch and me for supper? Well, well, thought Jack. Either she's very sociable – or what? It could have been just a working lunch. Why make anything of it? They were neighbours, they had a big event on. Did there have to be any more to it than that?

They were walking across the lawn, their footfalls squeezing water out of the short grass.

'There'll have to be a funeral,' went on the old man. 'I can't face that. All the people to phone up and whatnot. And a cremation or burial. What do you think's best?

'It's up to you,' said Jack with a shrug. 'When you're gone you're gone. What do you prefer?'

'If there's heaven,' said Mr Swift, 'then, surely, you need a body to walk up all those steps? I always feel with cremation, all that heat would burn up the soul.'

'Isn't it supposed to float off when you die?' said Jack. 'The body being just a shell. Mind you, I'm a heathen. When I'm dead, you can put me in the dustbin. I won't be around to gripe.'

'I got some savings.' The old man bit his lip. 'I think a burial with a marble headstone.. Maybe Liz could make a poem to go on it.'

'The funeral won't be a while yet,' said Jack. 'There has to be an autopsy when there's an unexplained death. And then an inquest.'

The old man went on as if he hadn't spoken. 'I was thinking of singing *Down by the Sally Gardens* at the funeral service... Do you think that would be suitable?'

'I do,' said Jack. 'Well, I enjoyed it. It's a song full of regret, for things that should have been done better.'

'So say all of us,' said the old man.

They were at the wall. Jack paced the gap.

'Do you think you could set your line up this side?' said Jack, 'while I bring the bricks out and then make up the mortar.'

'If I can get down to ground level, I can manage that.'

'There's no hurry,' said Jack. 'Do it at your own pace.'

'You'll never make a foreman.'

'And never want to be.'

He went into the yard, and to the tool shed. The wheelbarrow was there, neatly against a wall, his tools still in it from yesterday. Jack wheeled it out and over to the pile of

175

reclaimed bricks. He removed the tools and filled the barrow with bricks. Then laying the tools on top, set off back to the wall.

While dropping off the bricks, he noted that Mr Swift knew what he was doing, though he was a little creaky on hands and knees. The old man had set up a line, running from both sides of the old wall, across the gap, at one brick height.

'The first course of bricks is the important one,' said Mr Swift. 'Get that right and you've got a good level to work from.'

Jack left him, and returned to the yard with the wheelbarrow, to make up the mortar. It made a change to have a mate to work with, though he'd have to take care the old boy didn't push himself too hard. One death in the family was more than enough.

Chapter 38

They were seated round the mess hut table: Zar, Rose, Amy and Bill, with Liz at the head. She wasn't sure how to begin, but she had to tell them the news. Her hands were below the table trembling. She would keep the meeting short and get them all out working. And busy herself too.

'I've sad news,' she said, deciding there was no easy way in. They were all looking at her, wondering. 'Ian died this morning.'

'Bloody hell,' cried Bill.

'He can't have,' exclaimed Amy. 'He was right as rain when I left yesterday.'

Rose said, 'Who's been putting pins in him?'

'He was younger than my dad,' exclaimed Zar.

'Forty-six years old,' said Liz with a sigh. 'Jack took Mr Swift to the hospital this morning and they gave them the news. Ian had been in intensive care all night, but it didn't work. Sadly. Jack and Mr Swift were taken to the mortuary to view the body. So there's no doubt.'

'Do they know what killed him?' asked Amy.

'No,' said Liz. She would not mention poison, not with Zar here. Let it come out later, when she was more capable, when events were fuzzier, some time ahead, not now. 'There will be an autopsy,' she went on, 'and an inquest. But for now, it's an unexplained death.'

'Heart,' said Bill knowledgably. 'These things. Usually the heart. They find a weakness no one knew about. Living on borrowed time, I bet you.'

She might have stopped him, but he was offering other possibilities. Clouding the issue.

Amy said, 'Five o'clock yesterday, I was talking to him in the playground. I've never seen him so cheerful. So full of energy.'

'He was grinning all afternoon,' agreed Rose. 'I wondered what he was on.'

'Yes,' said Zar, 'he came in here when we were eating cakes. Remember? And for once, he wasn't looking at his watch all the time.'

'He made a little speech,' said Amy. 'Something about us all being like a family.' A tear rolled down her cheek. 'It's so sudden. I can't believe it. Dead.'

'We'll make up a floral tribute,' said Liz. 'It's the least we can do. Close the park for the day of the funeral.'

They were watching her; she wished they weren't. As if she had answers. And maybe she had, but none she wanted to give them. Amy was wiping her eyes with the back of her hand. Bill was Bill, no different it seemed. He'd been Ian's confidant. But then Bill always expected the worst, so perhaps was the least surprised of them all.

She said, 'We're a bit pushed today. We've lost a morning with the rain. I'm leaving the tennis courts shut. There's puddles in there anyway, and it's too much trouble to clear them. Let them dry out over the afternoon. Bill and Zar, you two carry on with the flowerbeds. Get them cleared and dug over this afternoon. I'll give you some overtime if needs be. Hopefully, we can get at least some of the flowers put in tomorrow morning before the Mayor and his party arrive. In fact, it will look good with the two of you working on the beds when everyone comes. Boxes of colourful primulas and all that. I'm going to be watering the plants in the greenhouses, and I have to test out the hose and connections for the cascade. Rose – you can go in the playground...'

Amy interrupted. 'That's my job, Liz.'

'Rose, you can go in the playground,' repeated Liz.

'That's mine, I always do that,' insisted Amy.

'Be fair,' said Rose, smiling at Amy. 'Share and share alike.'

'I'm the playground worker,' went on Amy. 'Ian *always* has me there. It has to be me.'

'No, it doesn't,' said Liz, angered by Amy's tirade. 'You can leaf vac this afternoon for once.'

Amy stood up and pointed at Rose. 'It's a family thing!' she exclaimed. 'Not even in his coffin and you're playing favourites.'

'How dare you speak to me like that!' exploded Liz. She stood up. 'You are an assistant gardener, the same as Rose. You do not tell me where you are working.'

'I always do the playground, Liz,' she said, visibly weakening.

'You do not always do the playground, Amy.'

Liz was determined not to lose this face off. She was either the manager in the park or not.

'I know where everything is,' insisted Amy, 'I know all the mums, they trust me.'

Liz stood her ground. She was boiling inside, but could see Amy was beaten.

'Amy, are you the manager of this park?'

'No. I'm not. But, Liz, it's my right.'

'I don't know what right you are talking about, Amy. Your contract of employment says you will work anywhere in the park as requested by your manager. That being so, it's Rose in the playground this afternoon. And you, Amy, on the leaf vac. And that is an end to it.' She gazed round at them all; they'd stayed like kids watching a fight. 'You all know what you have to do. Let's go.'

Bill and Zar left. Rose too, working to hide a grin. Amy stayed.

'Please, Liz,' she wheedled. 'I need to be in the playground.'

'You do not.'

'It's my job.'

'I have been telling you for the last few minutes, that this afternoon it is not. Maybe tomorrow, but not this afternoon. It's not for one person to assume they have a permanent position.'

'You have in the greenhouses.'

'I am qualified,' she said, knowing that wasn't quite true. At least not on paper. 'You are not.'

'Please, Liz. I beg of you.'

'I don't want to sack you, Amy, but you are pushing me to the limit. I have told you what to do. Leaf vaccing. Are you refusing to do it?' She waved a finger at her face. 'If so, I will dismiss you.'

Amy sagged like a pierced cushion.

'I'll do the bloody vaccing.' And she left.

Liz sank onto the bench. She was exhausted. She hated herself for going through that, but simply was being fair. Rose, sister or not, had been leaf vaccing too long. Jobs were to be shared. She could not let Amy take ownership of the playground.

Though her lie about qualifications made her realise her own weakness. She had to take the exam and pass it. Pass well. And hope no one else looked through her job application of three years ago.

She left the mess hut, as Amy was leaving the yard pushing the leaf vac.

PART THREE:
THE INVESTIGATION

Chapter 39

The man had come in the rear entrance from Balaam Street, and done a tour of the park, avoiding the grass as it was too wet for his almost new, brown leather shoes. He noted the layout with the two cottages side by side, the playground, the tennis courts, the bowling green, the lawn with the marquee in the middle, a couple of greenhouses, a yard. Two workers were on a flower bed digging it over, another two doing some bricklaying, one surely too old. A couple of people were walking dogs. A woman in the playground was wiping the seats of the swings with a large sponge.

He was black, tall, broad shouldered, late twenties perhaps. Someone who plainly took care of his appearance. His grey trousers had a sharp crease, his navy jacket was spruce, and under it a white shirt with a red tie.

Zar came near with a wheelbarrow of compost.

The man said, 'Excuse me. May I ask you something?'

Zar put down the barrow. 'Sure. What do you want to know?'

'Lots,' said the man.

They gazed at each other. Zar felt he should be looking away.

'Do I detect one of the chosen people?' said the man, his eyes widening.

'I beg your pardon?' said Zar.

'Do you want to go to the Promised Land?'

Zar shook his head. 'I'm sorry, but I'm a Muslim.'

The man laughed. 'Don't worry, I'm not a holy roller.' He paused for a second, his gaze not leaving Zar's eyes. 'Let's be direct, young man. Are you gay?'

Zar hesitated. 'A bit,' he stammered.

'Can I take that as a yes?' said the man with a smile.

'I don't know you,' said Zar.

'But do you want to know me?'

Zar was electric. It was clear what was happening. They had recognised each other. And it was in his court. He could say yes, he could say no.

'I'm not sure,' he said.

'It pays to be careful,' said the man with a nod. 'We could meet after work. Have a chat. And see where it goes.'

'We could,' said Zar. His neck was prickly. He was shivering; he knew the man knew. Was it so obvious?

The man had his phone out. 'Give me your phone number. If I'm bothering you, just give me a dud.'

Zar gave his correct number and name. The man tapped it in his phone.

'I'd better let you get back to work, Zar. That old geezer is watching us.' He indicated Bill who was standing on a garden fork looking their way. 'I'm looking for a Jack Bell. Do you know him?'

'That's Jack over there.' He pointed to the wall by the bowling green where Jack was working. 'Why do you want him?'

The man took out a card and gave it to Zar.

Zar read. 'Detective Constable Edward Thomas.'

'Eddie,' said the man. 'I'm not a poet.'

'You're a cop.'

'And we're meeting later on.' He put out his hand. Zar took it. The shake was longer than formal. 'Thank you for your assistance. Tell the old fella, I'm a cop investigating a crime in the park. And I didn't say what.'

'You didn't.'

'Then you won't have to lie. Never a good idea.' DC Thomas smiled. 'And now a word with Mr Bell. Hope to see you later, Zar.'

Zar watched him walking away. He was scared stiff, he was excited. But he was at work, later was later. He picked up the barrow and wheeled it in to Bill.

'Jack Bell?' said DC Thomas.

Jack put down his trowel. 'That's me. And who, may I ask, are you?'

DC Thomas flashed his ID.

'A bit slower,' said Jack. The man showed it again and allowed Jack to read it. 'You're a policeman.'

'I am. A detective constable to be accurate.' He looked about him and said in a low voice, 'Can we talk a little more privately?' He drew Jack along the drive, out of earshot from Mr Swift. 'I am investigating some suspicious circumstances concerning the death of Ian Swift who was the manager of this park.'

'Right,' said Jack. 'Now it's making sense.'

'And correct me if I am wrong, but you found him last night about 9 o'clock and took him to the hospital.'

'That's correct,' said Jack.

Thomas took out a notebook. 'How long had you known him?'

'All of...' he calculated, 'Fourteen hours.' The man jotted as Jack spoke. 'I met him when he opened the park first thing yesterday. Never seen him before then. Bit of a bully actually. He was having a go at me before I'd said a word.'

'You think he'd got enemies then?'

'He had a knack of rubbing people up the wrong way.'

DC Thomas nodded and jotted a note. 'The park was closed when you found him. So what were you doing here, Mr Bell?'

'Liz Parker, she's acting manager, said I could bring in

my telescope to look at the stars.' He shrugged, a little embarrassed. 'It's my hobby.'

'Not illegal, Jack,' said Thomas with a smirk. 'I can't get you on that.'

'Good,' said Jack. 'Anyway, I brought my telescope into the park, and was about to set up when I saw him. Over there, near the playground. Obviously in a bad way. Liz came out. She lives in one of those houses. And we decided I should take him straight to hospital.'

DC Thomas took some time writing this note.

'Excuse me asking,' said Jack. Thomas stopped writing and Jack went on. 'Is this to do with the poisoning?'

'That was not supposed to get out,' said Thomas.

'The doctor told me when I went in this morning with Mr Swift. That man there,' he pointed out his partner working on the wall, 'Ian's Swift's father.'

'I'd be obliged if you keep the fact of poisoning to yourself.'

'I've already told Liz.'

Thomas sighed. 'And who knows who she's told? Too late now.'

'If you don't mind me saying, you are somewhat junior,' said Jack hesitantly.

'We all have to start somewhere,' said Thomas. 'But I take your meaning. We're not going to come in with a scene of crime team and a dozen vehicles, if we are unsure there's been a crime at all. You, being a taxpayer, would be the first to complain.'

'I don't pay that much tax,' said Jack with a short laugh. 'I don't earn enough.'

'I never thought you were an eccentric millionaire, Mr Bell.' Then added, 'I'm here in a quiet way to find out if there is anything suspicious in Ian Swift's death.'

'Do you mean murder?' said Jack.

'Or an accident,' said Thomas. 'Let's not rush to

186

conclusions. Or nothing at all.' He bit his thumbnail thoughtfully. 'How many women work in the park?'

'Why women?'

'I'm asking the questions.'

'Ian must have said something about a woman...'

Thomas gave him a broad smile. 'You should be doing my job, Mr Bell. According to a nurse, his last words were: *she killed me.*'

'Which could mean anything,' said Jack. 'Or nothing.'

'Precisely.'

'Well, there's Liz Parker, the manager,' said Jack. 'I should say acting manager, then there's her sister, Rose Parker, assistant gardener, and there's Amy – and I don't know her second name, she's also an assistant. That's all the women workers.'

DC Thomas jotted the names and closed his notebook. 'Thank you for your assistance, Mr Bell. I'd be obliged if you could take me to Liz Parker.'

Chapter 40

Liz took the young detective constable into her office. His visit had taken her off guard. She excused herself and went to the toilet next door. Perhaps not a good idea as it showed her nervousness, but she needed to settle herself. She washed her hands and face in cold water. The police, so soon... This could be nothing. What could they know, after all? Give nothing away. Stick to the truth as far as possible. Liz took ten deep breaths, then held her hands out in front of her and stilled them, more or less. She looked in the mirror, her hair was somewhat straggly. Well, she was working and wouldn't be judged on that. Her face was pale, rings under her eyes from lack of sleep.

Take it slow.

She went in to join the policeman, her stomach rolling as if she had been called upon to give a speech to an audience of a thousand.

'Sorry for that,' she said. 'Policemen always make me nervous.'

'These are simply preliminary questions, Mrs Parker. Don't worry. There's a little concern about Ian Swift's death which we hope to clear up.'

'It's *Ms* Parker actually,' she said.

'My apologies. Must get these titles right. You're not married?'

'Single.'

'And your address?'

'2 Balaam Cottages. At the back of the park.'

He jotted her information down. She realised what he was doing. Asking simple questions to put her at her ease, and then dart in with a surprise.

'How long have you known the deceased?'

'Three years. Ever since I've lived there. Mine's a tied house, it came with the job.'

'You're a qualified gardener?'

'Yes, I am.' Oh, that question again. She must be able to answer it truthfully. But here, she had to go on with the lie.

'As a qualified gardener, how would you kill someone, Ms Parker?'

'I beg your pardon.'

'You must have poisons in your cupboard.'

'Well, some of the insecticides and herbicides are certainly poisonous. But I'd never consider them as a way of killing someone...'

'Why not?'

'Because it has never occurred to me.' Not true. She'd had suicidal moments, way back, and had considered the bottles and cans in the potting shed.

'But if you did,' he pursued.

'Well, in Agatha Christie mode let's say,' she said with a weak smile. 'Not a good idea. They'd taste vile. You couldn't disguise them in a cup of coffee.'

'What about a poisonous plant?'

'I'm not an expert on this,' she said, her neck prickly. 'There's monk's hood. But we'd never grow that in a public park. I've heard castor oil plants have poisonous berries, or there's laburnum seeds. But how poisonous they are, I've no idea. This really is not my field.'

'What about mushrooms?'

'Some of those are very poisonous. Yes. The amanitas for example... But I've never seen any of those in the park. Never. And if there were, I'm not sure how you'd begin...' She was floundering, hot. 'Try them on a cat perhaps, but then a cat is so much smaller than a human being...'

'Maybe a horse,' said Thomas with a grin. 'I'll be plain with you, Ms Parker. We don't know whether there is anything to this at all.' He waved a hand. 'It's simply possible. There's an autopsy to be carried out, and we'll know more then. Though another tack... If you were considering suicide, then might the chemicals in your cupboard be a way?'

'If you were desperate enough...' She shuddered. 'But imagine drinking creosote or petrol. That's the sort of flavour.'

'I wouldn't think there are many nice poisons, Ms Parker.' He consulted his notebook. 'There's a Rose and an Amy I'd like to speak to. Where might I find them?'

'Rose is in the playground. I'll take you there.'

They left her office. It's a long way to the playground when you're watching every word, and working to breathe an innocent breath. Why had she offered to take him? She had no small talk for a detective, or for anyone else. She could so easily have told him where the playground was and sent him off.

It was her native politeness.

The sky had cleared, leaving a few small cumulus clouds adrift in the blue. There were still lots of leaves in the trees, yellow and burnt brown, whose time was near. Where was Amy? She should be vaccing all those on the lawn. All that fuss earlier. She noted Zar and Bill side by side with their spades, digging over one of the flower beds.

'What's the marquee for?' asked Thomas.

'It's for tomorrow,' she said, glad to be on a safe subject. 'The Mayor comes every year to plant a tree, and in addition, this year, we have our local MP who's not standing in the election, coming too. A headache really. On top of everything.'

'Are you definitely the manager now?'

'Most likely,' she said, 'It's very sudden, you know... I've been told informally that it will be me, but they have to have their conversations.' She stopped and pulled his arm. 'What's that?'

There was yelling from the playground. Screams.

'Sounds like someone's killing someone,' said Thomas.

They speeded up as they passed the tennis courts, and saw in the playground two women in overalls fighting. Liz knew them at once as Amy and Rose, spinning round, clawing and kicking at each other.

'It's the two you want to see,' exclaimed Liz.

The detective put a finger to his lips and they continued silently. Rose had fallen to the ground and Amy jumped on top of her, pulling the hair of the smaller woman, who was barely visible under Amy's bulk, arms and legs flailing underneath her.

'Give me it! You bow-legged cow,' screeched Amy.

Rose's answer was a piercing yell. The few women in the playground, by the swings and monkey bars, were watching as if it were wild animals fighting, keeping at a safe distance.

Thomas and Liz dragged Amy off.

'She's stolen my money! The thieving bitch!'

Rose was splayed out on the ground, breathing heavily, eyes screwed up, hands to her head and hair, groaning.

'What's going on here?' said Liz to Amy.

'She stole my money,' screamed Amy. 'Four hundred bloody quid!' She turned on Liz. 'She should never have been here in the first place. Just 'cus she's your sister!'

Rose had struggled to a seated position on the ground, wriggling her neck, rubbing her hair. She took a bundle of notes out of her pocket and held them out. 'Here you are.'

Amy grabbed them and stuffed them in her sagging overalls.

'What's this all about?' said Liz.

'Women Fly Women,' said Rose weakly.

'Shut your ugly mug!' screamed Amy.

'What's Women Fly Women?' said Liz.

'It's her scam,' said Rose, stumbling to her feet. 'I was going to give you the money and tell you all about it, when she jumped me.'

Liz turned to Amy. 'How long has this been going on?'

Amy did not reply. Her lips suddenly gummed.

'Months,' said Rose, 'You pay her two hundred pounds and you get this junk perfume to sell and then have to bring three others in...'

'I know about this,' interrupted Thomas. He flashed his ID card. 'Police.' He turned to Amy, 'You a pilot or a captain?'

She did not reply, looking about her as if there might be help somewhere. Her overall buttons were undone at her hips, one brace hanging loose. There were scratches on her cheek.

'She's a pilot,' said Rose. 'This is her aircraft.' She swung her arm round the playground.

'What the hell's been going on in this playground?' exclaimed Liz in bewilderment. 'Pilots, aircraft, captains... Someone clue me in.'

'Catch up later,' said Thomas. He turned to Rose. 'Do you know who the captain is?'

'I've worked it out,' she said.

'So tell me what you've worked out,' said Thomas.

'I'll kill you,' screamed Amy jumping on Rose. 'I'll tear you limb from limb, you double-crossing bitch!'

Thomas and Liz were immediately on Amy, dragging her off Rose. They held her arms, spittle running down her chin. She fought against them, then subsided.

'You had something to tell us,' said Thomas to Rose.

'I've never been in the playground before,' said Rose,

'and I was thinking to myself just why is that, why is it always me on leaf vaccing?'

'Why?' said Liz.

'Because she's a pilot,' said Rose pointing at Amy, 'and she has to be in her aircraft to take the money. And the captain made sure she was. Every day.'

'Ian!' exclaimed Liz, her hand hitting her forehead. 'It had to be Ian. This is sort of making sense.' She turned to the policeman. 'And I put Rose in here today. And did Amy holler!'

Thomas moved swiftly. A pair of handcuffs were out of his pocket, one cuff slapped on Amy's wrist before she realised what was happening. He pulled her arms behind her back and thrust her other wrist in the second.

'Amy, I am arresting you on suspicion of being part of an illegal pyramid scheme, Women Fly Women,' said the detective formally. 'You do not have to say anything but it may harm your defence if you do not answer something you later rely on in court.' He held her arm, the caution done. 'Don't be more awkward then you've been already, Amy. Your best bet is to come clean, you're small fry in this. I'm taking you to the police station.'

He held her arm to lead her off. Amy jerked away and spat at Rose. A gobbet landed on the young woman's cheek, spray pitted her eyes.

'I'll murder you, you tosspot!' screeched Amy. 'You see if I don't.'

DC Thomas pulled her away and led her out of the playground.

Chapter 41

Jack and Mr Swift had laid two courses of bricks. Jack was working from one end and Mr Swift from the other. They each had a bucket of mortar that Jack topped up from the nearby wheelbarrow as needed. Swift had the expertise; in one movement with the trowel he scooped up exactly the right amount of mortar, while Jack took too much or too little and had to adjust.

'You're not a bricklayer, are you, son?' said the old man as they met in the middle.

'I trained as a carpenter,' said Jack. 'I don't do a lot of bricklaying.'

'Your work's OK,' said Mr Swift, looking at the bricks Jack had laid. 'You do your checking with the spirit level OK, but it's the knack you haven't got.'

'I never do it long enough,' said Jack. 'My last job was shop fitting. My next is some kitchen work. Don't know when I'll be a brickie again.'

'No offence,' said the old man, 'but I wouldn't have had you on site. Too slow.'

Jack shrugged. 'I'm self employed, so if I'm slow that's my loss. Long as it's good enough.'

'Good enough,' nodded the old man. 'The mortar's right, you cleaned the bricks well. You just haven't got a bricklayer's speed on the trowel.' The old man put his trowel down. 'Do you mind if I take a break?'

'Of course not.'

'You'll never make a foreman.' He laughed, cutting it

short with a wince. 'These old bones won't take it.'

'I'll get you a chair,' said Jack.

He went into the yard and to the mess hut. And brought out a chair. He put it down and helped Mr Swift on to it.

'That's better, son. Too low down those bottom courses.'

'Work to your own time,' said Jack.

'I know, I know,' said the old man with a laugh. 'It's not as if I'm getting paid.'

Jack was no longer listening but watching the detective constable and Amy coming down the drive. Her hands were behind her back and she was shuffling along, her clothes awry. DC Thomas was talking into his phone. Jack watched them come in, puzzled.

'What's up, Amy?' he called when she was about five metres away.

She grunted and turned half about, showing the handcuffs.

'What you been up to?'

She shrugged and came past with her minder talking into his phone. It was police-speak that Jack could make little sense of. He and Swift watched Amy and the detective make their way to the park gate.

'She's been arrested,' exclaimed Swift scratching his chin.

'Yeh. She has,' said Jack. 'I wonder what for.'

'Stolen goods, I bet you.'

Rose was coming towards them. She was wriggling her neck round and round, lifting her arms like a swimmer just before a race. She straightened her overalls as she neared, and did up one of her shoulder toggles.

'What's going on, Rose?'

'That fat cow would've killed me,' she exclaimed.

'Why?'

'She's been part of a pyramid scheme in the playground. Selling junk scent. Ian was her boss... She came on me like a buffalo charge. If that cop and Liz hadn't have come, I'd have been smashed to bits.'

'Why you?'

'Because I collected her money. I thought, screw her, I'll have a piece of this. But two ton Tessie wanted the lot...' She wriggled her shoulders and grimaced. 'You wouldn't like to give my neck a rub, Jack – would you?'

He held her shoulders, then massaged the back of her neck firmly.

'How's that?'

'Ooh, that's better. Carry on.' She gave a satisfied murmur. 'Liz came over with that cop, I didn't know he was a cop, but I guessed he was maybe investigating. I knew I had to get rid of the money I'd collected or I'd get done along with Amy. So I told them I was collecting the cash to give to Liz and to tell her about the racket.'

'You're smarter than you look, Rose.'

'Not just a pretty face.' She pulled away. 'I can't stay chatting, Liz is taking my place in the playground while I clean up. The cow spat at me.' She snapped her fingers. 'And oh yes, while we're at it...' She took out some notes. 'Your 30 quid, Jack.'

He took the money. 'I never expected to see that again.'

'Cheek,' she said in mock effrontery. 'Now, we can go out to dinner.'

Jack laughed. 'What, with the money you've just given me back?'

'No.' She patted her back pocket. 'I'm taking you out.'

'Nicked money.'

'Who's going to know?' she said with a wink.

Jack put the money away. Something at least. And a dinner date. Who knows what might follow?

Rose went to Mr Swift on his chair. She put an arm on his shoulder.

'I'm very sorry about your loss, Mr Swift.'

'Thank you, my dear.'

'I know Ian cared a lot about you,' she said.

'We were close.'

'Well, living together and all that. You're going to be very lonely in that cottage.'

'It won't be the same,' he said with a sigh. 'Me on my own in that place.'

'Would you like me to come and stay for a few days, Mr Swift? Cook for you and keep you company.'

Chapter 42

Amy arrested. At least it had got rid of the cop, for the time being. But she'd have to phone Mr Greene a second time today. First she'd had to tell him about Ian's death, and now about the Women Fly Women scam which she only half understood. Quite what she'd actually say to him... Did she need to tell him that Ian was implicated? The captain, presumably receiving money from Amy and most likely others... No, she wouldn't tell him. Let it come from the police. Speak no ill of the dead.

Just say Amy had been arrested. She would of course be sacked. No way out of that. Carrying out illegal activities in the park. And Rose was within a hair's breadth of getting done. She'd been collecting the money! But handed it over sharpish, and told the detective what she knew of the scam. Enough for him to be forgiving with any luck. He certainly wouldn't believe her tale that she was collecting the money to give to Liz in order to expose Amy.

But then he didn't know Rose. The more Liz considered it, the more she was sure that Rose would be alright. Not that she deserved to be, just that she would be.

When Rose returned to the playground, cleaned up, Liz left her, not wanting to talk.

'Phone calls to make,' she said and hurried away.

She went round the park, noting work as she contemplated where she was. Two people gone and Ian part of the Women Fly Women scam. She kept coming back to that. The man she had killed. If she had done nothing then he might well have been arrested today. The irony! And would have far too much on his plate to shop her to the police.

Presumably, he would have been jailed. Say a year, two, who knows? But then, when he came out, he'd still have the hold over her. On top of it, he'd be homeless, while she had her cottage and so all the more reason to insist on marriage. But in that time, she'd have her qualification. And now she was manager, it shouldn't be that difficult for her to get hold of her original application form and destroy it. So when Ian was out she'd have been manager for two years, be running an excellent park, have made all the connections, got hold of her application form and burnt it. Who'd listen to the ramblings of a jailbird, with no evidence?

In a different universe.

In this one, Ian was dead, and there were suspicious circumstances. When the detective had questioned her about poisons, she almost fell to bits, wondering how much he knew, how much he was pretending to know.

The leaf vac was abandoned on the lawn. She'd have to do it, there was no one else. After she'd finished her wander. The rose garden needed vaccing too. Swish the puddles off the tennis courts. And all before the bigwigs come tomorrow. She crossed to Bill and Zar. They'd dug three quarters of the flower bed.

'What's happened to Amy?' asked Bill.

'She's been arrested,' she said. 'She was running a scam in the playground, taking loads of money...'

'I thought she was flash,' exclaimed Bill. 'Bought that car two weeks ago.'

'She'll be sacked, won't she?' said Zar.

'Yes, and probably jailed.'

'Cor,' said Bill, 'we're going down like blackfly under the thumb.' He turned to Zar. 'You not about to get fingered?'

'As if I'd tell you,' said the young man with a grin.

'I'd like both beds dug today,' said Liz. 'If I give you a

couple of hours overtime, do you think you can finish? You'll be doing me a favour. You know what's on tomorrow.'

'I'm on,' said Zar.

'Extra money. Fine by me,' added Bill.

'Thanks for that.' She waved her hands in the air. 'What a headache!'

She left them. At least no trouble there. She'd need to start early tomorrow to get the cascade plumbed in, and have Rose and Zar help with the planting. The playground could stay shut. But maybe not, the Mayor would expect to see it open, kids on swings.

How? With whom?

She gave Jack and Mr Swift a wave as she crossed to the bowling green pavilion. She had no wish to repeat her moans to them. At least the green was fine. There'd be no play on it until spring. The pavilion might be needed tomorrow, though. She climbed the few steps to the verandah and took out her bunch of keys. They were all labelled. She opened up and stepped into the large open space.

Rather stuffy. She screwed her nose, some scenty smell somewhere...

Zar came in breathless.

'I saw you go in,' he said. 'And I thought I should explain...'

'Explain what?'

He scratched his hair awkwardly. 'I stayed here last night. I had to leave home in a hurry. I'm gay...'

'That's not a crime,' she said.

'It is in my house. With my parents.' He held his hands wide to show his need. 'I had nowhere to go, Liz.'

'I'm sorry about your parents, Zar.'

'They're strict Muslims. Gays should be thrown off mountain tops...' He stopped and changed tack. 'I saw you coming in here. You were going to find my stuff under the counter...'

'Enough,' she said, 'I haven't found anything. Besides, I haven't time to inspect the pavilion now, what with all the hoo-ha tomorrow. Though I will do a thorough inspection on Thursday. And I expect to find nothing here. Do you understand me, Zar?'

'Yes, Liz. Thank you.'

She flashed her open hands at him. 'Don't thank me. This conversation is about your day release starting next week. You know how short staffed we are? I expect you to work hard and justify your day's study.'

'I will, Liz. Promise.'

'Now. Go back and get that bed dug before you leave tonight.'

He ran off. She stood on the threshold; she wasn't inspecting any further. The less she knew the better. The pavilion would not be used tomorrow, she'd see to that. Drains, she'd say if she were asked. And she could take them into the greenhouse, show off the birds of paradise.

She locked the pavilion.

And now she had the phone call to make about Amy's arrest, then leaf vaccing, then... and then.

She was swept by weariness.

Chapter 43

That was the end of the mortar. No point making any more this time of day. Incredibly, they'd done two thirds of the wall. Jack had tried to slow down Mr Swift, but he worked on as if he were on a bonus. Now he'd have to stop. Buckets and wheelbarrow had to be washed out – and then knocking off time.

His phone rang. An unknown number. Might be some work.

'Hello,' he said, 'Jack of All Trades here.'

'Rose on the Swings here,' came the reply. 'Can you come to the playground?'

'What's it about?'

'I need your help. Right now. Too complicated to explain. Please. Right now!'

'Be there soon as.'

He closed the call. And told Mr Swift there was something in the playground that he had to deal with right away. And set off, wondering what could be so important that it needed him there, now.

The sun was low. His elongated shadow strode along the lawn, the boots fat and clumpy, legs pole-like, the body square and squashed with a tiny head like a plum on top. Quite apt, some might think.

Bill and Zar were busy digging, Liz vaccing the lawn, oblivious of the time. Even the manager hard at it. Not that he was against managers getting their hands dirty, but she was in a rush, as if every fallen leaf was a criticism of her park. Her park now.

As he entered the playground he saw Rose talking to a youngish woman in a headscarf who was waving her arms in agitation. She backed away as Jack came towards them.

'What'd she want?' he said.

'Her money back,' said Rose. 'I told her it's nothing to do with me.'

'Was she one you collected?'

'No. The few I took have gone. She's one of Amy's passengers.'

'I doubt she'll see a penny of it,' he said, watching the woman, who was talking to a friend at the swings, both keeping an eye on Jack and Rose.

'She could sell the scent,' said Rose.

'You said it was junk.'

She shrugged. 'Plenty of people buy junk. Anyway, I don't want to discuss the ethics of capitalism. Come into the playground office.'

'Am I safe there with you?'

She looked at him wide eyed. 'It's a kids' playground, Jack. I am not going to take advantage of you here.'

'Pity.'

He followed her to the office, wondering why it was necessary, especially when he found there was scarcely any room inside, as the small space was almost packed out with scent packs.

He picked up a box. 'Amy's been flogging this stuff for how long?'

'For months from what I gather. Two hundred pounds a throw to a load of mugs. But never mind that.' She took a bundle of notes from her back pocket. 'I want you to hold this for me.'

'Why?'

'I don't trust that woman and her mate. They might beat me up. Take it.'

'You need to learn martial arts,' he said.

'Not useful advice for the next hour.' She looked at her watch. 'Give or take. But I'm hoping having seen you, they'll think better of taking it out on me.'

'But I've got to pack away. I can't stick around here.'

'I've got this,' she said, and showed him a whistle. 'It's quite a piercing blast. If you hear it, come running.'

'Right,' he said. 'I'll race over and hope to get here before they garrotte you on the roundabout.'

He shoved the money deep into his overall pockets.

'Anything else?' he added.

'Yes. Tonight,' she said. 'Plans have changed.'

'I thought it was too good to be true, you taking me out to dinner.'

'I've moved,' she said with a half smile, 'to Mr Swift's.'

'I noted you doing the deal.'

She pursed her lips in annoyance. 'He needs looking after, company.'

Jack might have commented on the type of company he needed, but didn't. Being lower than the angels himself.

'So I want you to buy a takeaway,' she said, 'for say 20 quid of that money, and then join us for dinner in Mr Swift's house. About 7 o'clock.'

'I didn't figure this was going to be a threesome.'

'Just for dinner, Jack,' she said placatingly. 'We'll work something out afterwards.'

'Like what?'

'Wait and see.'

'Not sure about your surprises, after last night's abandonment, but I'll give you a final chance.'

'Thank you, Jack. I'll do my best.'

She threw her arms round him and they kissed, longish and it might have been longer, but she pulled reluctantly away.

'This is the children's playground, Jack,' she said with a

204

sigh. 'And I don't want to lose my job... so, I'm afraid, certain standards apply.'

'I bet those mums are wondering what's going on in here.'

'Get out of here then. This minute. I'll see you at seven with the grub. And bring what's left of my money.'

He left her, the two women on the swings watching him as he crossed the playground. He gazed back at them and waved a stern finger in their direction. Let them make what they would of that. He turned away and left the playground.

The sky was darkening, but almost clear, the sun low in the tree tops. What a perfect night for a man with a telescope. But short of that, he reflected, he could bring his binoculars. The Pleiades were a brilliant sight this time of year. Where was Jupiter? He'd need to look it up.

Liz was busy vaccing as before, head down pushing into the leaves, the machine grumbling and groaning. The two diggers had finished the first bed and were heading with their wheelbarrow and tools to the second. Plainly overtime was on offer.

Back at the wall, Mr Swift was seated on the chair, breathing heavily. Jack considered giving him twenty quid. Or would he be insulted?

'Ian'd be proud of that wall,' he said.

'We're a good team,' said Jack.

'Put it there,' said the old man, putting out his hand. They shook.

'I'll be coming over with a takeaway tonight, if that's OK.'

'Be pleased to see you, son.'

Chapter 44

Back at his flat, Jack showered and changed. He considered doing the washing up left from the morning. It seemed such a waste of time and hot water. The more you wash up, the more you have to wash up. Wait till the crockery runs out.

He made a cup of tea, using the one cup left in the cupboard. And while he drank, phoned through the takeaway order, to be picked up in half an hour. It was only once he'd come off the phone, that he considered whether it would be to Mr Swift's taste. It was from the Indian restaurant up the road. He had no doubt Rose enjoyed a varied palate, but you never know with old people.

Too late. It was ordered.

His phone rang. It was Mia.

'Hello, love.'

'He's back,' she exclaimed.

'Who?'

'Bloody Tony.'

'Language, please,' he said, the admonishment giving him an instant to consider his response.

'Tony is back,' she said with a sigh. 'Here. Now. In the flat.'

'What happened?'

'He came to get some clothes he'd left,' she groaned. 'That was supposed to be it.'

'And it wasn't?'

'He said how sorry he was about everything. And he'd packed up finally with Emily...'

'Or she packed him up.'

'Of course. He's a total liar. And then I was sent off to do my homework... And next thing I know they're in the bedroom. At it.'

Jack was torn. Although on the side of Mia, he could see it from Alison's perspective too, but it wouldn't do to say that.

'It won't last,' he said.

'Why not?'

'The man's an opportunist. Emily has thrown him out so he's gone back to your mother. Soon he'll find somebody else...'

'And lie his head off to Mum. Two-timing again.'

'And she'll find out and kick him out.'

'But that could take *ages*.'

What could he say? Alison's sex life in some ways was a mirror to his own, but at least he didn't have a twelve year old taking notes. Or rather, only one weekend a fortnight.

'What can I do, Dad?'

'Is there a counsellor at school you can talk to?'

'I'm talking to you.'

Good point. And it was better to be talked to than not, having been there, and all stations between.

'It's difficult, I know, Mia,' he said with some effort. 'But the relationship won't last. Your mother kicked him out once, she'll kick him out again.'

'Then he could come back again. And again!'

'You could try getting on with him,' he said warily.

'I don't like him. He's creepy.'

'Why don't you play some music, read a book, go on Facebook, instead of putting your ear to the wall.'

'Thanks for nothing.'

She'd rung off, obviously angry at his uselessness. He sat

in his armchair dejected for a few minutes. There was little he could do. Mia and Alison were in Brighton, he was over 70 miles away. Perhaps he should talk to Alison, not that he'd get through at the moment, and when he did – she'd tell him to mind his own business. But surely she could sense what their daughter was feeling.

Or maybe she just didn't want to.

He tried three times to send Mia a text. Some chin up words. Each time, he erased them. They were too rah rah. She wanted him to get rid of Tony, and he couldn't.

He had to send her something. And tried once more: *Try talking to your mum. I will as well. See you at the weekend. Dad xxx*

Jack read it through, changed the x's to capitals, 'as well' to 'too' and sent it. Then sprang out of the armchair. He picked up his binoculars and left the house to get the takeaway.

He had his own love life to consider.

Chapter 45

From outside the park gate, he phoned Rose. She buzzed the gate open. He entered with the carrier bag and his binoculars in their case around his neck. The park was shades of black, street lamps and houselights spilled orange at the edge. This was the city, there would always be light pollution, just less in the middle of an unlit space.

He halted near his wall and looked up at the stars. There were the Pleiades in the north west, close to setting. That was disappointing. They'd be gone by the time he would be out here with Rose. But there was the Square of Pegasus – and later, from it, he'd try to find the Andromeda Galaxy. At best a smudge, even with binoculars, but the thought of being able to see another galaxy, across impossible distances, always excited him.

The Summer Triangle was still up there, the three bright stars of Cygnus, Deneb and Lyra at its points. And yes, the Corona Borealis – the Crown of the North, like a set of golden false teeth through binoculars. And Cassiopeia, a spread-winged bat pointing to the Pole Star, and from there to the Great Bear. A good night for seeing.

Dinner first.

As he walked down the drive he heard it, and thought it must be coming from one of the gardens surrounding the parks. Then realised it couldn't be. The leaf vac. Seven o'clock at night. Surely not. He could not see where it was, somewhere near the end of the park. He had no doubt who it must be, vaccing in the dark.

He continued down the drive, the groan of the vac growing. Past the tennis courts, the fencing a solid black mesh against the deep purple, along to where the drive turned into the Mayor's Avenue. There, he could just make her out, an amorphous shadow in the rose garden. He'd not been in it. Where was the entrance? He brushed a hand along the hedge, going back and forth until he found the gap. Then headed for the growl.

'What the hell are you doing?' he shouted above the racket as he approached.

She continued vaccing, and for a second he was unsure whether she'd heard him or seen him at all. He put an arm on her shoulder and pulled her away from the handles. She didn't fight him but stood listlessly.

'Where's the damned off switch?' he exclaimed searching around the handles. She pressed it for him. The silence engulfed them. She had her hood up, her face a black mask.

'What are you doing vaccing this time of night?'

He grasped her arm and slid down to her hand. It was cold and lifeless.

'What are you doing vaccing this time of night?' he repeated.

'I have to do Amy's work,' she said wearily. 'The park must be clean.'

'But more leaves will blow in overnight,' he exclaimed. 'And it's not your fault she's gone.'

'She wouldn't be if Ian were still here.'

'You've lost me,' he said.

'I put Rose in the playground. He wouldn't have.'

'I don't see why you're torturing yourself about that. She and he were in a racket together. You're not responsible for her arrest.'

'Not even if I killed Ian?'

This struck him like a slap. 'What are you saying, Liz?'

'I poisoned him. Yesterday at lunch time.'

His hair was prickling, his legs hollow. He recalled Mr Swift telling him Ian had gone to Liz's for lunch.

'Are you telling me you murdered Ian? Seriously.'

'Yes, I am.'

He was choked, flailing. She had thrown it on him. The heat of the takeaway pressed through his trouser legs. Liz was confessing to murder. To him. Out here, in the rose garden.

'How did you kill him?' he managed to say.

'With death stalk mushrooms. I put them in a pie and a sauce. He was hungry. He told me it was delicious. So I gave him some more.'

Jack recalled the detective constable telling him Ian's last words – *she killed me*. What should he do? As if a cat had placed a half dead bird at his feet. His responsibility now.

'Leave the vac here,' he said. That was easy to deal with. 'I'll put it away.'

'The yard's locked.'

'I'll put it in the marquee,' he said. 'There won't be any giants tonight,' he added, surprising himself at his humour. 'But let's get you home first.'

Linking his arm in hers, he led her out of the gate of the rose garden. What on earth should he do? Call the police? Run away and put his head under a pillow? Did it have to be true?

They walked slowly along the path, the leaves slippery underfoot.

She said, 'It wasn't at all necessary. I didn't have to kill him. Amy didn't have to be arrested. He'd still be at home with his father instead of in the mortuary.' He felt her clutching his arm. 'It's a horrible way to die. Vomiting and cramps. I left him out there, doubled up in pain. I told him I'd phone the hospital.'

'But you didn't.'

'I left him there,' she said. 'It was you who found him.'

He recalled Ian's agony on the bench last night. The awful drive to the hospital as he retched and kicked on the seat beside him.

They were at her door. It was slightly ajar, passage light spilling out on to her path.

'Go in,' he said. 'I'll be along as soon as I can. I've got to deliver this takeaway next door. And I should eat some or they'll be suspicious.'

'Don't be long,' she said and kissed him lightly on the cheek. And went in, closing the door after her.

Jack remained on her path for a minute or so. In that cottage was a woman who'd confessed to murder. He knew what he should do, what law abiding citizens did in such circumstances. Call the police. Lay the half dead bird in their lap.

But he was stuck with the sanctity of the confessional.

It's up to you, she'd more or less said. Doom me or save me. Not that half an hour or so would make any difference. The man was dead. And he had hot food in a bag to deliver.

He breathed deeply and deliberately as he made his way next door. He knew too much. And felt resentful. Twice this evening, the impossible had been asked of him. Mia and Liz. As if he were a faith healer, a gentle touch on a cheek and the lame would walk.

At least he could deliver a dinner.

He rang the bell.

In the seconds before it was answered, he considered leaving the food on the step and running off. Then he wouldn't have to speak. Find topics of interest.

'Took your time,' exclaimed Rose as she opened up and pecked him on the cheek. 'Ooh, you're cold.'

'I was looking at the stars,' he said.

The heat hit him as he entered. He unzipped his coat.

'Leave your coat in the hall,' said Rose, taking the carrier of food.

Jack hung up his jacket and walked the few steps to the sitting room. Mr Swift was sat at the table where three places were laid. Rose was already taking out the aluminium trays from the bag and putting them on place mats in the middle of the table.

'Hello, son,' said Swift with a wave. 'I'm so stiff. I think I've overdone it, that bricklaying.'

'You were going like you were on double bonus,' said Jack.

'Nice job, though, isn't it?'

'Class bricklaying,' he said.

'What have we got here?' said Rose. All the trays were out, and she was taking off the cardboard tops. 'Smells lovely.'

'Indian food,' said Jack.

'And what exactly?'

He tried to recall. It had been so long ago he'd made the order. In another galaxy, a world like this one, but with one item altered.

'Pilau rice,' he said. And found it wasn't so difficult to recall, once he'd begun. He tended to go for the same things. 'Onion bhajees, samosas, sag aloo, vegetable curry, and chicken kurma.'

Rose was putting spoons in the containers.

'Do you like Indian food, Mr Swift?' she said.

'I do,' said the old man eagerly. 'Me and Ian would go up the Himalaya in Stratford sometimes, after we'd been to the pictures.'

'I'll get some water,' said Jack.

He went into the kitchen. It was thoroughly tidy. Nothing on the units, nothing in the sink. He sank onto a stool. There was food out there. He should eat. What on earth was he going to talk about? The stars had gone out. Brighton had disappeared. There was the wall. How much could you say about a wall? And there was a woman next door who had told him a secret.

Rose came in.

'What's up, Jack?'

'Tired,' he said.

'There's something more,' she said.

'Your sister,' he said with a flap of his hand. 'I saw her just now. She's in a bad way.'

'What do you mean a bad way?'

'I can't tell you.'

'Can't tell me what, Jack?'

He smiled weakly. 'More than I already have.'

Rose stared at him, biting a finger nail. 'It's about today, isn't it?'

'Might be.'

'It's about Ian.'

He stiffened involuntarily.

'It is about Ian,' she insisted. And when he didn't reply, she pushed him on the chest. 'His death wasn't heart or anything like that, was it?' He didn't reply. 'Someone killed him? Didn't they? And she knows.'

He looked at her. He should be denying this, heading her off somewhere, but he lacked the energy.

'Doesn't she?' she continued.

He said, 'She was out there, vaccing in the rose garden. And she told me that she killed Ian.'

Rose's hands went to her face. 'My sister! My perfect sister.'

'I said I'd go over there,' said Jack.

Neither spoke for a while. He'd told her. Was it a betrayal? Either way, it wasn't just him anymore.

'We'll both go over,' she said at last. 'But let's play normal and eat. Mr Swift is tired, he'll want to go to bed early, I'm sure. Then we'll both pop next door. Like good neighbours.'

Chapter 46

Zar and Eddie Thomas were in a pizza house on High Street North at East Ham. It was a quiet night, with only a few other customers at the tables. They'd finished their main meal and were drinking coffee. Thomas was in jeans and a check shirt. Zar had simply taken off his overalls. He had no other clothing, having left home with so little.

'We could go to a club,' said Thomas thoughtfully, 'or what do you feel about drag?'

'I don't know,' said Zar, excited and scared.

'I'd like to go back to my place, but I share with a straight cop – and it'd be all round the station if I brought someone back.' He laughed and lightly punched Zar on the shoulder. 'A bit like your parents.'

'Bring someone back?' said Zar, spluttering into his coffee. 'You must be joking. My mum was horrified at a few mags and some chat room stuff. I couldn't bring you back. Or if I did, I'd have to lie – and we'd all sit together in the front room watching TV while they puzzled out who you were.'

'Or how about a quiet bar?' mused Thomas. 'I don't want anyone else grabbing you.'

'I don't drink,' said Zar.

Thomas shrugged. 'Explore the fruit juices while I go through the cocktail menu.' Then added, 'Or perhaps we could go to your pavilion...'

'Liz wouldn't like it.'

'We're not exactly going to scream from the rooftops. Or are we?' He laughed.

'It'd have to be with the lights off,' said Zar.

'All the better to get the feel of things,' said Eddie with a smirk. His phone buzzed. He scowled as he pulled it out of his trouser pocket. 'I hope this isn't work stuff.' He looked at it. 'A text. No panic. They're releasing Amy.' He smiled. 'Small fry. Though she had a lot to say, once she realised she might get off if she sang...' He stopped and added, 'But she wasn't any help on Swift's death. And I'm starting to believe it had nothing to do with the scam.'

'How did Ian die?'

'Didn't I say? Poisoning of some sort. The lab report isn't in yet.'

'No, you didn't tell me.'

'I thought it would be all round the park.'

'What sort of poison?' said Zar.

'That's what I asked Liz. What poisons she kept in her greenhouse. She said nothing you could put in a coffee. OK for suicide, not for murder.'

'She had me collecting death stalks yesterday,' said Zar.

'What are death stalks?'

'Poisonous mushrooms. There's some around the park. Deadly.'

'I asked her about mushrooms,' mused Eddie. 'She told me there weren't any. I distinctly remember that. I've got it in my notebook. She said there's none in the park.'

'There are,' insisted Zar. 'Well, there were. Yesterday she got me collecting them all up. I gave them to her to burn. She told me not to tell anyone.'

'Why's that?'

'So there wouldn't be a panic.'

Thomas thought a while, scratching his chin. 'She lied to me, Zar. Now why would she do that?'

'Because you're a cop.'

Thomas drained his coffee and stood up. 'It's the little

things, Zar. Pick up on the little things. We're going to go and see her.'

'What? Me too?'

'She can't lie with you there.'

Chapter 47

Jack was hungry, surprisingly so. He hadn't eaten after work, deciding he'd make the most of the takeaway. Liz's confession had temporarily removed his appetite, but sharing the burden with Rose brought it back again. Rose too was hungry, though attentive to Mr Swift, making him up a plate.

They talked of the food, perhaps exaggerating, a safe topic they could share. The sweetness and coconut taste of the kurma contrasting with the vegetable curry.

'If only Ian could've been here,' said Mr Swift, with a shake of the head.

Jack and Rose looked at each other. Neither picked up the topic.

'Though he was never one for company,' continued Mr Swift, 'but that Amy used to come round after work. I never knew what that was about. She being married and the size of her.'

'Some men like big women,' said Rose. 'More meat.' She laughed. 'Or chicken kurma.'

'Ooh, but I am that stiff,' said Mr Swift, pressing his back. 'When I was twenty I could work like that for a month and feel nothing. Drink a dozen pints and go out dancing. Now, look at me. A few bricks and I feel like my back has broken in ten places.'

'Early night for you,' said Rose.

'You can say that again.'

'Thanks for your help today,' said Jack. Every word had

to be chipped out of ice. He'd forgotten how to speak, like Ben Gunn in *Treasure Island*.

'We started off on the wrong foot, you and me, son,' said Mr Swift. 'But you took me to the hospital and you didn't have to.' He was wielding his fork in a rather frightening way. 'And then came with me to the mortuary.' The old man sighed. 'He looked just like he had gone to sleep, did Ian. Dead hardly half an hour when we saw him.'

'I was glad I could do something,' said Jack. 'Pouring with rain, so I couldn't work anyway. Then you gave me a hand when the sun came out.'

'Fair's fair, mate.'

'I was surprised how much you remembered.'

'But didn't I need that chair!' He laughed, even as he winced. 'A lot easier working from the chair. It's all the bending that kills you.'

Jack and Rose's hands went for the last bhaji.

'You have it,' he said.

'No, you,' she said. 'My treat.' Then she mouthed, 'Got my money?'

He nodded, and said to her, 'I should go next door.' To Mr Swift he said, 'I'm a bit worried about Liz. She didn't look too well.'

'Why don't you take her a plate of food?' said Rose.

'Good idea,' said Jack.

Rose put some bits and pieces on a plate and covered it in foil while Jack put his jacket on.

'Good to see you, son.'

'And you,' called Jack, not knowing whether he'd be back or not. Though stargazing was out, but what might be in – he had little idea. The evening had taken a different direction.

Rose took the plate into the hall and said in a whisper, 'Let's have my cash.'

Jack dug into his pocket and took out the notes. They swapped, she the money, he the plate.

219

'I'll get Mr Swift to bed and join you,' she said.

Jack left her. Outside, he walked quickly next door, thinking it unlikely that Liz would eat anything, considering the state he'd left her in. But it was a sociable offering. The light was on in her kitchen, though the curtains were drawn.

He rang the bell.

This dinner was cooling quickly, even though covered with foil. Well, a minute in the microwave would revive it. Liz was taking her time. This was only a little house. He rang again. Perhaps she was in the bathroom. He felt silly with the plate at the door. An offering for the harvest festival. He rang a third time. He put his ear to the door, there was no sound in the house. She might be in the bath. He put the plate down on the step and took out his phone. He phoned her, going straight to voice mail. He left a message, feeling idiotic: *I'm at your door.*

He rang the doorbell once more, and stepped back. There were no lights on upstairs. What was going on? He quickly ran next door to Rose. He rang the bell and heard her coming almost at once.

'You're back?' she said. 'What's up?'

'She's not opening the door,' he said, breathlessly. 'I've rung half a dozen times.'

Rose thought for a second. 'I've still got a key,' she said. 'Wait a sec.' She took the food from him and went back in.

He stayed on the step, concerned about what was going on next door. And not wanting to chit chat to Mr Swift. The meal was heavy in his stomach. All this coming and going wasn't good for digestion. Nor the worry. Liz had been in a state when he'd got her back home. He should have stayed with her, left the takeout on Mr Swift's step. Liz could be hanging from a rafter or drowning in the bathtub, wrists slashed.

Rose returned with the key.

'I'm just helping Mr Swift to bed,' she said, clutching his hand for a second. 'His back is playing him up. I'll be over as soon as I can. The key's a bit tricky. Keep trying.'

Jack ran next door and put the key in the lock. It wouldn't turn. A bit tricky, she'd said. He took it out and put it in again. Again it wouldn't turn. Was it the right key? The trouble he had with keys he was left by customers... He eased the key out slightly and this time it turned. Jack opened the door.

'Hello,' he called from the hallway.

'Hello, Jack,' Liz called back. 'I'm in the kitchen.'

He strode in hopefully, her voice was confident at least. Though why hadn't she opened up?

She was at the kitchen table, the remnant of a meal on her plate.

'What are you eating?' he said.

She shrugged. 'Just an omelette.'

'What sort of omelette?'

'Mushroom.'

At once, he grabbed the plate and tipped it in the rubbish bin.

'I'm calling an ambulance right away,' he exclaimed.

'I will deny it,' she said with a wry smile. 'Look at me, Jack. I'm fine. Haven't the medical services got better things to do?'

'Death stalks?' he said.

'What else?'

He stared at her helplessly, knowing it was pointless calling an ambulance. She did look well, too well, her cheeks red, she'd brushed her hair and tied it back with a green ribbon. Nothing like the waif in the rose garden, pitiful and appealing.

'I'll put the kettle on,' she said. 'We'll have a coffee.'

'Rose'll be here in a few minutes.'

'Three for coffee then. That'll be nice.'

He watched as she filled the kettle. She was sprightly, the perfect hostess. Who wouldn't open her door for him five minutes ago.

'Why did you eat the mushrooms?' he said.

She shrugged, taking a cafetiere and coffee down from the cupboard.

'It's fitting,' she said. 'I needn't have poisoned Ian; he was in trouble anyway. But I was in a rush. Too desperate.' She spooned coffee into the cafetiere as if each spoonful were a defence. 'If only I had waited...' She shrugged, 'But I didn't. And that cop is suspicious.' She turned to him, waving the spoon. 'Every time I see Mr Swift, I think, what have I abandoned him to.'

'It's a horrible death. Death stalks,' he said, thinking of Ian's agonizing cramps in his van as he ferried him to hospital.

'I don't want to lose this house,' she said, as if he hadn't spoken. 'And fifteen years in prison – without this sky, the trees. I love this park, Jack. The rose garden in summer, the mist on autumn mornings, my greenhouses.' She turned to him. 'What will I see through prison bars?'

He struggled to find reasons for living, to counter those she'd given for dying.

'Think of your parents,' he said. 'Rose.'

'Don't worry about Rose. She's tough,' she said. 'She'll bounce back. But think, how would my parents deal with the trial and publicity?'

She leaned against the counter, awaiting his reply. The kettle was whooshing, the poison oozing into her blood stream. He was a lousy counsellor.

'There's always a reason to live,' he said. 'There's people, there's books. You can paint in prison.'

The doorbell rang.

'Rose,' he said with relief, someone to come up with better reasons. And went to the door.

But it wasn't Rose. Instead, standing there were DC Thomas and Zar.

'Good evening,' said Thomas with a smile. 'I was passing

and thought I'd drop in. I've a few questions for Ms Parker.'

'She's not feeling too well at the moment,' said Jack.

'Well, I won't be long.'

He pushed past Jack into the house. Zar followed.

'Oh, more company,' said Liz at the kitchen door. 'Stay in the sitting room. Make yourself comfortable. I'm just making coffee.'

Zar and DC Thomas sat on the sofa. Jack sat on the arm of an armchair. He needed a phrase book. Expressions to use when meeting people.

'Might I ask what you're doing here, Jack?' said DC Thomas.

'Social call,' said Jack awkwardly. 'I was having a meal with Rose and Mr Swift and thought I'd pop over.'

He noted Zar was fidgety. Cops made everyone feel guilty. Everyone has secrets.

'Hello, Zar.' He could manage that much.

'Hello, Jack.'

'Been out?'

Zar shrugged. 'Just for a pizza.'

Liz came in with a plate of shortbread which she put on the coffee table.

'Pleasant room you have here, Ms Parker,' said Thomas. 'Are they your paintings?'

'Yes, they are,' she said. 'That one's of the park. You probably won't know the others.'

'Hampstead Heath,' said Zar.

'Well done,' she said. 'You're very observant.'

'She's had a meal of death stalks,' exclaimed Jack. It burst out of him. The politeness. Biscuits and coffee. He had to say it.

'Don't be stupid, Jack,' she retorted. She turned to the others. 'I played a little joke on him. And he's been completely taken in.'

'Doesn't sound much of a joke,' said Thomas.

She shrugged. 'You're right. It wasn't. Totally bad taste. I made a mushroom omelette. What's that, said Jack when he saw me eating it. Death stalk omelette I said.' She chuckled. 'I have a silly sense of humour.'

'It's in the kitchen bin,' said Jack.

'Take a look, Zar,' said Thomas.

Zar went into the kitchen.

'She has taken them,' insisted Jack. 'They don't take effect immediately...'

'8 to 12 hours,' said Thomas.

'She's standing there, playing whatever game with us. And dying,' said Jack.

'That's enough!' shouted Liz. She turned to the detective. 'Men!' She threw up her hands. 'I told him I didn't want an affair... And now see what he's doing to me.'

'She's taken poison. Believe me,' insisted Jack.

'Get out!' yelled Liz. 'Out of my house, right now.' She pushed him off the arm of the chair. 'Out! I never want you here again. You forced your way in. Go, get out of my house. I'll release the park gate for you.' She continued pushing him, he backed off. She turned to Thomas. 'Will you help me get him out, officer?'

'I think you'd best leave, Jack,' said Thomas.

'I'm not lying,' he insisted, looking for assistance to the detective and Zar.

'Then I'll find out. But this is Ms Parker's house, and if she wants you out – then you'd better go.'

Jack looked at Liz, her face screwed in frenzy. He threw up his hands.

'Don't say I haven't told you.'

And left, slamming the front door.

In the cold night air, he wondered what to do. He'd told them about the death stalks, but not her confession. Perhaps he should have done. But he couldn't. Even when she'd turned on him.

He was going out the garden gate when Rose bumped into him.

'Jack!' she exclaimed, feeling his body in the gloom. 'You gave me such a shock. Sorry I've been so long. Had to give Mr Swift a back massage. Where're you going?'

'Home.'

'Oh, you can't.'

'Oh I can. Your sister...' He waved his hands in frustration. He'd lost the power of civil communication. 'She's poisoned herself and is pretending she hasn't.'

'What?'

'Go in and find out. No one believes anything I say.'

'Give me the key.'

He fished it out of his pocket. 'Take it. The cop's in there, and Zar. Your sister is dying. And I'm off home. That's if she's remembered to release the gate.'

He strode on to the drive. He must get home, straight home. Away from this mad world.

Chapter 48

Liz was bustling with the coffee in the kitchen, refusing any assistance. Rose joined the others in the sitting room, taking an armchair. Thomas was munching on shortcake.

'Last time I saw you,' she said, 'you were arresting Amy.'

The police officer held up a finger to denote a full mouth, swallowed and said, 'She's been released. They might still charge her, but she's being very helpful.'

Rose didn't comment, thinking of the large woman who'd been sitting on her chest and pulling her hair. She turned to Zar to change the topic.

'What's he like,' she said playfully, 'when he's off duty?'

Zar smiled. 'So far, so good. But we've only had a pizza together. Honest.'

'So far,' she said with a wink.

'This is worse than the station canteen,' groaned Thomas. 'Talk to anyone, go anywhere, and everyone knows before you do.'

'I like to see you young people getting on,' said Rose.

'Hark at Methuselah,' retorted Thomas.

Liz brought in the coffee mugs on a tray. And passed them round. When they all had one, she sat down in the remaining armchair.

'I don't want to spoil anyone's evening,' said Thomas, 'but I do need to get to the reason for this visit. Something's been bothering me, Ms Parker...'

'Liz,' she said. 'You can drop the formal.'

'Liz then.' He put down his coffee and went on. 'About

this afternoon. Specifically about poisonous mushrooms.'

'I'm all ears,' said Liz.

'You told me there were none in the park. And to be specific – no death stalks.'

'That's right,' she said. 'I did. I got Zar to collect them all up.'

'I think that was a misleading answer, Liz, as you led me to believe none grew in the park.

'I am sorry about that. I didn't mean to.'

'Hm.' Thomas chewed his lip, judging the importance of her reply. Then turned to his companion. 'Zar – you collected all the death stalks?'

'I did.'

'Do you think you might have missed any?'

'I went round the park a couple of times. Probably not.'

'Hm.' He thought for a second or two. 'And what did you do with the mushrooms once you'd collected them?'

'I gave them to Liz. She said she'd burn them.'

'Did she say anything else to you?'

'She said, keep it to myself. She didn't want to cause panic.'

'Do you agree with that, Liz?'

'Yes, I do. With a big ceremony coming up I thought best to keep it quiet. Death stalks in the park. And you never know, if children find them – they might experiment. You have to be aware of these things in a community setting.'

'Did you burn them?'

'Yes.'

'All of them?'

'Yes.'

He stared at her, trying to read her. She held his gaze.

'Do you know the symptoms of death stalk poisoning?' he said.

'Well,' she began, 'nothing for quite a while, which makes them so dangerous. Then vomiting and cramps. Then there might be a period of what appears to be recovery for a couple of hours. And then massive liver or kidney failure. Followed by death.'

'You seem to have that off pat.'

'I read it up yesterday,' she said. 'When I found out they were in the park.'

'Have you eaten any yourself?'

'No.'

'Zar – what did you find in the bin?'

'Remains of an omelette with bits of mushroom in – but I couldn't say of what sort.'

'So, Liz, why did Jack say you had eaten death stalks?'

'I had a bit of fun,' she said with a sigh, 'and then when he was horrified, I told him it was a joke. I know he believed me. We talked of other things. And then out of the blue, he came on to me.' She threw up her hands. 'I mean really, Ian dead, what sort of callous beast does he think I am? I told him forcefully that I wasn't interested. Men! You wouldn't believe it. He came tonight to see my sister, and then decided that I, a woman by herself, was a better bet. And when I wouldn't have it, he had to get his own back.' She turned up her hands plaintively. 'Why else come up with such rubbish?'

'Unless you have eaten death stalks.'

'I haven't. I don't know how many times I have to say it.'

Thomas sighed. 'I don't know whether to believe you or not, Liz. But I am a lowly detective constable just making a few enquiries to see if Ian Swift's death might be suspicious. The autopsy is tomorrow, so we can't even be totally sure that Ian was poisoned. It's just that Ian himself thought he was.'

'He could've been wrong,' said Liz.

'He could've been,' agreed Thomas. 'But the doctor seemed to think it the most likely explanation for his sudden death. And he did have lunch with you yesterday, Liz.'

'I didn't give Liz the mushrooms until mid afternoon,' interrupted Zar.

'So that's me off the hook,' said Liz.

'Unless you found them yourself earlier.'

'I didn't.'

'Lunch would fit the timetable, though,' said Thomas. 'He got sick 9 at night. It would have to be poisoning around lunchtime. Dinner would be too late.'

'How can you be so certain it is mushroom poisoning?' she said.

'You've got me there, Liz. I can't. Not till the autopsy is completed.'

'So isn't this visit rather premature?' she said.

Thomas scratched his chin. 'I am in a quandary here, Liz. If Ian Swift is found to be poisoned by death stalks – then you are the prime suspect.'

'And if it was something else entirely?'

'As may well be. It all comes down to the pathology report.' He took a sip of coffee. 'Let's put aside how Ian Swift may or may not have died. Zar gave you the mushrooms mid afternoon...'

'I agree, he did.'

'So you could have had them in your supper.'

'I burnt them.'

'If you did,' he insisted, 'you could be dead by the time we get the autopsy report.' He shook his head. 'I'm afraid I have no choice, Liz. I am taking you into custody.'

'I'm not going. You have to charge me.'

'You want to be arrested? Fine by me. Obstructing the course of justice.'

'But I'm not.' She appealed to the others. 'I am answering all his questions. How am I obstructing anything?'

He scratched his hair. 'This is way over my pay grade. I need to go to the station and get some advice.' He stood up. 'I may be back later. I may not.' He turned to Zar. 'Sorry, mate. But you could be an important witness in this case. Our relationship will have to stop at a pizza until this is cleared up.'

'I understand, Eddie.'

'Then I'll say good night to you all.'

He left them. Liz followed him to the door.

'What a pity,' exclaimed Rose, rubbing Zar on the back. 'He'd have been a real treat for you.'

'I thought it was too good to be true,' said Zar ruefully. 'Though he might be able to help me with somewhere to live. He knows people.'

Liz returned, and threw up her hands in relief. 'Thank God, he's gone. I thought he was going to arrest me then and there. That's enough day for me. I'm off to bed. And you need to make sure Mr Swift is alright, Rose.'

'I'm sure he is, but I'd best go next door and check. See how good I'm being?' She rose from the armchair. 'What about Zar in your spare room?' Adding, 'He's not me, Liz.'

'Yes, why not?' said Liz. 'Get your stuff from the pavilion, Zar. Rose, let him have your key. You don't need it. And let's all get some sleep. It's going to be an eventful day tomorrow.'

Rose gave Zar the key.

'I'll get my stuff,' he said and left them.

When the front door had shut, Rose held her sister by the shoulder.

'You didn't take death stalks, did you?'

'No. It's a load of rubbish. Look at me.' She broke away, swung her arms and did a pirouette. 'Bet you can't still do that, Rose. Not now you're thirty.'

Chapter 49

Jack considered phoning his Alcohol Halt buddy, Max. He hadn't spoken to him for six weeks. Nice guy, but really not that suitable, not for him. Max was having a God phase, and kept trying to persuade Jack to have one too. At their last meeting, he'd told Jack to pray.

'And if I can't?'

'Just try. It'll come easier with practice.'

Max had a soothing voice, but his nostrums weren't useful. God, or his stand-in, the doorknob, wouldn't work for Jack.

Weariness did. He was home. In order to get drunk, he'd have to go out again to search for a late night booze shop. Too far, too long. But he felt so alone. He'd walked out. Alcohol Halt said if a situation becomes too demanding – leave. You are always free to go, said the convenor. And so, Jack had left. No, he hadn't, he'd been thrown out. She'd told everyone he was harassing her, because she'd rejected him.

He'd failed to convince any of them that Liz had taken poison. She had so convincingly denied it, that he was beginning to wonder himself. Could it have been a simple mushroom omelette on her plate – that his own fears had read as death stalks with scrambled egg?

What more could he do?

He could've said that she had confessed to murdering Ian. But she'd deny that too. Say Jack was the bitter lover who'd say anything in revenge.

He strode about the flat. This was appalling. He felt so

useless, so taken over. Greg at AH swore by yoga. It took his mind off alcohol and his inner demons, he said all too often. It was his inner higher power, he claimed. Jack had tried it once at a class and couldn't stop looking at the attractive women in front of him, in clinging leotards. His own, inner, lower power.

He showered, and got into his pyjamas. Another step away from booze. He put on some jazz, closed his eyes and listened to the oozing trumpet and piano rhythm twisting round and round each other. Let the music swell. She'd done the dirty on him. Maybe she thought he'd done the dirty on her?

In the rose garden, she'd told him that she'd killed Ian. Then when he came into her house later, she said she'd taken death stalks. No, not quite like that. He thought back. She had told him she was eating a mushroom omelette. And he'd asked her – are they death stalks? And she'd said – what else? Then he'd thrown them in the bin.

He was sure then. Now, not so sure. She'd said why she'd taken them. Because it's fitting, she'd said. What on earth did that mean? He was tired, too tired. Examining every damn word. And so muddled. He'd forgotten half the words he or she'd said. But the sense of it was that she told him that she was eating death stalks. That was no joke. But then when the others came, she denied everything. Saying it was him getting back at her.

He didn't know what to believe. She was poisoning herself. She wasn't. She was. And there it stayed. She was. But what could he do? Calling an ambulance would be useless. She'd say, it's that dreadful builder. Look at me, I'm fine. Go and treat someone who's really ill.

His phone rang. Late for a call. Liz or Rose? To say they were coming over. Fat chance. He half laughed and looked at the phone. Neither of them.

'Hello, Mia.'

'They're having another row, Dad.'

Jack laughed. He couldn't stop himself.

'It's not funny,' she declared. Not the slightest bit.'

'Sorry, Mia.'

'Why are grown ups so stupid?'

'That's a tough one...' And totally apt. What does one say? Hormones, laziness, loneliness, but he settled for, 'Animal instincts pretending to be civilised actions.'

'What?'

'It's why the world is in such a mess.'

'And Mum?'

'She's a lonely animal pretending to be a deputy head. Mostly, she gets away with it.'

'Until Tony turns up. Oh, listen to them! Mum got hold of his phone again. And Emily hasn't gone. What can I do?' she wailed.

It's easier to give advice than to take it, he thought. No one had listened to him so far tonight. Why not make it a series?

'Go in and tell them to damn well shut up,' he said.

'I can't do that.'

'You can,' he said. Reminding himself of Max and prayer. His certainty. 'You won't know till you've tried.'

'She'll shout at me.'

'Shout back at her.'

There was a long pause.

'Are you still there, Mia?'

'I'm going to do it. I'll phone you back, Dad.'

That was better. Distraction Find another story to lock himself into. Of course Mia might walk straight into their lovemaking. A shock to everyone. The secrets of the bedroom. Except they were screaming their heads off, so unlikely to be in sexual throes. Unless a row was simply sex gone bad.

The jazz was still playing. He'd turned it lower during the

phone call. Now it was *'Take the A Train'*, Duke Ellington. And he segued into a train hoping to stop at a quiet siding, but there was none so he'd roll on – until... Acheson, Topeka and Santa Fe.

The metaphor didn't hold. Trains don't need love. Have rows, get drunk, have children.

The phone rang. He picked it up, expecting Mia on her own track.

'Jack.'

It was Alison.

'Hello,' he said carefully. 'I hear you were having a row.'

'Did you put her up to it?' she said.

'She was totally miserable,' he said. 'I don't know what you think you're doing. But stop it.'

He amazed himself by his forthrightness, but what the hell, what was there to lose?

'Tony's leaving,' she said and paused. 'There. That was the front door.'

'What are you doing in such a stupid relationship?'

'I don't know. I just wanted to believe him when he came back.'

'He's a rat.'

'Yes.'

'I can't believe you are agreeing with me. This never happens.'

'Oh, why can't you be in Brighton now!'

He laughed. 'You don't mean that.'

'I do at this moment,' she said. 'You never did the dirty on me. Just got drunk. And now you've sorted yourself out – I'm kinda sorry you've gone.'

The irony. Someone thought he was OK. On the phone. For the moment. Seventy miles away.

'It wouldn't last,' he said.

'It might.'

He'd never considered getting back together. Not

234

seriously. They always rowed. It was a pattern. The way they were. Blame v blame.

'Would you like to come to Brighton for the weekend?' she said.

'Are you serious?'

'I think so.'

Did he want to? You can't step into the same river twice, said some clever dick at AH. He was two years on. Older, but wiser? That was the question. And there was Mia to consider. The Fat Controller was throwing his switches. Which track to where?

'I'll come,' he said. 'Best behaviour.'

'Ditto.'

PART FOUR:
THE BIG DAY

Chapter 50

Liz gave Zar a shout in the morning to wake him. She informed him she'd left a clean towel in the bathroom. To help himself to toast, eggs, yoghurt or whatever. But wash up afterwards. She had to open up the park and get going. Busy day.

Left alone, he might've slept till noon. The night before, he'd found the pavilion floor hard, and, when he'd finally got to sleep, been woken up by Rose and Man Mountain. And though grateful for her company, she did chatter. Death and autumn. She was rather a loony, but he liked her. And she'd got him this bed tonight.

He mustn't call friends loonies.

As he showered, he wondered whether he could persuade Liz to make this permanent. He'd have to be a model guest. No mess, no noise. That wasn't his style anyway. And he didn't have any lovers to bring back. Eddie who might have been, wasn't.

No screwing of witnesses.

Somewhere to live came first. He would be so nice to Liz today and hope. Pay the rent and housekeeping of course, without any argument. The others might think it peculiar, him staying at Liz's place. He'd need to come out as gay. But then Liz knew, Rose knew. Amy was gone. That only left Bill. And he'd moan whatever Zar was.

He went down to the kitchen. It was as tidy as his mother's. What were they saying about him at home? Nothing much, he suspected, once they'd blown their tops.

Probably just glad he was gone and so couldn't disgrace them. At least, not in their house. Not so that the community would know.

He'd never cooked at home. Nothing more than toast, that is. The kitchen was his mother's realm. So he'd have a go now. Tea was just a tea bag in a cup. No problem. Toast in the toaster, simple enough. Dare he try fried egg?

Zar put too much oil in the pan. He broke the two eggs badly. They fried greasily, popping and spitting. He was glad Liz was out at work and so wouldn't witness his haplessness. He made the atmosphere worse by frying a slice of bread in the swimming oil. The kitchen steamed with greasy odour.

Zar ate hungrily. Then washed up, scrubbing the frying pan. He opened the window to release the smell. It was a warm, sunny day. Great. There was the builder already at work.

Jack was coming out the yard with a wheelbarrow of bricks when he bumped into Liz. He stared at her for an instant and would have ignored her, but she spoke.

'Sorry, Jack.'

He almost charged off, but instead stopped.

'That was a bitch thing to do,' he said.

'For which I can only apologise.'

She was in her overalls with a clipboard in her hands, her fingers grimy with peat.

'Did you eat death stalks?' he said.

'Change the subject,' she said.

'It's the only subject.'

'Then I didn't.'

'And did you kill Ian?'

'No.'

'So erase the conversation in the rose garden, erase what you said in the kitchen?'

'Yes,' she said, holding his gaze. 'I was depressed. I said crazy things. I'm fine now.'

'You look well,' he said.

She smiled at him. 'Wait till you see me in my suit.' She looked at her watch. 'Oh, I must rush. Such a lot to do before the nobs come. See you later.'

He watched her stride down the path to her greenhouse. Not knowing what to think. What she'd said, what she was. He'd agreed in the early hours to go down to Brighton to stay with Alison. Well, that could be cancelled. If anything happened here.

All this hedging of his bets. It was too Tony.

He unloaded the bricks by the wall, and went back with the wheelbarrow to the yard to make up the mortar. Rose was coming in. She gave him a peck on the cheek, so she wasn't mad at him either. So maybe he wasn't judged so badly. Or had Liz had a word with her?

She told him Mr Swift had overdone the bricklaying yesterday and was having a lie in. So he'd have no mate. And then she rushed off. Zar came across the lawn and hailed him. Even Bill had a good morning. Jack noted that Zar went out with the leaf vac. The lawn was priority. Bill had a two wheeled barrow of white, yellow, purple and red flowers. Primulas, he said. And had gone off to plant them.

The mortar made up in the yard, Jack took a barrowful outside and began today's bricklaying. The courses they'd laid yesterday were even. He simply had to keep to them with the spirit level. His action with the trowel had improved from watching Mr Swift. And he hit a rhythm.

Every so often he saw Liz, in and out the marquee with plants from her greenhouse.

He was surprised to see Amy. She came in the other gate, past the playground, and must've seen Rose there, but she didn't go in. Bill and Zar gave her a wave, she waved back, and went to talk briefly to Bill. And then went into the marquee.

She was in there, perhaps ten minutes, and came out weeping.

A closed lorry came into the park. Jack had to move his wheelbarrow for it to get by. Folding tables were taken from its interior into the marquee, along with plastic chairs and a large open box of white tablecloths. The two men were leaving the marquee when Liz came out yelling at them. Jack could hear her from where he was. Telling them how short staffed she was and she'd report them if they didn't set things up.

She won. But then he knew she would. He'd seen her in action a few times. The men went back into the marquee. He could still hear Liz, but muffled by the canvas.

He checked the course with the spirit level. Going well. Matching up at both ends. He should be finished by noon. Push on. Make up more mortar. He looked at the sky, with luck it should stay fine.

He was sitting on the wall for his tea break when Liz came along the drive in her suit.

'What d'you think?' she said, doing a twirl.

It was a navy blue dress suit, well cut to her figure. She wore a red scarf round her neck and was wearing smart flats on her feet.

'No six inch heels?' said Jack.

'I can't stand them,' she said. 'Useless to work in. Kill your feet. Scandalously overpriced.'

She'd put on light make up and a little perfume. Jack looked in admiration; she almost frightened him. What clothes can do. She'd leaped out of the working class.

'I prefer you in overalls,' he said.

She lifted her nose snootily. 'I'm in manager mode. Ah!' She indicated the gate. 'That's the Mayor's limo. I'm the reception committee too.' She wandered further up the path as the vehicle drove slowly in.

Over the next half hour, a few other vehicles came, and various less privileged pedestrians who'd left cars outside the park. Several remarked on the quality of his bricklaying, including the soon to be ex Member of Parliament, who Jack thought quite nice for a Tory.

The marquee was bustling. There were waiters and waitresses with trays of drinks to hand out to the besuited throng. Every so often, between people, he noted Liz chatting. She seemed at home, in demand.

Zar rushed past him into the yard.

'Liz wants me to come in. She wants me to talk about the Tree Map.'

He came out of the yard a minute later, indicating clean hands, and then ran towards the marquee. Deciding about ten yards from it, that he'd best walk. Jack saw Liz immediately draw him in and then he was out of sight in the mêlée.

He'd brought out the last of the bricks. There was enough mortar to see him through. He was on the top course, laying the bricks crosswise to finish off. A little later, he noted there was hubbub and motion, guests were streaming out of the marquee and heading towards the avenue. It was mostly men, but some women, all with high heels except Liz in her sensible shoes.

Every so often, as he worked, Jack looked over to the Mayor's avenue, but with the milling of people could see little of what was going on. There was a TV camera, the operator dancing about, here and there. The tree planting, Jack assumed, but could see only a wall of suits. Speeches too, he guessed, a few dainty shovels of soil from the chrome plated spade – and back to the marquee for a drink or two.

Though some with tight schedules were already heading

off to meetings about budgets and personnel. The Mayor came past in his limousine, off to his next port of call. The MP went, telling Jack to keep up the good work. The TV people had nothing to stay for, but had a drink or two and grabbed some sausage rolls and were off to another assignment.

Jack laid the last brick. And stood back to look. Straight and true. He'd only needed to use a few of the new bricks. And had separated them out, so they didn't stand out. Now to clean up. And job done.

In the marquee, Liz had a small audience of those less hurried. With a glass of red wine in one hand, she was pointing out and naming the flowers and plants down the sides of the waterfall in her cascade. Answering questions, when suddenly she doubled up, the glass and wine flying out of her hand and dropping into the rapids. She staggered, bashing into the side of her structure, and collapsed onto the bottom step where the gushing pool burbled through pebbles. She sat up brushing water off her hair, her hand among lilies at the side.

'How on earth did that happen?' she said with a smile.

An arm helped her to her feet. Liz clambered out, water dripping off her suit, her hair dank, lips trembling. She began thanking her helper, tottered a few steps as if the earth were shaking under her, and would have collapsed but a man caught her, now a dead weight, and laid her gently on the grass.

She was clutching her stomach, rocking back and forth, as the ambulance was called.

Chapter 51

Jack arrived home mid afternoon. He'd been oblivious to the fuss over Liz as he'd been in the yard, hosing down his wheelbarrow and tools. Zar came in yelling that Liz was being taken away in an ambulance.

He ran out. There was the ambulance, just beyond the wall, the back doors wide open. Two paramedics were carrying Liz on a stretcher across the grass. Rose was by the vehicle.

She said, 'You were right all along, Jack.'

'The last thing I want to be.'

'She collapsed into her cascade,' said Rose. 'She didn't want an ambulance, kept telling us she was alright, but it was obvious she wasn't. By the time they got here, she was frothing at the mouth, vomiting and thrashing about. She fought them off. Can you believe that? They had to give her an injection to pacify her.'

Liz was being slid into the back of the ambulance. A small crowd had gathered. The day had clouded over; there was a chill wind.

'I never believed you tried it on with her,' said Rose, taking his hand.

'I didn't.'

'Because she wouldn't have rejected you, Jack. If that helps your ego.'

'Not much.'

'Miss,' called a paramedic, 'if you're coming along then you'd better get on board.'

'You know my number, Jack. Keep in touch.'

They embraced, and quickly parted. And then Rose was in the back of the vehicle. The doors were closed, and in less than a minute the ambulance was gone from the park; a dying siren signalling its route to the hospital.

Zar was crushed. 'She was eating and drinking, had a crowd around her cascade, all asking her questions, when she dropped into the water. Out of nowhere.'

Bill was philosophical, as one might expect.

'You never know what's eating you up inside. Like termites.'

Jack had left soon after, though wondered how they'd manage the park, just the two of them and all the debris of the ceremony. The marquee to be packed up, tables and chairs collected. The playground run. Who was in charge now?

Several times during the afternoon, he'd tried phoning Rose, and had given up by the time DC Thomas arrived in the early evening. Jack invited him up.

'I've only instant coffee,' he said.

'OK by me, Jack.'

He made them a mug each, and they sat in the sitting room, his kitchen being a tip.

Thomas was back in his smart working suit. A plain clothes cop.

'Have you heard anything?' he said.

'No,' said Jack with a shrug. 'I've been ringing Rose on and off, with no luck.'

'Well, I'm sorry to inform you that Liz died about four o'clock this afternoon.'

'Oh God.' Tears filled his eyes. 'Excuse me,' he managed, rubbing his eyes with the back of a hand.

'Take this,' said Thomas, handing over a tissue.

'Thanks.' He wiped his eyes and blew his nose. 'I only knew her a few days; you'd think I was her brother or something. It's just... she touched me.'

'There's nothing wrong with crying, mate,' said Thomas patting him on the back. 'I've met bastards who wouldn't weep if their daughter's head was chopped off in front of them. Let 'em flow.'

'Thanks,' said Jack sniffing.

'You were right all along,' said Thomas.

'You're the second one who's said that to me.'

'She was so jolly last night,' said the detective. 'What d'you make of that?'

Jack thought this over. 'She'd settled what she was going to do,' he said at last. 'Taken the mushrooms and had no regrets.'

'We've had the preliminary post mortem report on Swift. And it's confirmed, death stalk poisoning.'

'Two in two days,' said Jack.

'There's no doubt in my mind,' said Thomas, 'that she killed Ian Swift. Do you agree?'

'Yes.'

'And then she killed herself because of guilt, fear of being caught, or whatever.'

'Or whatever,' echoed Jack.

'Did she tell you she killed Swift?'

'No,' he said. There was no point getting himself in trouble.

'There's one thing missing though,' mused Thomas. 'Motive. Why did she kill him?'

'I've no idea,' said Jack.

'He must have had something on her,' reflected the detective. 'Something in her past he was going to reveal.'

'I don't know anything about her past,' said Jack. 'Just who she was in the last few days of her life.' He took a sip of coffee. 'What happens now?'

'There'll be a post mortem to ascertain the cause of death. And we can be pretty sure what it will reveal. Then there'll be two inquests.'

'Might she be accused of murder?'

'As it stands,' said the detective, his tongue lolling in his cheek, 'No. There's not enough hard evidence. There's what she said to you – but later she denied ever saying it. Up three steps, down four. There's Zar and the mushrooms, but she more or less had an OK reason for wanting to keep them secret. Without the motive, she gets away with it.'

'Not quite,' said Jack. 'She's dead.'

'Point taken,' said Thomas. 'But I'd like to tie this one up. A neat bundle. Case closed. I don't like these half done things. I'm trying for promotion to detective sergeant...' He stopped and waved his hands, 'But don't let me start on my ambitions.'

'Will you pick up with Zar?'

'I hope to. But not till the inquests are over. Professional etiquette. He's staying in Liz's house for the time being. There's a good chance it could be permanent. They're impressed with him. He ran the park almost single handed this afternoon. The other man... what's his name?'

'Bill.'

'Useless. Zar took charge.'

'He showed them the Tree Plan at the ceremony. Liz brought him in.'

'I think the lad might've struck lucky.' He rose. 'Thanks for the coffee, Jack. I won't keep you any longer. I'd be obliged though if you could come to the station as soon as you can and make a statement.'

'I'm off tomorrow,' said Jack. 'I'll come in late morning.'

And with that Thomas left him.

Jack sat for a long time, reflecting. He'd been right last night. She'd confessed to him in the rose garden. And admitted in her cottage there were death stalks in her omelette. That was the sadness. Her willingness to die. Killing herself because she'd killed Ian, and couldn't stand losing her park.

But it was so unnecessary.

Ian would've been arrested today, or some time soon, for his part in the scam. Gone. Out of her life. For what? Why had she needed to kill him at all?

Did it matter? He had no paperwork to tie up.

He regretted not getting to her greenhouse. A tour of her patch. And wondered who would take it over? Presumably, they'd bring someone in. With three gone from the park, Liz, Amy and Ian; they'd have to. He'd phone Rose in a couple of days, suggest they did something or other. A meal, a movie. What would happen to her? In the other cottage with Mr Swift for the time being. Most likely they'd have to go when new staff came. Hopefully, they'd get enough notice to sort something out.

There'd be a funeral. Two in fact. But only one he'd be going to. Bring some flowers. What would Liz like? What's in season? The park would make a floral tribute from her greenhouse. He'd wear his one and only suit.

He thought of last night in the park. Her vaccing in the rose garden in the dark. The vroom across the lawn; he hadn't known who was doing what or where it was exactly. And found her, barely visible in the gloom doing needless work. Sweeping leaves even as they fell.

And would fall for another month or more. Piles and piles of dead leaves to crackle under foot and be vacced away. And put on heaps. He'd been struck by one of the pictures in her sitting room; the red, brown and yellow leaves floating on the pond. October days. But dark skies too, that he'd wanted to share with her. The lozenge of Auriga, the Pleiades, the Square of Pegasus.

This weekend was Brighton. There might be change and change about. Take it slow. Too much had happened too quickly. Don't walk in to be thrown out again.

Rose sat on the bed, exhausted. Too many nights on the razzle, and the hours and hours in the hospital, waiting for news of Liz. How could she die? Even though she'd been charged into intensive care, how could she die on her? Rose had always known that in spite of the fact that Liz was five years older, that she, Rose, would die first. It was her preordained fate. From childhood.

How could her sister cheat her!

Rose was fated to be the tragic heroine in the family. Instead she was the survivor. She'd wanted to be the dead sister, the one causing grief, the one everyone exclaimed 'so young, so young' over, as they stared at the body on the river bank with strands of algae in her long hair. Still weeping, as they sorted out her memorial and funeral with eight limousines in a cortege covered in wreaths. Now she would have to organise all that. Imagine! Rose Parker having to mastermind a funeral. She'd need to contact Mum and Dad. Give them the details. Go through Liz's phone book.

What a task!

Not a role for the clubbing girl, the wild thing. This had been Liz's area. Her older sister who knew all the plants and flowers, who could tell the difference between a field mushroom and a death stalk.

She loved her. She hated her. The sister who had thrown her out. Who half protected her. Who didn't live in the cottage next door any longer. Though her things were there. Like a museum of Liz's life. Her books, her paintings, all the little bits of arts and crafts scattered around the house. Her clothing, shoes, bedding and towels. All to be sorted out. By Rose – the organiser.

What a legacy!

At least Zar was next door. Her mate. He was acting manager in the park. He'd never handle it. Not tough enough. Bill would mess him about and whatever replacements were taken on, they'd have a field day with too-nice Zar. Except she'd be his bully boy. Yell and browbeat them into shape. Push them about. And maybe Zar would get the job permanently.

What was her chance of staying in this house? She did work in the park. They couldn't just throw out Mr Swift. There'd have to be some notice. And if it came to that, and if Zar got the manager's role, then she could prevail on him.

You have to think of yourself. Even at a time like this.

Especially at times like this.

She couldn't evade the call to their parents. Go visit them. Talk about funeral options and so forth. Oh, how responsible she'd have to be! Making up lists of undertakers. Caterers. A memorial some time, somewhere.

Maybe Zar would come with her. That would confuse Mum and Dad. No. She'd have to go alone. Phone them tonight.

Something was pushing into her backside. Was there nowhere comfortable in the world? This constant itch. She pulled back the bedclothes. Nothing but the sheets. Then she lifted the corner of the mattress. There it was. Her discomfort.

Bundles and bundles of banknotes. Seven tidy bundles to be exact, each bound with an elastic band. Must be £1000 in each.

Ian had been commendably tidy.

Rose knew at once what it was. The proceeds of Women Fly Women. Amy's daily deliveries and who knew who else's? Taken in by Ian and hidden under his mattress for the time being. Nobody knew of it. They were all getting arrested, from the bottom to the very top. This was buried treasure. The pirate captain was dead, the crew in clink. Finders keepers. Plenty to pay for a funeral. Though Liz had enough, and to spare, in her bank account.

Rose had a thought.

It was she who'd brought Man Mountain to the park. The great wrecking ball who'd toppled over the cascade and knocked over Jack's telescope. It was she who'd led him to the marquee. To get him out of her way, so she could get some sleep.

She had a debt to pay. Not that such things usually bothered her, but then pirate's loot didn't often come her way. She flicked the notes. Smelt them. Filthy lucre. Do something useful with it.

In a couple of days, she'd turn up at Jack's door. See his face when she handed over the hefty cardboard box.

'Special delivery for Jack of All Trades!'

Thank you!

I am grateful to every reader who finishes one of my novels. I have taken you on a journey which I hope you have enjoyed. There are plenty of things you could have been doing, other than reading this book. So, thank you for your time.

If you liked **Jack By The Hedge**, here's what you can do next:

I'd appreciate a review on Amazon. In that way, you can help me tell other readers about my books. Without reviews authors get few sales on Amazon. So I'd be grateful for your review to help this series get on the move.

You can get a **FREE** ebook of **Jack of Spades** if you sign up for my readers' list. You may give it to a friend if you wish. Every month a lucky reader from the list will be sent a **free**, signed paperback of their choice from the series. Sign up using this link:

http://eepurl.com/buAh5H

When you sign up for my readers' list you will receive my regular newsletter. This will give you news about me, what I'm reading, tell you about my future books, PLUS a variety of giveaways.

Books by DH Smith

DH Smith is the name I use for my Jack of All Trades series. The books are all standalone novels and can be read in any order.

Out Now:
- Jack of All Trades
- Jack of Spades
- Jack o'Lantern
- Jack By The Hedge

Coming Soon:
- Jack in the Box
- Jack on the Tower
- Jack Be Nimble

Mystery/Crime
Murder at Any Price

Books by Derek Smith

All my books, other than the Jack of All Trades series and Murder at Any Price, are written under the name Derek Smith.

Fantasy
Hell's Chimney
The Prince's Shadow
Elektra

Other
Strikers of Hanbury Street (short stories)
Catching Up (poetry)

Young Adult Novels
Hard Cash
Half a Bike
Fast Food
Frances Fairweather Demon Striker!

Children's Novels
The Good Wolf
Feather Brains
Baker's Boy

For Younger Children
The Magical World of Lucy-Anne
Lucy-Anne's Changing Ways
Jack's Bus

About the Author

I live in Forest Gate in the East End of London. In my working life, I have been a plastics chemist, a gardener and a stage manager before becoming a professional writer. I began with plays, working with several theatre companies, and had a few plays on radio and TV, as well as on the stage. In the early 80s I became involved in running a co-operative bookshop and vegetarian café in Stratford, learning to cook, and having my first go at writing a novel. The first was a mess, and, after too many rewrites, binned. The transition from drama to novels took me a couple of years to get to grips with. My first success was a young adult novel, Hard Cash, published by Faber. Buoyed up by this, I stuck with children's work, did school visits, and made a hand to mouth living as a full time author, topped up with some evening class work in creative writing at City University and the Mary Ward Centre in Holborn. A few adult fiction titles appeared from time to time, between the children's list, and I have since been working more in that direction with my Jack of All Trades series.

My full name is Derek Howard Smith. I write as DH Smith for my Jack of All Trades series; all other books appear under Derek Smith. Earlham Books is my own imprint.

www.dereksmithwriter.com

The book you're holding was designed by Lia at Free Your Words...

Contact lia@freeyourwords.com for a quote

www.ingramcontent.com/pod-product-compliance
Lightning Source LLC
Chambersburg PA
CBHW061955170626
46813CB00006B/2649